W9-CBB-430

I

Kissed

Alice

I Kissed Alice

ANNA BIRCH

WITH ILLUSTRATIONS BY
VICTORIA YING

【Imprint】
MAKE YOUR MARK
NEW YORK

[Imprint]
MAKE YOUR MARK

A part of Macmillan Publishing Group, LLC
120 Broadway, New York, NY 10271

I Kissed Alice. Text copyright © 2020 by Anna Birch. Illustrations copyright
© 2020 by Imprint. All rights reserved. Printed in the United States of America.

Library of Congress Cataloging-in-Publication Data is available.

ISBN 978-1-250-21985-5 (hardcover) / ISBN 978-1-250-21986-2 (ebook)

Our books may be purchased in bulk for promotional, educational,
or business use. Please contact your local bookseller or the Macmillan Corporate and
Premium Sales Department at (800) 221-7945 ext. 5442 or by
email at MacmillanSpecialMarkets@macmillan.com.

Book design by Carolyn Bull

Illustrations by Victoria Ying

Imprint logo designed by Amanda Spielman

First edition, 2020

1 3 5 7 9 10 8 6 4 2

fiercereads.com

Beware the jabberwock, o thief
Should herein you pillage or plunder
The beast descends in spite of your shrieks
The vorpal blade tears you asunder

To Daniel:

Till a' the seas gang dry, my dear

— ROBERT BURNS

To Levi, Rhys, and Parker (in no particular order!):

I love your hearts!

CHAPTER 1
ILIANA

Hate is a complicated word.

Some people believe hating is wishing death on someone.

Others think it's three-minutes-in-a-dark-broom-closet away from True Love™.

If this is the case, I don't hate Rhodes Ingram at all: I don't hate her, and I would rather die *myself* than be alone with her *anywhere*.

But, oh, it feels good to say it:

I hate Rhodes Ingram.

I hate Rhodes Ingram.

I. HATE. RHODES. INGRAM.

We're standing in the doorway of the dorm room Rhodes shares with Sarah Wade, my best friend since we were kids, and I never have any idea what's happened here. She doesn't tell me when she fights with Rhodes, or when Rhodes makes her feel small, or when Rhodes bites her head off for turning on the overhead lights too early in the morning. Sarah only Velcros herself to my side, and then I have to needle around for details until I can finally pull everything out of her.

And oh my God.

I *despise* Rhodes for it.

I've memorized every square inch of Rhodes's face—her dark, full eyebrows, the way her hair hangs in long sheets past her shoulders, the wisps that curl at her temples, too short and too new to be forced into submission. I've blended shades of orange and pink watercolor until I could find the precise shade of her cheeks when she flushes either from embarrassment or anger, and I find myself comparing sticks of soft pastel to match the blue of her eyes.

Every day, we take seats across from each other in Drawing III. We spend seventy-five minutes in uncomfortable eye contact over the tops of our sketchbooks instead of working, ignoring the endless blathering of our drawing teacher, Benjamin Randall.

Which is exactly what we did today—*literally* nothing.

Nothing at all, but glaring and fuming and whispering snide remarks over the tops of our sketchbooks at each other. And now we're here, two hours later, standing three feet from each other while she scrambles—because that's the only thing she knows how to do— flushed and shoving dirty clothes into a hamper.

"I can't believe you talked me into this," I whisper to Sarah.

Her face pinches up in that way that it has since childhood, a little red and a lot ugly.

She doesn't respond—she doesn't have to.

Her texts in our messaging app earlier today said more than enough:

Its_sayruh_17 6:13a: look you don't have to talk to her ok

Its_sayruh_17 9:42a: it's my birthday

And

Its_sayruh_17 10:46a: don't you think you can just like pretend to get along for five minutes

And

Its_sayruh_17 12:15p: you're both my best friends??? Clearly you both have good taste??? Like?

And

Its_sayruh_17 1:52p: ANSWER

lts_sayruh_17 1:52p: YOUR

lts_sayruh_17 1:52p: TEXTS

lts_sayruh_17 1:53p: BITCH

So, here we are.

Thirty minutes later leaving than we had originally intended.

Rhodes's *things* are nice enough—I recognize her quilt from the cover of a Pottery Barn Teen catalog I saw in my orthodontist's office. She has one of those boutiquey burlap-tufted headboards and crystal bedside lamps that are completely ridiculous paired with the cinderblock walls. Her curtains match her bed skirt, a preppy kelly-green-on-white lattice print.

But six half-empty water bottles litter Rhodes's shelf over her bed, and two have plummeted between her headboard and the desk. Her office supplies match, too, all the way down to a cup filled with unsharpened pencils that have sat there as long as Sarah and Rhodes have shared a space, but today they're scattered willy-nilly across her desk.

Meanwhile, Sarah's side of the room is meticulously tidy. She possesses a kind of ingenuity I don't see from the Conservatory kids who come from money: She's broke, the *other* sophomore-year transfer besides me, and she's only here due to one of a handful of scholarships the school extends to the area's talented poor. Whereas the girls down the hall order their room supplies from places like West Elm or Pottery Barn, Sarah has upcycled literally everything she owns from thrift stores, dumpsters, and her grandmother's attic.

There are three rows of bins on the shelves that hang over her bed, spray-painted white and fitted with DIY tie-dyed liners. She braided the rug that sits on the linoleum floor between the two beds from old sweatshirts and crocheted her shower bag with strips of old plastic bags from the grocery store.

I like Sarah's side far better.

Rhodes has moved on to stowing dirty bowls spirited away from the dining hall beneath her bed, cursing under her breath, so I direct my attention to Sarah instead. She nudges me toward her bed; I duck under Rhodes's long arm, which is flailing out to grab a dining hall mug from where it sits on top of the microwave, and hoist myself up onto Sarah's mattress. "Well? What do you want to do first, Birthday Girl?"

"I think we should read tarot cards," Sarah says. "Did you bring yours?"

"Oh, give me a break." I dump my bag onto Sarah's homemade quilt, an uncharacteristic hodgepodge of every monogrammed article of clothing she's owned since birth. Three decks tumble out, each safe in tiny, hand-sewn silk pouches. "I always have them with me."

Sarah takes each deck from its bag and turns the cards out.

First, the original Rider-Waite deck, with a pretty tile pattern on the back that makes it impossible to tell if a card is upright or reversed before it's been flipped—a detail that could change the meaning of the card if the picture on the back is upside down or right-side up. Second, a deck influenced by the art deco movement from the early twentieth century that shimmers with touches of gold leaf. The last deck—and my favorite—my Sacred Feminine deck.

Even if we go through this little ritual every time I've read for her, she always chooses the same deck. She glances over to where Rhodes lies sprawled across her own bed, then places the Sacred Feminine deck in my upturned palm.

"What makes you think you can see the secrets of the universe with a deck of cards?" Rhodes drawls. She's lying on her side, her head propped in her hand. "Why do *you*, Iliana Vrionides, think *you* possess a sixth sense for the unknown?"

We've been through this eight hundred times.

Every single God-dang time she sees my cards, she asks the same question.

I always give the same answer, and I recite it now as if I'm reciting a Bible verse in church:

"Tarot cards are mirrors, not windows. I don't practice tarot to see the future; I practice tarot to see myself."

"Yeah," Sarah echoes, frowning. "It's not about trying to see the future."

Rhodes sniffs. She rolls onto her back and stares up at the ceiling. "I don't see why you can't just, I don't know, look in a mirror. If it takes a deck of playing cards to 'know yourself,' *Iliana*, you've got bigger problems."

I don't like the way my name rolls around in her mouth: It's pure, old-fashioned, rural Alabama drawl, with consonants conveniently forgotten and every vowel delicately stretched into its own kind of music. It sounds like a secret; I've wondered what it would sound like to hear my name whispered like that.

Sarah shifts and uncrosses her short legs and stretches them out in front of her. She's gone from a pleasant, excited flush in her pale cheeks to an all-over crimson that even screams pink under her bleached hair. We make eye contact; she shakes her head, and I drop my eyes to the cards between us.

This girl is the person I called when I experienced my first orgasm on accident two summers ago, leaning up against the washing machine during the spin cycle to reach the box of fabric softener on the top shelf. I was the one she called for advice the three months she hid having her period from her mother, an overly emotional, sentimental woman who Sarah had caught searching phrases like "moon sister" and "first period party" on Pinterest the week before.

Sarah's my best friend in the whole world, since we were little girls, and I absolutely hate watching Rhodes tear her apart.

Rhodes watches this wordless exchange from her bed with an air of boredom.

I lose track of time running through the myriad things that may or may not cool the burn in Sarah's cheeks: that new horror movie coming out over Thanksgiving weekend she's excited about, the buy-one-get-one sale at the bubble tea place on Richard Arrington Jr. Boulevard, whatever nineties Christian metal band she's ironically-slash-unironically obsessed with this week.

"Oh!" I dig down to the bottom of my bag to retrieve two small, gift-wrapped rectangles. I hand them over, beaming. "Open your birthday present!"

I have the decency to wait to throw Rhodes a look of pure victory until after Sarah turns her attention to the careful task of unwrapping each gift without tearing the paper. Sarah's been my best friend for as long as I can remember, but *this* is also what today is about: a carefully choreographed dance demonstrating each of the eight million ways Rhodes and I are the better friend to her.

Rhodes stares at her nails. She knows me well enough to feign indifference, and I know her well enough to identify that the little twitch in one corner of her generous mouth means she isn't indifferent at all.

Sarah gasps, and holds up a cassette tape with both hands as if it's the Holy Grail. "Antestor! I don't have this one!"

"Lucky you," I say, "apparently somebody dropped off their old cassette tape collection at the flea market last week."

Sarah cries out again as she opens the next. "The Finnegans Wake LP! I've been looking for this everywhere."

"Is there really an entire album named after that God-awful James Joyce book we had to read in Lit Two last block?" Rhodes will never be able to match my gift, and the fact that she categorically refuses to glance up from her hands tells me that she realizes the same thing.

"I loved it." Sarah takes on the snotty, poised mannerisms we've seen in Rhodes more than I ever care to admit. When Sarah does it, it looks more like a little girl clodding around in her mother's heels.

"I read that Joyce wrote the whole thing in six weeks, and for some reason he was proud of the fact that he never changed any of it," Rhodes says.

"I doubt that any of the guys in the Billy Saunter Band ever actually read Joyce, Rhodes." I hope to God this isn't the way the rest of our night will go. "If I remember correctly, *you* didn't even read Joyce for Lit Two."

"I'm pretty sure that was *Ulysses*," Sarah says, as if it matters.

Joyce is a dick. It doesn't matter. I have no idea if she's right.

Rhodes pulls a small, professionally gift-wrapped box from under her pillow. She hands it over to Sarah with a sigh.

A small box that looks like it contains jewelry. My face reddens.

I looked at a few jewelry counters at the flea market for Sarah's gift, too, but I couldn't afford anything she would have actually liked. Aesthetic comes with a premium, apparently.

A moment of something soft passes between them.

I don't like how it makes me feel.

It's so easy to forget that their friendship is a real, live thing.

I can't watch anymore.

My phone suddenly becomes a heck of a lot more interesting.

To my relief, a single tweet of a bird signifies a notification from the fan fiction website Slash/Spot, an old-as-the-world fandom data-

7

base from which every queer ship pairing has set sail since the early days of Harry/Draco. The website itself is some kind of web 2.0 relic—the header looks like someone's mom made it in Microsoft Word, and the color scheme reminds me more of a doctor's waiting room decor than any of the professionally developed branding you see in higher-budgeted corners of the internet.

Normally this is a small detail that would bug me enough to deter me from ever using it.

But I came to understand what it meant to be queer on Slash/Spot long before I understood what that meant to my own identity, and who I would love, and the person I would ultimately grow into—someone I'm *still* growing into.

"Look!" Sarah whacks me on the arm. She holds a plastic rectangular cartridge out to me in her palm. "It's a guitar pick punch!"

"Yeah!" Rhodes says, beaming. "I found it at a record store the last time I went home. You can even use it on old records."

"Awesome," I say.

Rhodes doesn't know that Sarah sold her bass guitar at the beginning of the school year to cover her share of the school's required art supplies. The thought either hasn't occurred to Sarah yet, or she doesn't want to tell Rhodes her gift is functionally useless until Sarah saves up to buy another one.

My attention goes back to my phone.

There's a notification at the top of the page: user I-Kissed-Alice has shared a document with me. If there were a time on Slash/Spot before I-Kissed-Alice—Alice, as I call her, and she calls me Cheshire after my own username—I don't remember it. There was no life before Slash/Spot, and the rest of it barely mattered before I met Alice.

It's not just *any* document, though: She's sent back the script that will be the next installment of our Alice in Wonderland fan fiction comic, complete with in-line notes and a few sketches for me to check before she starts laying out the panels.

I curl up into the headboard and position my phone so neither Rhodes nor Sarah can see.

This is a part of my world no one knows about, and Alice is at the center of it.

I want to be alone with my thoughts, and with Alice's beautiful words.

When I see my Alice's incredible pencil sketches of the Red Queen falling in love with her Alice, I want to pretend it's actually *us* falling in love. Maybe it isn't pretending at all.

With a flick of a thumb, the direct messages feature appears on my screen. My chat with Alice is at the top.

Curious-in-Cheshire 3:41p: Incredible.

I hit send. I'm not finished gushing.

Curious-in-Cheshire 3:42p: This is even better than I could have imagined.

Curious-in-Cheshire 3:42p: I won't be home tonight, but let's talk tomorrow, okay?

Alice isn't online, so there is no answer.

Sometimes she'll pop online a second or two after I message her, but she doesn't this time.

With an overdramatic *swoosh*, Rhodes swings her long legs over the side of the bed and pushes herself to standing. "If we want to get dinner before we go out tonight, we should probably get going."

She doesn't wait to see if we're following her. One minute she's standing in the middle of the dorm room, and the next the door is slamming behind her and she's already halfway down the hall with her eyes on her phone.

"You sure you want to do this?" I ask Sarah, who remains frozen in her spot on the bed next to me.

Sarah flicks at her septum ring with one chipped black thumbnail. "You're both my best friends. I don't want to think about my birthday without either of you."

I hand Sarah her dad's Walkman cassette player—the small, simple connection between Sarah and her obsession with terrible music from the nineties. With a quiet glance at the door, Sarah takes a second to pop the Antestor cassette into the cradle before she clips it onto her hip.

I'm the first to march to the door. Sarah's reflection in the closet door mirror breaks my heart: She rubs her face with both hands and swipes under her lower lashes with her middle fingers to tidy the liner rimming her eyes. Her shoulders tug toward the floor, and with a frown, she grabs her keys from on top of the microwave to lock their dorm room door behind us. When my phone finally pings again with a Slash/Spot notification on the way to the car, I'm in no position to answer it.

CHAPTER 2

RHODES

We all have that one friend we make poor choices with, one who gives you permission to leave your problems in the rearview mirror and only focus on what's in front of you. The kind that wouldn't know a good decision if it slapped her in the face, that pulls you into her vortex of weird ideas, and family drama, and cassette tapes of nineties Christian metal bands because they're the only topic she and her dad know how to talk about.

She's my roommate and my "manic pixie dream girl."

It isn't flattering for either of us to admit I think of her that way, even if it's only a 99 percent *platonic* MPDG situation and I'm not *actually* objectifying anyone.

But still: I know it.

She knows it.

And I also know that tonight I chipped off a little piece of her "manic pixie dream girl" heart earlier. I don't know why I did it. I don't know why I act that way, and I don't know why I lash out at her when it's Iliana I hate, and I don't know what I'm doing here tonight at all.

I don't deserve to be her friend, and I wish she would have just done what I feel like she probably wanted to do (and the thing I know Iliana would have wanted): to tell me to stay home.

Sarah's eyes are rimmed in heavy black liner that screams against her pale skin, and she seems to have largely forgotten about our three-way suckfest back in the dorms before dinner. She's a peroxide-bleached blur in the dark, running and laughing with the handles of painter's buckets swung over each arm, her dad's red-and-blue flannel button-down billowing behind her with each blast of chilly autumn wind. Iliana Vrionides's short legs pump twice as fast to get her half as far as the rest of us, and her body practically vibrates with tension: Her shoulders are tense, and her hands are balled where they swing at her sides. She's Venus of Willendorf, short and strong and feminine in shredded jeans and a shirt that reads "unapologetically fat." Ninety-seven percent humidity has given her honeyed curls sentience.

I don't need to be Iliana's friend anymore to know what she's thinking: *Not again.*

She's eighteen now, and trouble will stay with her forever.

On the other side of the fence, crowds press into metal bleachers, against concession stands, through parking lots. The sky is as wide as it is dark over our heads, spangled with stars, like diamonds scattered in blue velvet. A perfect night for a high school football game—even if neither football team belongs to the Conservatory, since we don't have one at all.

This is the song of the South: cheerleaders chanting, trumpets blaring, and a referee's whistle punctuating another down.

It's Sarah's birthday, and it's homecoming at the high school Sarah—and Iliana—left after their freshman year for higher ground where we all go to school now, the Alabama Conservatory of the Arts and Technology. According to Sarah, Iliana left Victory Hills High School like she leaves everything else: scorched earth, dousing every bridge with gasoline, and dropping matches on her way out. Sarah told me once that she doesn't know which came first: Iliana hating, or being hated.

Sarah's experience was different, and tonight feels more like catharsis than birthday shenanigans.

"Rhodes!" Sarah calls to me from the field house. "We're going to get caught! Come *on*!"

Iliana is a smaller shadow to Sarah's left, stooped with her hands pressed into the tops of her thighs and panting. I fast-walk to keep up, but the very thought of running is exhausting on an existential level.

My therapist likes to tell me there are two kinds of exhaustion: one for your body and one for your soul. I like to tell her she's full of crap—I'm just *tired*.

I don't care where my exhaustion comes from. I want to go home. I want to work on the next update for my Alice in Wonderland fan fiction comic, *Hearts and Spades*. I want to spend the night talking with Cheshire—my coauthor—about everything and nothing. I don't feel much these days, but I *ache* for this.

"This is a terrible idea, Sarah—" Iliana's nasal-heavy voice carries down the hill. "I can't—"

When I finally reach the top, Sarah is squatting with both buckets positioned in front of her, and Iliana's stooping over the top of Sarah's head. The field house is spectacularly unspectacular as far as school architecture goes: It's cinder blocks on four sides, built like a little LEGO house complete with rusted metal doors. At the bottom of the hill, the game continues.

The first bars of "Dirt Road Anthem" echo up from where the football field recesses into the valley below. A glance at the scoreboard, and we have five minutes of play before halftime—more like fifteen, given the fact that both teams are playing dirty and the referee's throwing penalty flags approximately every eleven seconds.

Sarah pries the lids off the painter's buckets and pulls a paint roller for each of us from the bag slung over her shoulder.

"We're going to get arrested," Iliana says.

Her lips are pressed together, and her brows are high on her forehead, and everything about her is the fly in this night's chardonnay. Her eyes shift to me, then to the thin, rectangular profile of my phone in my front pocket.

"Good thing your brother's an attorney," Sarah says. Iliana makes a face.

It wouldn't be the first time Iliana's oldest brother has gotten any of us out of hot water.

I wish I'd thought of the barb first.

Instead, I dutifully take the roller from Sarah's hand. Our eyes meet.

That thing between us—the wildness in her and the numbness in me—finds where it puzzles together, and before I know it, her grin spreads across my face. I grab a handful of the stuff that sloshes in the bucket and sling it into Sarah's hair; she lets out a shriek of a laugh and dumps a handful of the slimy substance down the front of my shirt. Iliana and Sarah share eye contact for the slightest of moments, Sarah grinning and Iliana frowning, but after a split second Sarah slings the substance onto the wall instead.

"What *is* this?!" I yelp, pawing at my cheeks and squinting in the dark for a better view of the grit that covers my hands.

"It's, like, blended-up moss," Sarah says, dipping the roller into the mixture. She applies it to the cinder blocks, instead of me, this time. "And liquid fertilizer."

I follow suit, rolling behind her. Sarah begins painting on the petals of a flower, and suddenly the side of the field house isn't a wall anymore—it's a blank canvas. "So I guess it will grow back as . . . moss?"

"I included some little wildflower seeds, too." Sarah's grin is wicked.

"They'll just pressure-wash it off," Iliana says. After a moment, she dips her own roller into the mixture. "If you're going to commit a felony, it should at least be somewhat permanent."

"It's not a felony, grandma," Sarah says, grinning.

Whatever is happening between them is over as soon as it starts.

Some people would just want to do dinner and a slice of birthday cake at Olexa's Bakery, but not Sarah. She needs to do something bigger and more ridiculous.

"My dad and Principal Hoffman go to the same Masonic temple," Sarah says. She turns to Iliana, frowning, and rests her hands on her hips. "He wouldn't press charges; I'd just come wash it all off. Chill out, all right? You're harshing my mellow."

"Who *says* that?" Iliana snaps.

"I just did, obviously."

Iliana sneers, and paints the illusion of a cat around the wide smile.

"We should make this Alice in Wonderland themed," Iliana says. "Flowers growing out of the walls feels very *Alice*."

It's my turn to sneer.

Alice in Wonderland belongs to *me*.

My laptop is completely covered in Alice in Wonderland stickers—Tenniel's original illustrations, and Disney's Alice, and even Mia Wasikowska bearing the White Queen's suit of armor.

Ever since I was little, the idea of being able to shrink down to the size of a thimble and enter an entirely different world—no matter how wild or wonderful it would be—has always been tantalizing. As a child, the stories meant escape—escaping my mother, escaping my problems, escaping myself. The thought of Wasikowska's delicate, lovely Alice bearing the vorpal sword has always given me strength.

It was Wasikowska's Alice that inspired *my* Alice in the fan comic I coauthor. Curious-in-Cheshire—my partner in crime—loves this version of Alice, too. She says she sees this version of Alice in me and reminds me almost daily that being brave simply means doing the hard thing—even if you're terrified.

I don't know if she's right, but I want her to be.

All of this is a universe that Iliana doesn't belong in—a wonderland of its own kind, with no tiny bottles of potion at hand to usher her in through its tiny doors. No one can stop her from enjoying it, but it doesn't exist for her like it does for Cheshire and me.

No, Alice in Wonderland doesn't exist for Iliana—not at all.

"No, I want to write something." Sarah swipes through Iliana's cat with one hand. "I don't want it to be just a picture."

"Guys! We don't have time!" Iliana gestures to the board. When she turns back to face us, her words are for me. "We have, like, two minutes of play left."

Iliana whirls on me. "Rhodes. Just *draw* something! Jesus!"

Draw something.

Draw something.

The easiest thing on the planet, right? Wrong.

I've been screaming at myself to *just draw something* for days. Weeks. Months.

The blankness of the wall itself is an assault, and the only kindness is that the sky is too dark for the burn in my cheeks to be known by anyone but me.

Draw something. Draw something. Draw something.

Just a week ago, I was standing in the back of the auditorium balcony, and the students crammed around the stage could be one hundred miles away. Like the rest of campus, it's the sort of place built specifically to photograph incredibly for the school's promotional literature with no actual consideration for basic human comfort: Everything is a variation of the color "oatmeal." Beige walls; pops of an earthen green in the curtains and chair upholstery. Ugly backless benches under our bottoms and hardwood floors gleam under our feet.

"The Capstone exists as a stepping stone for the best and brightest in the Southeast," June Baker said from the stage, a withered frame hidden under layers of pastel cashmere, "a rite of passage for young people who exhibit the kind of artistic excellence that has become synonymous with who we are as the Ocoee Arts Festival."

June, who sent me a card and a sweet little painting for my eighteenth birthday, has been a juror for every Ocoee Arts Festival ribbon I've won since my first time in the show as a nervous thirteen-year-old. I know her money's on me for the Capstone, and I know it's something she's focused her energy on because she considers my success a reflection on her insight as a mentor and a member of the board.

"As an extension of the Ocoee Arts Festival, the Capstone Foundation Award is more than a scholarship: It's a yearlong seat on the board of directors, a guaranteed placement at Alabama College of Art and Design, and a yearlong fellowship with the Birmingham Museum of Art following graduation. It's a bedrock for a résumé, and exposure. The first step of the rest of one fortunate student's life as a career artist."

The Capstone was supposed to be my birthright, but instead it's the final nail in a coffin I never thought I'd build myself.

"The award season will take place in three parts, starting with an essay declaring intent, due November first. Those who are selected in the essay round will be invited to participate in a public project proposal on December seventh. Students whose projects are selected by jury will compete in a final show on December twentieth, where a winner will be awarded on-site." June smiled and adjusted her glasses on the bridge of her nose. "The requirements are simple, as we do not wish to stand as a barrier for students in need: a grade point average of three-point-seven or higher and a record in good standing with your educational institution."

Three-point-oh would be a reach. Three-point-five, a pipe dream.

Three-point-seven, a snowball's chance in hell.

Besides, what would I do if I could make it in?

It's not like I've painted or drawn anything new since the last Ocoee Arts Festival.

I don't think I even know how to do that anymore.

Draw something. Draw something. Draw something.

I'm irreparably broken—my brain, my hands, my heart—and no one knows it.

Or maybe *everyone* knows it, and this is all some cruel machination for Iliana to make me feel like crap. Both are possible.

"Oh, give me a break." Iliana's grumbling is barely audible over the sound of the band warming up just off the field—the football game continues, but the percussion line sounds like a warning call that halftime is around the corner. She swipes a broad, arching vertical stroke upward. Then another, perfectly complementary, creating a long, rounded teardrop.

"*Iliana!*" Sarah claps her hand over her mouth.

"I don't—" I cross my arms, red-faced again.

This time, it's an inside joke I'm clearly not meant to understand.

Iliana adds a second shape inside the first that looks like a rosebud, with its petals pressed together. By now, the two girls are laughing riotously—loud enough to get us caught—and I feel like crying all over again. I drop my roller into one of the buckets.

She swipes a small circle into the highest point of the—*flower? Fruit? Some combination of both?*—and Sarah is hunched over, crylaughing.

"*Rhodes!*" Sarah cries out. "You don't know what you're looking at?!"

I want to get in the car and go home. This is terrible—*everything is terrible*—and I should have never let Sarah convince me that the three of us could spend the night together without *somebody* getting hurt. I *would* get in the car and go back to campus, except I drove us here. Even if I'd strand Iliana without batting an eyelash, I can't do it to Sarah, so I'm stuck.

"Tell us what you think it is," Iliana says.

Her grin is the Cheshire Cat's, brilliant white against the dark. As soon as the thought hits me, I strike it away. It's sacrilege to think of the Cheshire Cat—not to mention, *my* Curious-in-Cheshire—and Iliana at the same time.

"No."

"Oh, come on, Rho," Iliana says. "It's okay. It's funny. I just want to know what you think it is."

"Don't call me that," I say. "That nickname's not for you."

I would give anything to be Iliana right now. If the shoe were on the other foot, and if it were Sarah and somehow me making Iliana feel like this, she'd have laid us all to shreds. She'd raise her sharp brows and bare her sharp teeth, and in a matter of a dozen words, we'd both be crying. And with a toss of all that wild, curly hair, she'd march off without so much as a look behind her.

But I'm not Iliana. I'm me, and I'm terrible at this sort of thing.

"It's a mango," I say.

"Well, apparently, this will be educational for you *and* the entire Victory Hills athletic program," Iliana says. With her hands, she swipes an arrow pointing to the small circle at the top of the teardrop-flower-fruit.

In wide, crude letters, she writes:

NEWSFLASH:
THIS!
IS!
A!
CLITORIS!

Oh.

The moment reframes itself, and I'm embarrassed again, for entirely different reasons.

"I knew that," I mumble, but the girls are lost to giggling again.

It's not so much that I've never heard of one before. Sarah told me once that Iliana has been with a lot of girls—well, not *a lot* a lot, but more than Sarah, who has never actually disclosed her number but strongly implied that she's had sex more than a few times—and I've physically been with exactly *zero*.

I mean, I've kissed girls. But I've never actually *seen* a clitoris that belonged to someone else, and I've never been brave enough to use a mirror to take a look at my own.

Not to mention—in my family, sex isn't something we talk about at *all*.

I don't know how to even begin talking about it so casually; a part of me wishes I could. The rest of me still squirms with discomfort.

The announcer's voice echoes up to us, declaring the end of the first half. The score is tied, the air is thick with tension, and an entire platoon of shiny helmets and shoulder pads are marching toward the backfield gates below. With a shriek, Sarah and Iliana slap the lids onto their buckets and toss the rollers into the woods.

We're running again—this time the long way across the back of the field and out toward the parking lot.

I have no idea if the girls are going to remember tonight five years from now, or what they did, or what I said. It's hard to know where my thoughts ended and the stuff that came out of my mouth began—only that everything felt personal, and then it wasn't, and that I didn't know something, and everybody else did.

I pull out my phone when we get back to the car, and while Iliana and Sarah are loading the trunk, I get in and swipe past eight bajillion notifications to open where a Slash/Spot shortcut is saved to my home screen. I have an entire afternoon's worth of direct messages waiting on my phone.

The relief is so palpable, I could cry with it.

Cheshire knows me. She knows my heart, and she knows that these kinds of conversations terrify me, and she doesn't judge me for any of it. It's okay that I've never been with anyone. It's okay that I'm still a little bit afraid of how everything works.

It's okay that I don't want to talk about it until I do.

And when I *am* ready, when I'm burning with want for her, she's always ready to catch me. I open the direct message feature on my phone and reread Cheshire's messages from earlier:

    Curious-in-Cheshire 3:41p: Incredible.

    Curious-in-Cheshire 3:42p: This is even better than I could have imagined.

She loved my concept sketches for our next *Hearts and Spades* update.

I could cry with relief—this is the only thing I have left. The only piece of my creativity I have left that isn't broken.

It's also the only thing I won't let anyone else in the world see.

Iliana's and Sarah's voices are echoing through the windows from outside the car. I don't know what they're laughing about, and I don't really care—of course I care, I hate being left out of anything—but I hurry to fire back a response before I lose my phone for the rest of the night.

    I-Kissed-Alice 8:41p: yes, tomorrow <3 let's go over the script one more time after you get off work, okay?

"Let us in!" Sarah yanks on the handle of the locked passenger-side door. Iliana is propped against the car behind her, eternally uninvested in Sarah's plight.

My heart is wild in my ears.

All I want is to curl up next to Cheshire and listen to all of her theorizing face-to-face, find some kind of a keyhole I could squeeze through into another life and another world where anonymity and distance doesn't separate us. Sometimes I'm afraid that all she sees of me is a computer screen—to me she's real, and she's perfect. She's all I've ever wanted.

But I belong to Sarah tonight—not Cheshire—so I allow myself one last message before I put my phone away for good.

I-Kissed-Alice 8:42p: I have to go. More soon. <3

With a kiss popped onto my darkened phone screen, I throw the thing into the console and unlock the car doors.

"Petty much?!" Sarah shrieks when she falls face-first into the front seat. "Jesus Christ on a cracker, it got chilly fast."

In the rearview mirror, I catch Iliana glowering at the seat warmer controls.

"Don't use the Lord's name in vain, Sarah," Iliana snips. She squints at the numbers on my dashboard. "Besides, it's just sixty-seven degrees. It's only *comparatively colder* than it was before the sun went down."

I turn on the radio, and Sarah turns it off. We ride back to Sarah's house in utter silence.

The car may be quiet, but tension screams in the air around us.

Comment 11: **I-Kissed-Alice** 11:43p: OH MY GOOOOOD.

Comment 12: **I-Kissed-Alice** 11:43p: You literally lifted that word for word from our direct messages the other night

Comment 13: **Curious-in-Cheshire** 12:15a: Are you ok? Was I not supposed to use that? You didn't say . . .

Comment 14: **I-Kissed-Alice** 12:15a: It's fine. It's perfect.

Comment 15: **I-Kissed-Alice** 12:15a: I'll be in my bunk

I-Kissed-Alice 5:42a: last night was a nightmare

Curious-in-Cheshire 5:42a: it's in the water, apparently

I-Kissed-Alice 5:42a: you too??? Jesus Christ, what gives?

Curious-in-Cheshire 5:43a: you know the saying, "you don't pick your family"?

I-Kissed-Alice 5:43a: yup

Curious-in-Cheshire 5:43a: you ever feel like you don't pick your friends, either?

I-Kissed-Alice 5:44a: all the fucking time

I-Kissed-Alice 5:44a: wait why are you up so early

Curious-in-Cheshire 5:44a: work.

Curious-in-Cheshire 5:44a: why are *YOU* up so early

I-Kissed-Alice 5:46a: I snuck out for my therapy appointment because I didn't want interested parties to know what I was doing. So.

Curious-in-Cheshire 5:46a: therapy isn't until eight, I thought.

I-Kissed-Alice 5:46a: mom likes to grab breakfast first

Curious-in-Cheshire 5:47a: ah. Well tell your therapist I said hello.

I-Kissed-Alice 5:47a: tell your boss I said to suck it

Curious-in-Cheshire 5:47a: xoxo

CHAPTER 3
ILIANA

Username: Curious-in-Cheshire
Last online: 3h ago

It was the end of our junior year when everything between Rhodes and me came to be as it is now.

It was May, and we were at a pop-up installation on the edge of campus. Clouds of heavy, weed-scented smoke hung up around the light fixtures of an old gas station with bars on the windows, and rain was falling in through a spot where the roof had caved, leaving puddles on the dirty tiled floor.

Behind each ancient cooler door was an installation: women with tape over their mouths. Women with their hands bound. Women dressed like schoolgirls, and dressed like moms, and dressed like frumpy old ladies with curlers in their hair. There was a gas station attendant behind the dilapidated old counter, a girl barely older than us with shiny red lip gloss and breasts begging to escape from a Playboy Bunny costume. Word around campus was that participants had to be eighteen so they could sign the liability waiver provided by the lead artist.

Men wandered from one cooler to the next, shopping quietly, selecting someone to take with them along with six-packs of beer and packs of beef jerky.

Rhodes and I had become friends, sort of.

We weren't talk-on-the-phone friends, or even text-on-occasion friends.

But Sarah had been my best friend since the third grade, and Sarah and Rhodes had become completely symbiotic during their first and second years as roommates at the Conservatory. It had taken weeks of begging for Sarah to even suggest to Rhodes that I come along—no matter what I did, Rhodes thought my work was "pedestrian."

She didn't think I'd understand the show—called *Quickies at the Kwickee Mart*, clever them—or that the art installation would speak to me the way it spoke to her and Sarah.

But by some force of nature, *I* had been the one to win a scholarship at the Savannah College of Art and Design only a week before. My art wasn't an existential crisis played out with paint and canvas, and it didn't make any grand political statements, but it was going to pay for my college—and apparently it meant I was allowed to play with the big girls now. Only two days later, Rhodes invited me along herself.

A week after that, we stood side by side, stoned beyond belief and attempting to make sense of the little theater that played out in front of us. Some of the girls in the cases were seniors at the Conservatory, and I knew about half of the people standing around us from campus as well. The rest were unimaginably sophisticated, worldly looking artist types—people with ink-stained hands and tattoos that crept up from under the collars of their shirts and onto their necks.

If my perception hadn't been *completely* altered, I would have thought to be a little embarrassed by my own clothing choices. I felt so *metal* sneaking out in my tattered-on-purpose Slipknot T-shirt and my tattered-on-purpose acid-washed shorts and my tattered-on-purpose pink-and-white-striped tights.

"It's, like, feminism—" Rhodes said.

Her brows were knit together; her cogs were turning.

She didn't understand. I didn't want to tell her otherwise, to ruin the night like I always do. It wasn't enough to say it was about "like, feminism." Anything can be about feminism, because in everything there's an imbalance of power. There will always be one person in the room that has more privilege than the rest, and that person is almost *always* an Ingram.

It didn't surprise me that Rhodes didn't understand then, and it doesn't now—she doesn't really know what it means to be a little further down the food chain than everyone else. I'm not much further down than she is—I'm just as white, Christian-adjacent, abled, and straight-passing as she is—but I'm *aware* of it.

"Yeah, just, you know—" Sarah's pupils were blown out. She held on to me for dear life, the way Rhodes's barely younger brother and then-dance-track student, Griffin, clung to Rhodes's arm. Sarah liked Griffin then—she was infatuated, really. I think she thought he'd be an easy segue into being a fixture in Rhodes's life forever.

She thought wrong.

"The motherfucking patriarchy," said Griffin.

The motherfucking patriarchy. As if that phrase in and of itself wasn't the purpose of the installation, the fact that women are continuously victims of sexual violence in Western culture, so much so that it has permeated our patterns of speaking and even the way we curse.

Rhodes sighed, and nodded appreciatively.

Sarah sighed, and nodded appreciatively.

Griffin sighed, and nodded appreciatively.

This is art, they communicated, with stoops in their shoulders and ennui-burdened frowns. *This is life.*

This is suffering.

Pot only ever makes me *more* philosophical. Everyone around me was melting into puddles, and I was practically writing ninety-nine theses on third-wave feminism on the back of a fifteen-year-old Kwickee Mart napkin that had been stuck to the bottom of my boot.

Griffin wobbled on Rhodes's left. He was transfixed by the swirling lights against the far wall—reds and whites, then blues.

I stumbled, and then tripped over myself, even though I hadn't taken a step in minutes.

Whatever was in the air was strong, and apparently it was all part of whatever the lead artist was trying to communicate to the audience. It occurred to me in a detached way that maybe I should be afraid I'd be next in the cooler.

Around us, the installation shifted quickly. The women in the coolers broke character, made eye contact with their would-be purchasers. The girl behind the counter turned to whisper to someone dressed in all black, invisible where they stood in a dark corner. People began to scramble, and unbind themselves, and dart for doors that led into back offices and alleyways.

"This is so realistic," Rhodes mused. "I wonder what the shift means."

"This must be the end of the second act," Griffin said. As a dance-track student, he wasn't watching the installation like an artist. He was watching it like a performer.

The pulsing music overhead squealed to a stop, but tinny, familiar sirens continued—a higher pitch than those on a police cruiser, or any kind of emergency response vehicle. It felt like an entire lifetime later that I recognized the sirens from the Conservatory security team's safety vehicle.

"Rhodes." It sounded like my voice was coming from outside my body.

She didn't hear me.

Somewhere on the surface, I was panicking. I knew my stomach should be falling through my butt, and my hands should be shaking, and I should be screaming in the faces of the girls next to me.

There was a Savannah College of Art and Design scholarship with my name on it, and the ink had barely dried. It had been the kind of *deus ex machina* blessing that only happens in the movies and never to the people who need it in reality—people like me, whose parents were filing for bankruptcy literally the same day as the scholarship winners were announced.

This couldn't be happening.

To my right, Rhodes and Griffin had disappeared. Sarah was gone, too, and when I ran out the front doors of the old gas station, their car was empty. They left me. All that was left was the panicked-looking Conservatory security officer blocking my view of the parking lot.

From that moment on, everything was different.

Sylvia's Diner has always been exactly what it sounds like.

Everything is oak veneer. *Everything.* The walls, the ceiling, the Formica countertops, the fronts to the refrigerators and stove.

Every. Thing.

The menu is relatively small, and half of the items are sold out in perpetuity because Sylvia (the woman who owns the place) refuses to order the random ingredients she needs for us to throw it together. None of us have food permits, and the only reason the health board hasn't shut us down is because they like Sylvia's sweet potato pie too much.

Sarah and I have been working here since the summer before we transferred to the Conservatory, and in two years *nothing* has changed—even if everything else in our lives *has*.

"You can't hate Rhodes forever," Sarah says, for what feels like the eight millionth time. "You didn't hate *me* forever, so I know you've got it in you."

She turns to check her lipstick in the microwave door behind her, a shade of magenta-purple rendered ungodly against her ashy-pale skin. "It wasn't on purpose—you were behind us, and then you weren't. Her parents paid your legal fees. Are they supposed to pay for your college, too?"

I don't want to answer her.

She isn't wrong—I *did* forgive Sarah.

I know Sarah wouldn't have left me behind on purpose.

But Rhodes has been trying to get rid of me for as long as she and Sarah have been friends, and I really have a hard time believing that Rhodes was innocent, too. It would have been too convenient for her if the Conservatory had succeeded in kicking me out.

And plus? I just don't like her.

I don't *want* to like her.

I don't want to forgive her, because I don't care about my relationship with her.

"Tubes of lipstick aren't lollipops. You aren't supposed to suck on it." I poke her cheek, and she swipes the extra lipstick off her teeth with the hem of her apron. I don't say this to her, but I'm *so pissed* she's even talking about this right now.

This morning before work was such a weird, delicate thing—we found Rhodes getting ready to dash out the front door at 6:30, mumbling something about chores and darting off to where Griffin was idling at the curb before we could ask any questions.

33

Sarah was desperately hurt.

I couldn't decide if I was angry for Sarah or happy for myself.

The rest of the morning has been a gauntlet of keeping Sarah's spirits up—we painted each other's nails before we left the house this morning, and I promised that we'd give each other DIY facials and pedicures after work. We're going to back to my place, where my mom will be babysitting my little nieces and have a tea party.

We're going to listen to Sarah's God-awful new music as much as she wants.

I was already exhausted from all the planning by the time we got to work, and yet Sarah was *still* defending Rhodes's honor.

"*You* can suck on it." She slides me a smile, then turns to open the dishwasher seconds before it starts to beep.

Behind us, an old man sitting at the counter chokes on his country fried steak. His eyes drift downward—down, down, down—and rest on Sarah's ass as she bends to pull the dishwasher basket out to heft it onto the prep counter against the wall.

The man still has his fork in his hand when I swipe his half-full plate and chuck it into the sink.

"Hope you enjoyed your meal." I stare at him with as much fire as I can muster, and it takes exactly three seconds for him to lift his eyes from Sarah's ass to my face.

Pervert.

I don't say it out loud, but I think it loud enough that it drips from my words.

I smack his receipt onto the counter and turn my attention to Sarah next to me. "How did you even know I was thinking about Rhodes?"

"Because you get this look in your eyes whenever you think about her," Sarah says, oblivious. She wipes one coffee mug after the next with a damp washcloth. It's already wet, so it's doing nothing to wick the condensation from the mugs before she stacks them one at a time on the shelf over our heads. "It looks like you're thinking about murder."

"Maybe I am," I say.

The man and I are nothing but eye contact now—him with his mouth opening and closing like a goldfish, me with my hands on my hips and swelling to every centimeter of five whole feet tall. He's eavesdropping on our conversation, and he deflates a little.

The man tosses a five and two ones on the table, then a dime and three pennies.

Exact change. He stands, placing an old black-and-white houndstooth fedora on top of his head before he turns for the door.

"Hey!" I call after him, "Are you tipping or not?"

"I didn't finish my dinner. Ain't nothin' to tip, young lady."

"We've gotta eat around here!" I shriek. He's the only one in the restaurant right now, so it only serves to rattle the dusty blinds that hang over the windows. "You old bastard!"

The tip wouldn't have been mine. It would have been Sarah's, if she hadn't forgotten about him in favor of clean dishes. But still, she's been buying her own toothpaste lately. If she doesn't get tipped because of *my* mouth—and the loss of his dinner—I won't forgive myself for the rest of the night.

"Here's your tip, sweetheart—" he says with a flourish. "Do something about that attitude."

I throw him a short, pudgy middle finger. The sleigh bells clattering against the glass are a cry for help when the front door crashes back into the frame, and the man disappears into his crusty old Buick.

"His check was, what, seven bucks? Eight? It doesn't matter." Sarah turns to lean against the counter, frowning. "I'm gonna live another day without a dollar-fifty."

The frustration scatters over my skin like electricity. "It's the principle of the matter—"

"'The principle of the matter' doesn't matter," Sarah says. Her palms are warm and moist when she presses them against my cheeks, and she says it again: "*The principle. Of the matter. Doesn't matter.*"

This isn't just about the old man with the money. I *know* what she's saying to me:

Please, for the love of God, *let it go.*

Let Rhodes go. Let the past go.

Let. It. Go.

"You can't keep making everything about . . . *her*," I say, and bat her hands away from my face. She blinks once, twice, then returns to the dishes.

I don't have to say *her* name; it hangs around my neck like an albatross in perpetuity.

"We don't even have a year left," Sarah says. "It's going to be November soon. We have eight months together, tops. Quit making me split my time."

"I'm not making you split your time." It's easier to have this conversation without looking at Sarah, so I turn my back to sling a bleach-soaked washcloth up onto the counter. I work at where I imagine the man's fingerprints to be, as if I'm clearing a crime scene. "I'm making you *choose*."

"Choose. *Really?*" I don't need eyes in the back of my head to know she's scoffing at me. "She's my roommate, I can't just—"

"I got fucking arrested, Sarah! I lost my scholarship because of her! You can *absolutely* ask the school for a new roommate."

It's the right thing to do.

It had been less than forty-eight hours since The Incident the first time I said it when Sarah showed up on my front porch crying off her eye makeup onto her hands as if we were all equally victim to some great existential plight. She'd been grounded for the rest of the school year and the entirety of the summer; Rhodes's family had gone radio silent, and rumor had it both Rhodes and Griffin were being shipped off to one of those high-end rehabilitation centers set up in a McMansion with a live-in caterer the minute classes were over.

They all managed to get away, and the worst of their problems was dealing with their parents.

I hadn't heard from the Savannah College of Art and Design yet, but I knew the other shoe would eventually drop: They'd read about it in the newspaper, or the school would be required to inform them, or someone would read about it on social media and tip them off. My parents wouldn't take my computer away because I used it for homework, but I spent the entire summer on house arrest.

Rhodes, Griffin, and Sarah left me behind, and I had the most to lose.

I don't like the way Sarah watches me as if I'm about to rip her face off. I don't like this conversation, and I don't like the fact that by *not* choosing, she's making a decision every day to choose someone, the very person who hurt me.

"She doesn't choose you, you know." I snatch off my apron and toss it onto the counter. My shift doesn't end for an hour, but I can't stand to look at her anymore. Dad's supposed to come get me, but I think I'd rather walk home. "Do you *really* think her mom needed her help cleaning out the garage at 6:30 this morning? Why did *Griffin* come get her? Why didn't he stay—aren't y'all 'besties'?"

"You're just jealous, okay?!" Sarah's voice echoes off the walls, and her face goes from ghostly white to fire-engine red. "You're *jealous*. You've always wanted to be friends with her—"

"I've *never* wanted to be friends with her—"

"And I honestly think it blows your mind that she'd choose *me* and not *you*."

"Fuck off, Sarah." I march exactly ten paces to the ancient punch clock that hangs on the wall, snatch my card from the top, and slam it into the slot. The date and time prints across the card with a satisfying *cha-chink*, and I drop it back into the metal organizer that hangs by the old rotary phone I have no idea how to use. "You can fuck right off with that. I have *never* wanted—"

"You know why I still choose Rhodes?" Her eyes are the brightest topaz-honey-hazel I've ever seen, smudged with dark eyeliner spilling over to stain her cheeks. "Because *she* doesn't ask me to choose anyone."

"She doesn't think she did anything wrong," I say. I plant two hands on the counter and hoist myself over.

"That makes two of us," Sarah says.

It'll be an hour before Dad's idling in the parking lot to pick me up from my shift.

Hell will freeze over before I call and actually *admit* to him that I left work early over an argument with Sarah. I already know exactly what he would say: *Vrionideses are known for their work ethic! You have to think of the name you're making for yourself.*

Consider what you want people to think when others speak of you.

Think of the way I've worked to establish a name for this family, too, and ask yourself if you're adding to my work or taking away from it.

I shove earbuds into my ears and crank up the music on my phone as loud as it will go, in hopes that it will drown out the guilt clawing at my subconscious.

The boulevard that stretches in front of Sylvia's bustles with activity in both directions; the sky overhead feels low enough to touch, with clouds threatening rain, snuffing out what's left of the light with sunset around the corner.

Two by two, streetlights flicker on and a cool, resin-scented breeze tosses the curls around my face. It's going to rain soon.

I have an hour alone—Dad thinks I'm working, and Sarah won't have the nerve to come hunt me down for another day at least. I might as well be invisible, and the thought is *delicious*.

One hour in the back of a coffee shop with *Hearts and Spades* is more than I could ever ask for. The one on the corner—a sedate, locally owned place that's been around since the nineties—is perfect.

I duck inside just before the first drops of rain hit the sidewalk.

With a swipe and a tap of my thumb, the Slash/Spot app—and Alice—is waiting and ready.

Before I know it, I'm pouring my heart through the screen and out into the stratosphere.

I-Kissed-Alice 11:22a: I posted H&S update 48 before I left for therapy this morning

Curious-in-Cheshire 6:18p: I don't know what's fucking wrong with me

I-Kissed-Alice 6:18p: hello to you too

Curious-in-Cheshire 6:19p: hey. sorry.

Curious-in-Cheshire 6:19p: Every time I work with bff, it turns into an argument

I-Kissed-Alice 6:19p: oh. uh oh. What happened

Curious-in-Cheshire 6:19p: we argued

I-Kissed-Alice 6:19p: don't get tart with me

Curious-in-Cheshire 6:20p: sorry.

Curious-in-Cheshire 6:20p: Just. Like. I should know by now, right? I need to just. Idk. Refuse.

I-Kissed-Alice 6:20p: my therapist always says ~arguments are invitations, but you can decline them~.

I-Kissed-Alice 6:20p: or something.

I-Kissed-Alice 6:21p: idk how the saying goes, but you get my point

Curious-in-Cheshire 6:21p: how has that worked for you

I-Kissed-Alice 6:21p: well, considering the fact that 75% of my problems with people are because I'm too afraid to piss them off to say anything at all, I don't really think that's my issue. But theoretically I think I understand how that could be the case.

I-Kissed-Alice 6:22p: catharsis, and stuff.

Curious-in-Cheshire 6:22p: in the moment, that's all there is: screaming at someone. It's like popping a zit.

I-Kissed-Alice 6:22p: def know about *that* life. There isn't enough Accutane on the planet

Curious-in-Cheshire 6:23p: I should probably text dad and tell him I finished work early. Gotta go.

Curious-in-Cheshire 6:23p: <3

CHAPTER 4

RHODES

Username: I-Kissed-Alice
Last online: 2h ago

According to Instagram, Snapchat, *and* Twitter, Sarah and Iliana's fun didn't begin until long after I left this morning.

There's proof in discreet pics of their matching blue-black DIY manicures with Sylvia's oak-veneered wonderland in the background, and a thousand puppy-face selfies, and videos of Sarah singing along with the music playing over the restaurant speakers in the background.

It shouldn't matter—they're friends in their own right, of course. *I* was the one who left early. But it didn't stop me from spending the entire ride to Atlanta scrolling their feeds, witnessing a version of Sarah I've never met.

It's all beginning to feel intentional.

It makes my bones hurt; it gives me a headache and makes me tired.

The woman who sits across the table from me is the very epitome of a child of the seventies. Graying hair falls in waves past her shoulders, earrings fashioned from feathers hang parallel to her long neck, and a vintage Lilith Fair T-shirt peeks out from under a Very Professional (and Very Out of Character) black blazer with the sleeves rolled to her elbows. She plucks at a banjo during sessions sometimes.

I don't tell Mom that she smells like pot, even if I hate the two-hour drive across state lines to play craft time and talk about my feelings.

She's the best art therapist in the Southeast—or at least that's what her website *heavily* implies. This was more than enough for my mom, who wants the best of everything: cars, clothes, estheticians, and, apparently, even therapists.

Dusk—yes, her name is literally *Dusk*—runs a long needle through the binding of a book in her lap, tugging purple string high up over our heads. It's very much an extension of who she is: a hand-pressed-paper cover in plums, and cranberries, and saffrons with gold leaf sprinkled throughout to catch the light. Inside, the pages are thick, creamy white. I haven't gotten close enough to smell it, but it's probably pot-scented too.

Dusk is supposed to fix me, but it's hard to take anything she says seriously.

She loads her needle with half a dozen iridescent seed beads and runs it through the other side.

Irony of ironies—we're making art journals.

Her logic is that the creativity we pour into making them will manifest itself in the work that fills their pages.

My logic is that creativity doesn't work like that.

Her experience is that creativity ebbs and flows.

My experience is that I haven't lived on this earth long enough to find that out for myself, and I don't have the time to sit and wait for it to reappear on its own.

"What did you decide about the Capstone thing?" Dusk asks. "That scholarship, I mean."

This is the third session she's asked me about the Capstone. I stab a needle into the handmade paper in my lap hard enough to accidentally poke myself in the thigh. I don't curse, but I want to.

"I'm not doing Ocoee," I say.

"Oh?" Her brows hike up.

She presses the needle back through the binding. Another cadre of beads.

"I know what you're thinking—that I'm just giving up," I say.

She glances at me appraisingly. "Is that what I think?"

"I'm *not* giving up." My face is hot. "I just . . . I don't have anything to submit. I used everything from my junior year in the show circuit *last year*. The Capstone won't let you submit something that has medaled in another competition in the last year, so I'd have to create something new."

Might as well ask me to open my veins and bleed gold.

The field house wall from Sarah's birthday stretches in front of me, empty. *Just* draw *something*—like it's ever that effing easy.

It's like everyone around me thinks it's just a matter of me deciding to do it.

Mind over matter!

Quit being lazy, already!

I sling the handmade paper in my lap across the table and fold my arms.

"Tell me what you see right now," she says. She pushes a thick pad of white paper across the table. "Or draw it."

More blank paper.

Blank everything.

I push the pen away, too.

"A wide, blank wall," I say. "Last night, I celebrated my best friend's birthday and—*err*—her best friend came, too, and—"

"Sarah," Dusk offers.

I nod.

"The other is"—she picks up a tablet from her left and swipes up and down, skimming her notes—"Iliana, right?"

"Yeah."

Dusk makes a delicate face. "We talked about seeing Iliana outside of school."

"I couldn't avoid it," I say, back on task. "Anyway, Sarah wanted to moss bomb the field house where she and Iliana went to school before the Conservatory. Things were okay at first—they could definitely have been worse—but then Iliana yelled at me to *just draw something.*' And then it went from this ridiculous, like, prank, to . . . I don't know—"

"Emotional labor," Dusk says. "They're asking something from you, instead of letting you come to it on your own."

It sucks that Dusk was the first person to find the words for whatever this is, but—*yes*.

This feels right, but giving it a name doesn't solve anything.

People will never stop asking for things. If I want to spend my life as an artist, I'll spend my life creating what other people expect of me.

Inevitability doesn't make Dusk any less right, though.

"I couldn't do anything," I say. "Iliana ended up taking over, and, well—"

My face goes hot.

I couldn't identify a perfectly well-drawn clitoris, I would say, if I could find a way to say the word *clitoris* out loud without laughing like a fifth grader. It wasn't long ago I found my own, much less anyone else's.

I don't know how Iliana and Sarah are so effing *casual* about it.

"How did you feel about it?" Dusk scribbles into her tablet with a stylus.

"Clearly, not great," I say. "It was so *blank*, like it was going to suck me in. It was screaming at me, almost. Then Iliana was screaming at me, and Sarah was giving me *that look*—"

"Well, to be completely transparent—" Dusk says. She retrieves her banjo from the floor and plucks out something soft. "Your mom is paying me good money to make the Capstone happen. Extra money. A lot of money."

"Okay." This doesn't surprise me.

The Capstone Award means the world to Mom, and sometimes it seems like Mom doesn't even try to pretend that matters more than what I might actually need to make progress in therapy.

Suffice to say, it's not the first time my mom has been shady with my therapist, but Dusk has always been very open with me about it happening. I don't really understand what Dusk hopes the outcome will be, but at least I know I can expect honesty from exactly one adult in my life.

I hope, anyway.

Dusk's words are soft, and then she bends over the fretboard. Music hangs around us, mellow and plaintive, and I lean back in my chair.

"The Capstone Award isn't just about status, right? It's a yearlong ride at Alabama College of Art and Design. You get a fellowship at the Birmingham Museum of Art. It's an *opportunity*."

"Right." Every conversation I've ever had with Randall hangs like a ghost over my shoulder.

It's an opportunity, but it isn't the only one I have left. Yet.

"What do you think about just . . . doing it? You said it yourself: You'll be creating for other people for the rest of your life." Dusk glances up from her finger-work. "Creating at will is a skill—you won't be able to wait until the mood strikes forever."

You won't be able to wait until the mood strikes forever.

I understand the concept in theory, but I can't wrap my head around it.

Just . . . make something. Pull it out of my God-knows-where and smear it across a canvas for everyone to fawn over.

It would be crap. Literal, actual crap.

People may love it, but at the end of the day, it's still just *crap*.

"The thing I don't understand"—I pick my journal back up from where it lies across the table and run my fingers over its half-finished cover—"is how I *used* to be able to do this exact thing. The world told me to jump, and I'd only ask how high they wanted me to go."

The cover is crafted from a copy of *Alice in Wonderland* that was falling apart on Dusk's bookshelf, embroidered all over with teacups, and keyholes, and a March Hare with long, floppy ears. Alice is only a peach-hued face and half a hair bow at the moment, the rest of her a faint pencil sketch where I want her body to go.

As per usual, this is when Dusk goes quiet.

Her eyes follow my fingers, but I know she's listening close.

"That's why I'm here, right? Because something broke in me, and even if I know the *when* of it, I don't really know the *why*. And the *why* of it is what's going to fix me, right?"

"You can't think about therapy in terms of 'broken' and 'fixed,'" Dusk says. "It's more of a spectrum—surviving to actually thriving, with every little benchmark a success in between."

But that's not why I'm here. *This* is the thing that overrides my system: I need someone to fix me.

I feel like I'm crumbling inside, and Dusk is going to sit here and tell me that being here isn't about being fixed?

Why the heck is she wasting our time?!

"Don't look at me like that," Dusk says, smiling.

"I just can't believe, after everything we've talked about today, you're *asking* me to do something. To create something. For the sake of making someone else happy." It all jumbles out of me butt over kettle. My cheeks splotch and I swallow what's left of my anger. "Even if you're going to pick apart the semantics over *broken* and *fixed* and *surviving* and *thriving*, I *just* told you how much it hurt me when someone else did the exact same thing twenty-four hours ago."

"Rhodes, listen to me: I'm asking you to evaluate all of these high and lofty ideas you have about art, and I'm *telling* you to think about what it is you *actually* need right now—another chance—and whether it's worth milking the cow one more time in the name of going on with the rest of your life."

We blink across the table at each other.

I may have swallowed what was left of my anger, but it never actually left me—everything roils in my chest, wild and burning, and I honestly cannot believe this wannabe Joni Mitchell is telling me to sacrifice the very heart and soul of my work in the name of *money*.

Without a word, I hand my half-constructed journal across the table one last time.

Dusk holds it in both of her hands as if it's something precious.

"Follow the White Rabbit," it says across the bottom.

"I'd love for you to tell me more about your Alice thing sometime," Dusk says.

Embarrassment comes over me suddenly—painfully—and I don't really have the words to explain what it *is* exactly I'm embarrassed about.

"I'll explain it when I figure it out myself," I say.

47

"Well," says Dusk, "the time has come, the walrus said, to talk of many things—"

Of shoes, and ships, and sealing wax, I would usually respond, *of cabbages and kings.*

And then she would say: *And why the sea is boiling hot, and whether pigs have wings—*

We do this every week, almost as if it's some sort of religious call and response. Today, though, there is only silence.

I stand, and so does she. Our fifty minutes are up.

"I'll see you in two weeks," Dusk says. "Remember—seek out the people and things that give you joy."

Yeah, whatever.

"I'll try," I say.

She smiles.

"Let's get you back to your mom." With her banjo strap slung across her shoulder, Dusk guides me out to the waiting room.

♥ ♥

The therapy office parking lot looks more like a scene from a creepy video game—fog hangs in the trees, cutting off our line of vision to the busy I-85 below. It's otherworldly, almost as if we could walk in any direction and plummet off the side of a cliff into the great wide nothing below.

Mom's chemical-peeled skin is still red and swollen; she grimaces down the barrel of the green straw that sticks out from the clear cup in her hand. Wind rattles the thinning dogwood branches that ring the parking lot, and I pull my jacket tighter.

"So, Dusk told me you're thinking about the Capstone Award after all," she says, eyeing her reflection in the driver's-side window. With a flick of a polished thumbnail, the car beeps twice and the doors all unlock at once. I start to cross over to the passenger side, but Mom hands me the keys. "You need the practice."

I sigh and slide into the driver's side instead.

Translation: *I'm exhausted from my morning with the esthetician, and I'd like to sleep off the Bloody Mary that's still in my system before we get back to your dad.*

"I'm not doing the Capstone," I say.

My position has only galvanized between Dusk's office and Mom's car: I would be selling my soul to the devil. I'm not ready to count it as my only option just yet.

"We all agreed that the Capstone Award was a part of your outcome goals." Mom shoves a pair of oversize designer shades onto the bridge of her nose and then cringes. She fans her face with an old church bulletin off the floorboard. "I've got the document on my phone—"

"You can't just stick your kid in therapy because she's not doing what you want her to do." I jam the keys into the ignition and start the engine. "That's literally not even how therapy works."

Merely surviving versus fully thriving . . . But only when it's convenient to the adults in the room.

Mom reclines her seat as far back as it can go and fastens her seat belt.

I throw the car into drive and descend the hill through the fog, stopping to merge onto the frontage road. The traffic doesn't relent—the fog is thick, and one car after the next flies up with their brights screaming through my rear window.

I have no option: I have to go forward. There's no escaping, no turning right and finding a back road onto the interstate.

I'm stuck here, with no fewer than twenty cars behind me, and now they're all starting to blare their horns, waiting for me to merge. Stuck. Always effing *stuck*.

"Mom—"

"I'm just saying, you did wonderfully in the Ocoee Youth Arts Awards last year. It's so good for your résumé, and *this* is your year for the Capstone Award—"

"No." I breathe through the tightness in my chest. I'm going to pull out in front of one of these wild Atlanta drivers, and then we're both going to die. "I need you to tell me what to do—"

"Just send something they haven't seen yet. Surely you have *something*—" She pulls her sunglasses down the bridge of her nose to peer up at me. "Send them drawing homework. They *love* you."

All of the cars are honking now. All of them.

Thirty cars blaring their horns. To my left, the interstate is hemorrhaging midsize sedans. "No, I mean, I need help pulling onto the road—"

"Ugh, Rhodes honey, just wait for a break and then gun it."

"There are no breaks—"

"Sure there are. Just *go*."

Around me, cars all cut each other off. They jump in front of each other, and honk at each other, and fly around each other with middle fingers waving out their driver's-side windows.

With a deep breath, I throw us into traffic.

Behind me, a car swerves onto the shoulder. The car behind them slams on their brakes, and I hear a telltale metallic *crunch* three cars back—nothing life-altering, by the sound of it. A second later, the drivers are out of their cars and arguing.

They're fine by the looks of it, thank God.

"Go!" Mom says.

I rocket off toward the Alabama state line.

I won't stop shaking until long after I step out of the car.

"Just think about it," Mom says, oblivious. "Win the Capstone, and the world is your oyster."

I-Kissed-Alice 9:55p: Holy crap, update 48 is EXPLODING. Has your phone stopped buzzing at all?

Curious-in-Cheshire 9:59p: My phone's died three times. I don't think we've ever actually had this kind of a response before.

I-Kissed-Alice 9:59p: The comments are the best part: "It was so authentic." "I really felt their connection." "I ship it."

Curious-in-Cheshire 9:59p: Of course it felt authentic . . .

I-Kissed-Alice 10:00p: I mean I'm still surprised you used our sexts from the other night

Curious-in-Cheshire 10:00p: Was I not supposed to? I always thought that was kind of the idea

I-Kissed-Alice 10:00p: Oh I mean yeah. Of course.

I-Kissed-Alice 10:00p: It's the first time you've actually used a scene we workshopped like that. It feels a little, like . . . voyeuristic.

Curious-in-Cheshire 10:07p: :(Should I take it down?

I-Kissed-Alice 10:07p: . . . I like it.

Curious-in-Cheshire 10:08p: I do too

I-Kissed-Alice 10:09p: check your email for the #49 rough draft

Curious-in-Cheshire 10:09p: !!

I'VE NEVER SEEN THESE AREAS OF THE INTERGALACTIC UNDERLAND.

GRRRROOANN

OH GODS, THE SOUND... I CAN'T STOMACH IT. IT'S LEECHING THE LIFE FROM MY BONES.

IT IS HORRIBLE, BUT IT IS STILL A LIVING THING, QUEEN. YOU HAVE TAKEN YOUR CURIOSITIES TOO FAR...

YOU THINK OF ME AS SO CRUEL, ALICE. I DID NOT CAPTURE THIS JABBERWOCK; I FOUND HIM HERE.

THEN LET HIM GO.

ROAAR

IT IS AFRAID. I HAVE TRIED TO PENETRATE THE LOCKS, BUT HE HAS LIVED IN FEAR FOR SO LONG, I AM UNABLE TO FREE HIM.

IF I AM GOING TO ESCAPE THIS PLACE ALIVE, I MUST PLAY ALONG WITH THIS GAME OF HERS UNTIL I CAN FIND ACCESS TO THE ESCAPE POD—OR, I'LL BE LEAVING BY WAY OF THE REFUSE HATCH, THE ONLY SOUL THAT EVER CONTRADICTED THE QUEEN.

IT CONTROLS... COLD? THE ELEMENTS?

THE HEAT, ACTUALLY. COLD IS THE ABSENCE OF HEAT. IT CONSUMES EVERYTHING.

PERHAPS I AM SAFE WITH HER ... FOR NOW.

Comment 1: **I-Kissed-Alice** 10:44p: what do you think

Comment 2: **Curious-in-Cheshire** 10:44p: soooo how is therapy going

Comment 3: **I-Kissed-Alice** 10:44p: that obvious, huh?

SEVEN WEEKS UNTIL THE CAPSTONE AWARD

CHAPTER 5
ILIANA

Username: Curious-in-Cheshire
Last online: 3h ago

The rest of October flew by as fast as the wind could carry it.

In that Alabama way, it was still sort-of-summer until it wasn't—green, eighty degrees, and sunny one day, blustery and brown the next.

Sarah and I figured things out in that careful, uneasy way we always do.

She doesn't apologize, and I don't expect it anymore.

I apologized two weeks ago.

I suppose Rhodes and Sarah made nice as well, but who ever really knows what's going on with them? Sarah knows better than to bring Rhodes up with me at all anymore, but the fact that they're tagging each other in memes on social media again seems to be a decent indicator that they're back to getting along.

Hungover students wander the halls like zombies, armed with oversize sunglasses and nursing neon-blue sports drinks because people say it's the next-best thing to the proverbial "hair of the dog that bit you." I didn't go out for Halloween this year—I didn't have time. We might have seven weeks left until the Capstone finals, but the project proposal is in five. Our declaration of intent essays are due by "close of business" today, which Mr. Randall says means six p.m.

Close of business can mean a lot of different things when your parents fit pipes for a living. Mom and Dad didn't know what it meant, either. And for that matter, I had no idea what a declaration of intent essay even *was*, so while everyone else got drunk and toilet-papered houses in Mountain Brook, I worked my ass off.

We have three weeks until Thanksgiving break, and then a month until Christmas.

Five weeks until the Capstone Award project proposal, if we're so lucky to be invited, and practically zero hours until our declaration of intent essays are due. Maybe more like eight-hours-and-something, but it *feels* like zero. I still have no idea if this thing I cobbled together is what the Capstone board is going for, but I don't have time to start over.

I feel like I'm going to die.

Suffice to say, the energy in the visual arts wing is *peculiar*.

"No, not midnight tonight," Mr. Randall is telling Sarah—and probably fifteen others—at the front of the room. "Close of business means six p.m."

Randall is all tweed and elbow patches because it's November, even though it's sixty-two degrees outside because this is Alabama. Somehow, inexplicably, he loves what he does.

A blessing, I guess, because I've never been impressed by any of his work.

I lay sprawled on the polished concrete floor of the makerspace—a fancy word for what someone might have just called a *studio* five years ago—with a large crimson-red sheet of paper just under my nose. A long, narrow L-square—an L-shaped ruler used to draw right angles—lies under my chin, and notches have been scratched into the paper with a white colored pencil in regular intervals. A forest of legs stands around me, students draped over the tables, and standing at the printmaking equipment, and stretched out on the floors wherever they know they won't get trampled.

I don't think about the tight quarters when I'm working with the X-Acto knife until I jab myself in the thumb for the fifty-leventh time. I'm too tired to stand and drag myself across the studio to grab a bandage from my work locker, so I suck on the throbbing, swollen wound instead.

Sketchbooks, large and small, are strewn *everywhere*.

My own sketchbook is full, but I'd never let anyone else see what's inside: Rhodes at an angle, with her prominent nose in a stark, almost caricatured contrast to the softness of her mouth. Cubist Rhodes, with her features distorted as if she'd appear in Picasso's sketchbooks instead of my own. Rhodes slaying Holofernes, anguished and dragging a double-edged sword through Benjamin Randall's windpipe.

(Randall was not amused by my brief foray into the stylings of Artemisia Gentileschi).

It's locked away, with the couple pages filled with concept sketches for what's under my hands ripped from the spiral binding and cast just to my left.

It's an opportunity to catch up on my DMs from Alice rather than work, and I regret nothing.

> **I-Kissed-Alice** 9:31a: headed to go talk to my advisor next period.
>
> **Curious-in-Cheshire** 9:31a: fucking yikes
>
> **Curious-in-Cheshire** 9:32a: did you ask to meet or did he
>
> **I-Kissed-Alice** 9:33a: he emailed me. Copied mom on it. She has to be there
>
> **Curious-in-Cheshire** 9:33a: that's ominous

I have no idea how to tell her how bad this really sounds.

It's one thing to have scheduled meetings with your advisors. It's something else entirely when they bring your parents in for it—and it's rarely anything positive. Not that I'd know from personal experience—my grades have always kept me out of hot water with both the school *and* my parents.

We've purposely never actually discussed where we go to school—internet safety and all that—but I imagine our schools are pretty similar.

She goes to studio art classes like I do and deals with the same kind of asshole faculty advisors. I might have thought she attends the Conservatory, too, except there is no one here remotely like her.

There's only one Alice, and I'd know her anywhere.

I-Kissed-Alice 9:33a: nah. It's fine.

I-Kissed-Alice 9:34a: We have these all the time.

"Who are you texting?" Sarah is nothing but a pair of Christmas elf socks peeking out from scuffed Doc Martens when she appears to my left. She drops a bandage onto the screen of my smartphone.

"Where did you find this?" I yank the bandage free from its packaging and wrap it tight enough that the tip of my thumb turns purple.

"I grabbed it from your locker," she says.

I forgot she knew my locker combination. It isn't worth the stink to ask her why she was poking around my stuff. Or how she knew I even cut my finger, she's been on the other side of the room since class started.

It's easier to tell myself she was just trying to be helpful.

I know Sarah's hovering over me, but worry brings me back to Alice instead.

Curious-in-Cheshire 9:35a: but your mom was copied on email this time, right? She's going to be there

59

I-Kissed-Alice 9:36a: why are you so convinced this is something bad

I-Kissed-Alice 9:36a: quit being negative for christ's sake

This is bad.

Nervous-craps bad.

Gonna-barf *bad*.

Sarah nudges the phone from my hands with the toe of her boot. One of the elves on her socks winks at me. "Hello?"

"It's nobody important." I stuff my phone under my arm, but my cheeks tell Sarah otherwise. "We have an entire holiday before Christmas. Your socks are literally killing me."

She gives me *a look*. "Did you get your essay in for the Capstone Award?"

I've been working diligently on the essay every night since the Capstone Award presentation. The topic came to me, clear as a bell: Tarot imagery as archetype. The way such archetypes can be utilized in a creative process, and how each arcana carries its own arc, like a story. I'd been waiting for this all summer, more than I've waited for anything else. Not only for the opportunities it would give, but for the message it would send. If I won—*when* I won—Rhodes would *have* to see me as a Real Artist. She'd have to acknowledge that I deserve to be at the Conservatory, that I deserve the Capstone, and that art doesn't have to be soulless intellectual snobbery to mean something to people.

Most important? She *owes* me this.

I roll over onto my back and peer up into Sarah's face. My curls scrawl and skitter across the paper. I haven't sent in my Capstone declaration of intent yet or pitched the proposal—the next step, if my declaration of intent is accepted—but I'm already working on my project for the finals round. I have no idea if the other potential participants have started working on theirs as well, but the idea is apparently entirely foreign to Sarah.

No one worthy of winning is going to wait until two weeks before the finals round to begin working on their final project. Even if I don't make it in, at least I'll have created something that isn't Composition III homework.

"I sent it in yesterday," I say. This is a lie.

It sits unfinished on my laptop right now, two tables over. The thought of it sends my stomach into uneasy somersaults. I wanted it to be finished three days ago.

How the hell do I know if I'm even doing this thing right?

Why is it so hard to explain this to Sarah, who only ever seems to understand things *after* they've been hand-fed to her like she's some kind of defenseless baby animal?

I'll hit send as soon as open studio is over, when I get the chance to finish moving commas around without her looking over my shoulder.

But if I tell her the truth, it will be the same variation of the arguments she's already made a thousand times:

Let me see what you wrote for your essay. I need ideas.

And

You're the one that begged me to transfer here with you, so you need to help me keep my grades up.

And

Rhodes believes that formal education only prepares us for fitting comfortably in society's boring, square pegs, and she lets me use whatever I need because we're doing the only work that matters in the studio—

And so on and so forth, followed by an entire calendar week of Sarah climbing up Rhodes's ass and refusing to speak to me until I apologize for hurting her feelings by refusing to let her poach my work. But our eyes meet, with her hovering over me, and there's nothing nefarious in her features: They're held open wide and framed by brows arched in question.

"Oh. Okay." She frowns for a moment, processes, and drops down onto the floor next to me, criss-cross applesauce. "Want to hear a secret?"

"Sure." I stick my pencil behind my ear and wait.

"Rhodes didn't send in an essay at all." Her face is all expectation: She ducks her chin, and crosses her arms, and sort of looks like one of the elves on her socks.

I need to process.

I had heard rumors that Rhodes wasn't planning on doing the Ocoee Arts Festival at all this year, much less go out for the Capstone Award—she didn't participate in the informational meeting, even though she's juried into the Ocoee Arts Festival and has medaled three years in a row. Her silence was super obvious, even to the Ocoee Arts Festival chairwomen who came to give the presentation. Rhodes was meant to be an example for all of us, and she merely watched the whole thing unfold from the balcony.

It sent a message, loud and clear: Rhodes Ingram is too good for the Capstone.

"So, Rhodes isn't going for the Capstone after all." Disappointment rings in my voice. I fight the urge to clap a graphite-stained hand over my mouth. "What, are her parents flying her to France for college or something?"

Sarah shrugs.

Her face is still contorted into something sour, but it's quickly losing its heightened coloring.

"She didn't say anything to me about France." She's oblivious to sarcasm. It sounds like she's admitting to a crime. "She doesn't tell me anything."

"So, that's what this really is," I say. "You guys are fighting again."

This back-and-forth with them is exhausting. I thought they were fine.

"Is it fighting if you haven't really been talking?" Sarah fidgets, picking at the hem of her denim skirt and flicking the hole in her tights with a thumbnail.

"I don't know. Is it?" I ask.

Rhodes really doesn't seem to understand what the Silent Treatment™ does to Sarah. I want *so, so* badly to tell her I have zero desire to hear any of this.

It's sixty-two degrees outside, twenty degrees too warm for Sarah's "winter aesthetic" wardrobe choices. Her hairline is damp around her ears, and her DIY finger-knit scarf lay cast aside across the back of the chair where she sat typing into a computer only moments before.

She hikes her sweater sleeves over her elbows and turns her eyes to the wide, single-pane window past my shoulder.

"Look, about Sylvia's"—Sarah pulls her bottom lip through her teeth—"just . . . I don't know. I'm not sorry for what I said, but I'm sorry for how it made you feel? I don't know."

"Wow, some apology," I say.

Truthfully, our argument hurt more than I would have ever told her.

There's so much I never say to her. In spite of how used I feel, I'm not saying anything about this, either.

I need her, too. Aside from Alice, she's all I have.

Personal responsibility is not something Sarah has ever attempted to figure out for herself, though, and it would just become something she put back on me: I'm *jealous* of her relationship with Rhodes. I'm *jealous* of Rhodes's talent. I'm *jealous* of Rhodes's opportunities *and* Sarah's opportunities because she's in Rhodes's orbit.

Still, I need *something* from her so I can put it all to bed once and for all.

"Are we okay?"

"Yeah." I lie. I'll need another week before I'm *really* over it.

She smiles and leans around my hair to take a look at my work. "What are you working on?"

"My Capstone project."

I want so much to sound nonchalant about the award, but my voice gives me away: Each syllable drips with pride. Pride, and fear, and longing, and excitement, and God only knows what else I'm transmitting that I'm not aware of.

The way Rhodes talks about these things is always so sophisticated, and I know Sarah sees the difference between us. I want to crawl under something and hide.

I want this too much. I want everything too much.

"You don't even know if you'll make it in," she says. "What is it?"

"Well, it'll take a while." I roll back onto my stomach and run my hands over the paper. Seventy-eight rectangles marked in white pencil, waiting to be filled with seventy-eight tiny vignettes. "I need to get a jump on it. It's something I've always wanted to do, so I won't regret it."

I don't mind telling Sarah about *this*. She'll never be able to replicate it.

"It's a paper-cut, Alice-themed tarot deck. I'm going to mount the cards in a grid between sheets of glass." It isn't hard for me to picture: A lacy, delicate cups suit featuring the Mad Hatter and the March Hare. A swords suit detailing the slaying of the Jabberwock, one card at a time.

Alice, the fool.

Cheshire Cat, the hierophant.

Just like I wrote in my essay, each minor arcana suit is a story arc of its own kind, and it won't be hard to use this medium to illustrate each of the arcs in the universe Carroll built in Wonderland. I just hope those old biddies will understand that I'm exploring the myriad ways we can use art to tell a story—and not attempting to summon the devil himself.

"I can't picture it," Sarah says with a shrug. "I guess I'll have to see it when it's finished."

"I figured," I say, but really I want to stretch myself over the paper so she can't see the preliminary sketches already filling some of the rectangles under my arms. Something about Sarah's tone makes me want to wad it into a ball and try something else.

Instead, I focus myself on sketching in the Knight of Swords card—Alice, wielding the vorpal sword—and ignore Sarah's presence to my left until she finally gets up and walks away. It's all an act, though: I can't focus on my work, or the pencil in my hands, or even the very conceptual basis of what it is I'm trying to accomplish.

Alice might be on the verge of an academic disaster, but now all I can think about is Rhodes.

Removing herself from the scholarship means she's won in an entirely different way.

I-Kissed-Alice 10:14a: I still don't believe this is something bad

I-Kissed-Alice 10:14a: Do you really think I'm that bad of a student? Do you think I'm just not trying?

Curious-in-Cheshire 10:15a: Of course not.

Curious-in-Cheshire 10:15a: But you said yourself that you haven't been turning stuff in. Your advisor is calling in your mom to talk to you. It doesn't take a stretch of imagination . . .

I-Kissed-Alice 10:15a: wow

I-Kissed-Alice 10:16a: w o o o o w

I-Kissed-Alice 10:17a: I just can't believe you think this about me

Curious-in-Cheshire 10:18a: can we please just talk about this?

I-Kissed-Alice 10:18a: gotta go. Mom's here

Curious-in-Cheshire 10:18a: Alice.

I-Kissed-Alice has logged out of the system.

CHAPTER 6

RHODES

Username: I-Kissed-Alice
Last online: 30m ago

Cheshire really hurt me today.

She was supposed to be the voice of reason outside all of this.

She was supposed to be the one who believed in me, even when people like Randall and Mom don't.

Instead, she joined the chorus of literally every other person in my life right now: You are failing. You only have as much value as your work.

The vultures are circling over your head. You're *done*.

"Have you been crying?"

Mom has only two volume settings: incoherent mumbling and the kind of pitch that projects halfway down the hall. Today, Mom's loud. Every single senior in the hall stops in their tracks to stare back at us as we walk toward my advisor meeting with Randall.

They're staring at me, because artists who forget how to create are the stuff creative horror stories are made of. We're only three months into our senior year, but it's still enough of a contrast from my output as a junior to scare our entire graduating class. What if this is contagious? Can I pass it to someone by sharing a straw?

If nothing else, it's scaring me.

"No," I say, swatting her hand away long after it's gone.

We both know I'm not telling the truth, but Mom doesn't press the issue.

Have I given up on myself?

Surely, if I just made my craft more of a priority, I'd get back in the swing of it, right?

I wonder if this is what Randall is going to tell me: That I could be an artist again if I tried hard enough. That my grace period here is over, and if I can't paint, I can no longer attend the Conservatory.

Cheshire's scared me, and it isn't fair.

This is so like her: She sees a fight *everywhere*. Everyone she encounters has a chip on their shoulder.

I've been telling her as long as I've known her: If you're looking for crap, you're eventually going to step in it.

"Do you know what this is about?" Today, Mom is in all of her blown-out, lipsticked Hot Mom glory: Soft fabric. Touches of lace. Too much eye makeup. Fresh highlights in her naturally dark hair. Skinny jeans and beachy wedges I'd break my neck in. Her breath smells a little bit too much like the white wine she likely downed with her lunch, but she seems to have no problem teetering about in her OTBT-brand wedges, so we're dealing with a manageable *tipsy* rather than full-out *drunk*.

Besides, Mom is a "lady."

According to Mom, ladies know exactly how much wine they can tolerate when they day drink. She'd *never* show up somewhere full-on wasted.

Dusk wonders how much my mom—and women like her—hide poor coping skills in the woo-girl, mommy-loves-wine identities they've constructed for themselves.

I think Dusk has a point.

Mom's out of place in the visual arts wing—around us, the entire senior class is a haggard, disheveled mess, shuffling between classes and slipping down to the nurse's desk for Tylenol and a nap. Sarah's curious, watching from a distance.

If Sarah's in the hall observing, then Iliana can't be far away.

Cheshire's prediction—*omen?*—whispers in my ear like a cranky ghost, and suddenly all I want is to blend into the walls, but Mom is making *blending in* entirely impossible. Her sweater eases off her shoulder on one side, and I move it back into place. She looks like she belongs at a bar, honestly. Or on a date, maybe with Dad, more likely with literally anyone else.

I don't think she realizes I can read right over her shoulder when I'm home and she's thumbfucking her phone. But none of this matters now, except that wine-flavored dishonesty seems to be the very thing that drives my mom-flavored ire.

She shimmies until her sweater slides back off her shoulder. "It's supposed to fall this way. It's *fashion*."

Mom says this like she's speaking a language I've never heard before.

Mom isn't entirely wrong.

"Who are you trying to impress?" I put it back onto her shoulder a second time, and she allows it to drop again. "You can see your bra, by the way."

I can *feel* people watching us. It's everything I can do not to make a quote-unquote "bathroom run" and hide in my dorm room until long after the meeting's over.

"Jesus, you're edgy. Normally Griffin's the one acting like he doesn't want me here." Mom frowns. "You *do* know what Randall wants. You're not telling me."

"I really have no idea," I say. "Swearsies."

Randall appears in the doorway behind a throng of sci tech–track kids, cradling a laptop in his arms like a stack of books. He looks as disheveled as the rest of us, with his pouf of dark hair bouncing in a curly mess over his forehead and horn-rimmed glasses. He makes accidental eye contact with Mom and rakes a frizzy curl out of his face with one hand.

"Y'all ready?" He gestures us toward an unmarked door between two studios, then tips forward to grab it and pull it open to usher us inside—a mundane shock after the visual arts wing's wild, artwork-loaded walls.

We normally meet in the library. Something about this is especially ominous.

We're meeting in Randall's office instead.

I recognize the names on each of the little plastic plaques outside the cubicles—history teachers. Math teachers. Science teachers. English teachers.

There are names I don't recognize, too, but the ballet crap covering their cubicle walls gives them away as dance-track teachers. From somewhere in the recesses of the giant, open room, classical music starts, stops, and starts again at half speed.

Randall's cubicle is precisely what I would expect it to be: The shelves over his laptop's docking station are open, stacked to the hilt with spiral-bound sketchbooks. The walls are papered with sketches I recognize from exercises he's guided us through in drawing class over the past four years, rudimentary versions of what he eventually foisted upon us in class. It's clear he worked hard at all of them, that we didn't appreciate them at the time like we should have.

Somehow, I always manage to forget that Randall is an artist first.

Was this what he wanted for himself, to set his own craft aside in the name of equipping other people? The room begins to spin, and I drop into one of the chairs in his cubicle before I'm invited. Randall settles down next to his docking station to plug in his laptop, and Mom carefully lowers herself into the seat on my left.

"How are you, Valerie?" Randall smiles. Mom blooms.

"Oh, you know. Blessed." Her smile is cautious.

She's nervous too.

"Let's just get to it." It tumbles out of me, hard and loaded with sharp edges.

"Rhodes!" Mom whacks me on the arm. Not hard—she's never spanked me, not a day in her life—but enough that her fingers *smack* against my skin.

Randall takes a long, ragged breath. He grabs his pant legs in bunches on the tops of his thighs and adjusts his position in his seat.

"We need to talk about your progress, Rhodes."

"We've talked about my progress," I say.

"No," he says gently. I don't like his tone. "We *need* to *talk* about your *progress*."

Mom transforms in front of us: One minute she's blushing into her hair and batting her lashes, the next her back is ramrod straight. Her eyes are wide, and she grits her teeth.

Randall squirms under her undivided attention.

"Well?" Mom pulls a pad of paper and a pen from her bag.

"Everybody knows your senior year doesn't matter," I say. I don't like how my voice shakes. "It's all about your grades your junior year, right?"

"No." Randall pushes a piece of paper back and forth on his desk with one finger. "Rhodes, you'll be lucky if you walk at graduation at all."

"You're just trying to scare me." I cross my arms to stuff my shaking hands into my armpits.

"You don't understand how bad this is!" Randall's face is red, and his eyes dart from me to my mother. "I really don't know how else to communicate this with you, Rhodes. Given your current coursework, your best bet is starting out at junior college, getting your GPA up, and transferring into a state school from there."

All the blood is rushing to my ears.

"There's nothing wrong with that," he's saying, "I mean, I started out at junior college, lots of people do—"

I would be the first Ingram in four generations to go to a *state* school, rather than one of the sweet little New England private schools my dad's family favors, and I'm barely going to have the grades for *junior college*.

What the hell have I *done*?

"Mr. Randall, remember that you are speaking to a *child*." Mom's voice is doing that thing where it's only rail-thin and quivering because screaming isn't socially acceptable.

"With all due respect, Mrs. Ingram, I'm not speaking to a child. Rhodes is almost eighteen, and she's made choices for herself that are affecting the rest of her life." Randall straightens his tie.

None of the other teachers wear a tie.

Why does he wear a tie?

"Seventeen is barely considered adulthood," Mom says.

"And as someone who spends more time with your daughter than you do, I am going to assert that she does not respond well to being coddled. Child or adult, she needs to hear it straight." Randall swallows. "Ma'am."

"Excuse *me*—?"

Mom is honest to God going to have an aneurysm. She's just good enough of a mother to recognize when her parenting skills are being criticized. *Almost* good. Satisfactory.

Randall looks like a squirrel about to be run over by a car.

I think I'm going to vomit.

"Mom—stop." I'm trying to remember how to breathe. "He isn't wrong. I see him every day, and you've been working in Nashville for months."

She's sitting here getting offended because he's not farting rainbows, but maybe Randall has a point—this is *my* life.

"Why didn't you tell me this three months ago, Randall?"

"*Mister* Randall, Rhodes." Mom throws a sharp elbow into my ribs.

"Mrs. Ingram, Randall is fine." He waves his hand. "I did tell you three months ago. And I warned you at the end of the last school year, too, when you ended the year with a D in Composition II because you didn't turn anything in for the last two weeks of class."

He hands over the white sheet of paper he was pushing around his desk moments before. It's a log of some kind, names and dates.

A list of every one-on-one interaction we've had since the eighth grade.

The last four dates are highlighted:

One dated around May, another in August.

One dated in the middle of October.

Today.

Mom snatches it from my hands, and I let it go without a fight.

"So, what now?" Her eyes dart from the paper to the side of my head, but I don't *dare* make eye contact. Instead, I watch her evolve from cherry red to an ugly, apoplectic plum from my peripheral vision.

I won't need to worry about college, because she is going to *kill* me.

Randall shifts in his seat. "You won't be happy with me, Rhodes."

"I'm already not happy with you."

"The only person you can be angry with right now is yourself," he deadpans. "June Baker called me at the beginning of the week."

Mom flicks her glare over to Randall again, and he shifts in his seat.

This is it. She is literally going to have a coronary and die.

"To paraphrase our conversation, she wanted to know why you didn't participate in the Capstone Foundation Award informational meeting a few weeks ago."

Mom cuts her eyes to me, again.

I slide farther back in my seat. "I was there, Mom."

In the balcony. Doing my best to hide.

But I was there.

"And *what did you tell her*?" At this point, Mom's words are only leaving her hissed through her teeth.

Randall has no idea what kind of relationship our family has with June and the rest of the Ocoee board members. He will never understand what kind of hell he hath wrought if he has somehow damaged our family's reputation in all this.

"That I couldn't discuss the academic performance of a student." Randall shrugs. "I think she got the picture, based on the conversation between the two of us that followed."

I want to crawl inside myself and hide forever.

Embarrassed is an understatement.

I don't think there's a word for what this is.

"June is willing to waive the GPA requirement for Rhodes," he says simply.

Again, Mom shape-shifts in front of our eyes: The color fades from her cheeks.

She takes a deep breath.

Mom doesn't smile, but she looks like she could again.

Meanwhile, every bone in my body screams in protest.

NO. Nonononono. No.

I can't.

It's not even that I won't—I literally *can't.*

I have nothing left to give them.

"I've already told you—" Tears well up and spill over onto my cheeks before I can check them. Mom moves to *tut-tut* and put her arm over my shoulders, but I shove her away. "I *can't—*"

"Yeah, you've told me. Artistic integrity, yadda yadda yadda." Randall takes off his glasses and cleans them on the edge of his shirt. "You have to take advantage of your connections, Ingram. You put in your work for six years with June and the Ocoee Arts Festival—don't leave any opportunities on the table. Know what I mean?"

Mom sits back in her seat, visibly relaxed.

She knows she's won this battle. What the hell else am I even going to do?

"I don't have an essay," I say. "Today's the deadline."

Even if we all know I'm going to do it, I don't actually *say* it.

They can't have this from me.

It seems small, but I won't give Mom the benefit of hearing it from my mouth.

"You have makerspace next block, and I have prep block." Randall lifts his laptop back off the dock station. "Let's go to the library and crank one out."

"I hate you for this," I say.

This feels like betrayal, and I don't know who's responsible—Randall, negotiating something terrible with June?

Mom's happiness over my God-awful circumstances, if it means she's getting what she wants? The specific feeling of being saved by the thing that so many artists are desperate for—financial stability, and connections, and people around them who can solve their problems—when all I want to do is be able to save myself?

Me, placing myself in the position where this is the only option I have left?

"If this works out for you, you won't hate me anymore," Randall says, smiling. "That's a promise."

I-Kissed-Alice 12:15p: so it was fine

Curious-in-Cheshire 12:16p: oh wow

Curious-in-Cheshire 12:16p: that's great

Curious-in-Cheshire 12:16p: So what was the big deal? why did your advisor pull in your parents?

I-Kissed-Alice 12:17p: just the usual stuff.

I-Kissed-Alice 12:17p: also I decided to do the Capstone Award, too. My advisor thinks I have a shot.

Curious-in-Cheshire 12:17p: The Capstone????? Like?

Curious-in-Cheshire 12:17p: Ocoee Arts Festival?!

Curious-in-Cheshire 12:17p: The Capstone Foundation Award?

I-Kissed-Alice 12:18p: yeah.

Curious-in-Cheshire 12:18p: Alice.

Curious-in-Cheshire 12:18p: The project proposal is in Nashville. If our essays are accepted, we'll be in the same city at the same time.

Curious-in-Cheshire 12:18p: WE COULD MEET.

I-Kissed-Alice 12:18p: I can't do this right now

I-Kissed-Alice 12:19p: I love you, but I don't have the bandwidth to even think about this

I-Kissed-Alice 12:19p: you really hurt me today about the meeting with my advisor. It feels like you don't believe in me

Curious-in-Cheshire 12:19p: Are you serious right now??

I-Kissed-Alice 12:19p: I need to go finish my essay.

I-Kissed-Alice 12:20p: I'll have your notes back for #49 tonight

I-Kissed-Alice 12:21p: I think I need to unplug tonight. I'll talk to you tomorrow

I-Kissed-Alice is no longer logged into the system.

SIX WEEKS UNTIL THE CAPSTONE AWARD

ILIANA

Username: Curious-in-Cheshire
Last online: 3h ago

To say my nerves are shot would be the understatement of the century.

The turnaround for the Capstone essay round finalists to be announced was supposed to be relatively short—a day or two, max, and then we'd have a month to prepare for the project proposal.

It's been seven days.

A lot will happen between now and the project proposal: Thanksgiving break, and the Alabama/Auburn college football game the following Saturday that serves as a state holiday in its own right (the *Iron Bowl*, every resident in the state will whisper in reverent tones). We'll miss an entire week of studio time at the school.

It's been seven days since I've talked to Alice, too. An entire week of waiting with bated breath, flipping between my email app and Slash/Spot until I bleed my battery dry, waking up in the middle of the night to the sound of notification dings that ultimately meant nothing important.

I've been stretched about as far as I can go, and the only thing left is for me to snap.

The Birmingham Museum of Art's Wedgwood Collection sprawls around us all, brilliant yellow with ornate white trim, a sitting room straight out of an Austen novel plunked in the center of an otherwise minimalistic series of galleries. Wedgwood china, blue-on-white sets of antique dishes, sit in scattered rows behind glass. The room itself is arranged like an Edwardian sitting parlor, but there's no denying that we are still inside the hallowed spaces of an art museum.

Randall stands just in front of an entire wall of antique cameo pendants the size of my fist.

Sarah, Rhodes, and I are here with the other senior mentors, Randall, and his eighth-grade exploratory art class. The mentorship program at the Conservatory is a time-honored tradition: Rising seniors are "tapped" by faculty to shepherd entering eighth-grade students around during their first year on campus, assisting them in mundane tasks such as setting up the digital portfolio they'll contribute to during their entire tenure at the school and serving as de facto chaperones on field trips.

Being a mentor is yet another reminder of the kinds of things I missed out on by transferring in as a sophomore. I often wonder what kind of artist I would be if I had the same opportunities our new eighth graders have.

"If you forget that you're looking at a room full of plates and shelving, what you'll see are lines—lines *everywhere*. And what do lines do?" Randall is walking backward as he speaks. He flicks the tablet in his hand with one finger, then points to Charlotte Carmichael, an eighth grader I've never spoken to.

The questions aren't for Sarah, or me, or any of the other seniors present. They're for the eighth graders we're supposed to be mentoring.

Fortunately for me, *my* assigned mentee doesn't need me: Etoria Marshall is a whiz all on her own, and I honestly have no idea what *I'm* supposed to teach *her.*

"Uh, um—" Charlotte's eyes move from Randall to one of the girls on her left, then Rhodes, *her* mentor.

"*Ingram?*" Randall turns his attention to Rhodes—a caricature of herself, crumpled in the corner with her sketchbook, her hands knotted in her dirty black hair.

Caught in the existential crisis of the day, apparently.

"Yeah?" Rhodes is nothing but a set of wide, light eyes, peering over the top of her sketchbook. "Oh—um."

"*Your* mentee—"

Charlotte, the mentee in question, is visibly uncomfortable.

Oh, how the mighty have fallen.

"Lines denote space, Randall." Sarah holds a pencil in front of her as she studies an angle in the architecture, shifting it millimeter by millimeter as she moves her line of vision down a column in the distance until her eyes fall where it meets the floor. When she drops her head and marks the paper, the angle still isn't right, and as a result, her drawing looks like the world through a fun-house mirror.

"Yes, *Sarah*, lines denote space." As if Randall weren't already in a crap mood from having to take a gaggle of spoiled eighth graders on a field trip, the fact that he's having to deal with our Capstone nerves isn't helping a bit.

I'm not sketching the Wedgwood Collection at all—the assignment is for the eighth graders, so those of us who are seniors are free to work on our own projects until our mentees need us. My sketchbook is littered with concept sketches for a Queen of Swords card, the *pièce de résistance* of my Capstone project. It's hard to imagine a more important card for the deck than Alice bearing the vorpal sword, and even if it isn't *actually* the case, I can't let go of the idea that the entire deck hinges there.

Randall opens the sketchbook under his arm to show us a sketch he completed of the exhibit at some point before class began—months or years ago, apparently, judging by the differences in the placement of the Wedgwood pieces on display in the cases. Where there's an empty wall in real life, there was an oversize curio cabinet on paper; what was once a row of plates is now a single urn.

When was the last time he created something new?

"So," he says, gesturing to faint perspective lines with the point of a pen, "this sketch appears to be a fairly accurate representation of the space, right? Except the page is still flat; it's merely the *perception* of space."

"Perception," Sarah whispers emphatically, mimicking Randall's nasally vocal fry.

I drop the length of my pen along the center line of her paper. Sure enough, her perspective is just a little off. She frowns up at me.

"*Perception,*" I say.

Randall breaks from his lecture to wander from student to student, covering his eye with one hand and using his pen to measure angles, encouraging them to do the same. Soon, hushed voices become a cloud of noise, and a break from the lecture turns into independent study. Twenty-five eighth graders splinter into groups of two and three, gesturing and measuring and sketching and gossiping.

My phone dings in my pocket.

All three of us jump: Sarah, Randall, and me.

I pull it from my pocket, but I'm scared to look.

It could be an email announcing the Capstone finalists.

It could be Alice, for the first time since our disaster of a conversation about meeting face-to-face if we're both in Nashville for the project proposal.

It could be my mom, tagging me in something ridiculous on Facebook again.

I don't know if I want it to be the Capstone announcement or Alice more.

Sarah pulls *her* phone from her pocket; at the front of the exhibit, Randall flicks his tablet to life and scrolls through his notifications with two fingers.

Nothing times two. They both put their devices away and return to their work.

I can scratch the Capstone announcement from the list, and I don't know if I'm relieved or disappointed.

My notifications just show a *Hearts and Spades* update from Slash/Spot: seventy-five new views. Twenty-three new comments. One-hundred-sixteen kudos. But nothing from Alice. I can't take it anymore. It's been seven long days of wondering if I'll ever talk to her again, of being angry that she's freezing me out, of worrying that something serious is going on. We've never gone this long without chatting before.

My pulse roars in my ears. My gut flops.

I flick over to my direct message conversation with Alice. It shows that she's active now, and the last notification is a slap in the face:

I-Kissed-Alice 12:21p: I think I need to unplug tonight. I'll talk to you tomorrow

Tomorrow was *seven* days ago.

I take a deep breath. I don't know what else to say, so I just start like I always do.

Curious-in-Cheshire 8:58a: hi

It's marked as "seen" almost immediately.

The typing indicator bubble appears at the bottom of the screen, then disappears again.

An entire minute goes by before she starts typing again.

Then it flashes at the bottom for another minute.

This goes on for what feels like an eternity, typing and pausing, breaking, typing and pausing.

Finally:

I-Kissed-Alice 9:00a: hi

I have no idea what to say next, so I just start typing.

Where have you been?

Nope. I shake my phone to clear the text field.

I've missed you???

Delete, delete, delete.

Curious-in-Cheshire 9:01a: how are you

I-Kissed-Alice 9:01a: my nerves are shot. I've been refreshing my email for three days

I allow myself a little relief. This feels like our normal.

Curious-in-Cheshire 9:02a: I get that

I-Kissed-Alice 9:02a: I'm an absolute mess over the project though

I-Kissed-Alice 9:02a: I have no idea what I'm going to submit yet

There's something terrifying about this, that I didn't completely comprehend until now: Alice is going to be a competitor.

It's a cruel twist of fate, to have Rhodes out of the way and then be forced to face down Alice to get what I want. My conscience had no issue with sidestepping Rhodes for the scholarship—her parents' money has solved every problem she's ever had, so there's no doubt they'd have any trouble paying for her college. But Alice doesn't have any options left—her depression has left her grades in shambles, and the world deserves to see everything she's capable of.

Alice needs the Capstone every bit as much as I do.

> **Curious-in-Cheshire** 9:04a: Alice. Your work on Hearts & Spades has been incredible. Illustrate something.

> **Curious-in-Cheshire** 9:04a: What if you proposed a series of Alice in Wonderland illustrations, set in space? Hearts & Spades style.

> **Curious-in-Cheshire** 9:05a: Intergalactic Alice(TM)

> **I-Kissed-Alice** 9:05a: You know I can't do that.

I sigh.

This argument is old news.

> **Curious-in-Cheshire** 9:05a: You can't hide this part of who you are from the world forever.

> **I-Kissed-Alice** 9:05a: you don't understand what it's like to have the world expect something from you

I lift my eyes from the screen of my phone to glance up at the recessed lighting over our heads. We've had this conversation a hundred times.

I tell her to teach the world to expect something different.

She tells me it's never that easy.

I remind her that there's nothing harder than living in a world where people expect someone other than who you really are.

This has never been an issue for me—the world has only ever gotten exactly who I am, no compromises or apologies: Being an artist. Being bisexual. Being a loud, obstinate, angry girl. My parents have always affirmed who I am, but they've never been able to cope with the sheer amount of space I consume by merely existing. I've always sensed that I should make myself smaller around them, easier to deal with, but it's something I've never actually accomplished.

Meanwhile, people like Rhodes take a lot of joy in turning up their noses at people like me, enumerating the myriad ways I'll never have the couth to navigate *their* corner of society.

Alice is too concerned about what other people think, though.

It'll ultimately be the thing that kills her.

Three phones and a tablet all ding in unison, and my train of thought is long gone. The sound echoes fractious down the wing, reverberating off every shiny, angled surface. Over the tops of younger, smaller, inexperienced heads, Sarah, Randall, and I find each other.

This is it.

I expected that it would be an individualized email from the Capstone Foundation—*Dear Iliana, Your Declaration of Intent was the best essay we've ever read*—but instead it's a form email copied to God knows how many other people, with nothing but "Re: Declaration of Intent Essay" in the subject line.

My heart drops.

Sarah's scream on the other side of the exhibit is ice in my veins.

"Randall! Iliana! The email!" Sarah is jumping up and down, clutching her phone in her hands. "I'm in! *I'm in!*"

There's no way in hell Sarah made it in and I didn't.

I can't even wrap my head around it.

I scroll past a block of text—*"The Capstone Foundation has existed as an auxiliary of the Ocoee Arts Festival since . . ."*—and find a column of twenty-five names, listed one at a time. I don't recognize any of them:

Xuewen Miao

Marquetta Oliver

Tia Leath

Marianna Walters

Adelaide Lyu

None of them are Conservatory students. I make a mental note to find each of these people on Facebook and keep scrolling.

Marianna sounds like a great "real name" for Alice.

I imagine myself whispering *Marianna* in someone's ear.

Next, *Tia. Marquetta. Adelaide*.

It could really be anyone.

Sarah's name finally appears farther down the list, and it's the first I recognize. Even farther, a girl named Kiersten Keller from the Conservatory's theater-track program—someone I didn't realize was an artist at all. Judging by the scroll bar, I don't have much email left.

I want to cry.

I scroll, and scroll, and it won't be long until I reach the end—

Finally: *Iliana Vrionides*.

I look up from my phone, grinning, searching the exhibit hall for Randall and Sarah.

I want them to be happy for me, too.

It takes me a second to find where they are, kneeling with their heads together.

They're smiling, and laughing, and hugging . . . *Rhodes*.

They're celebrating with *Rhodes*. But before long, they're pulling me into a huddle, too, hugging me and patting me on the back, eighth graders I don't know and Randall in that awkward, endearing way he tries not to make too much physical contact.

Sure enough, I find her name listed at the very bottom.

When our eyes find each other over the tops of Sarah's and Randall's heads, it's every bit the confirmation I needed:

Rhodes Ingram's going for the Capstone Award, too.

Curious-in-Cheshire 9:21p: did you make it in

I-Kissed-Alice 9:23p: yep

I-Kissed-Alice 9:23p: did you?

Curious-in-Cheshire 9:23p: yep

I-Kissed-Alice 9:24p: looks like we're meeting whether we like it or not

Curious-in-Cheshire 9:24p: jesus.

Curious-in-Cheshire 9:24p: don't get too excited, Alice.

Curious-in-Cheshire has logged out of the system.

FIVE WEEKS UNTIL THE CAPSTONE AWARD

CHAPTER 8

RHODES

```
Username: I-Kissed-Alice
Last online: 30m ago
```

There are only two Saturdays between now and the project proposal.

Dusk and I can't find a way to make our schedules work for a face-to-face appointment before I head to Nashville, so we settle for therapy-session-by-video-chat instead. The rooftop garden seems to be the safest place for this—if someone climbs the ladder I'll hear it long before their head appears over the side of the rooftop wall, and this time of year there's hardly anyone in the mood for gardening.

The kale is overgrown now.

A cold snap last week means the pea vines are withered and brown.

My laptop is open next to me, set carefully on top of my backpack to protect it from the dirt below. The sky threatens rain like it always does this time of year, but it'll give way to blue skies by the time the morning is over. The only other person in the rooftop garden is my younger brother, Griffin, but he doesn't count: He's the only person who gets a rundown of my appointments with Dusk after they're over. He's the only one who knows how bad this *really* is, and the only one who believes me when I say there's no way I'm going to pull myself out of this.

"It just feels like the universe is conspiring against me," I say to Dusk through the computer. I'm lying flat on the ground, and the little rectangle on the corner of the video chat screen only shows a view of dying vegetation. It feels good to be invisible, like I'm not really here.

Dusk is in her preferred state, rambling pseudoscience-y psychobabble to the kale since she can't see me on-screen. Her hair hangs in silvery black waves around her face, and in lieu of her usual artistic piddling during our sessions, she's plucking at a ukulele.

"I can't see you. Can you sit up, please?"

"Nope, I'm good," I say.

"Okay, then." An awkward not-quite-note twangs through the speakers. Dusk adjusts a knob and strums again. "So you think the universe is conspiring against you. Why?"

"Because Mom has been shoving Capstone down my throat all summer—it's such a status thing for her. And then you told me I should do it, and that Mom was paying you extra to make it happen, which is *super-effing-unethical*. Then Randall tells me June called to check up on me, and honestly it felt like a huge way out—"

"But now June's given you an option you can't refuse."

"Exactly. I wanted to refuse it, too."

"I think . . ." Dusk strums again, then begins to pluck something soft, "adults think about this a little differently. We can all look at these things and pick out times in our own lives that we lost out on something because we didn't *feel like doing it*."

I sit up to glare into the camera. Dusk visibly jolts.

"This isn't a matter of 'not feeling like it,' Dusk. It's a matter of 'can't.' You can't squeeze blood from a turnip."

"'Can't' is such an arbitrary concept for you," Dusk says. "*Can't,* really? You physically *can't* come up with something? Your hands won't cooperate? Use your feet. Paint with your nose. There's a person that uses their breasts to paint fruit, for crying out loud. Do you see what I'm saying?"

I honestly can't believe I'm hearing this right now.

Griffin eyes me from over the top of my laptop screen, wary. He's a boyish mirror image of me, blue eyes and soft face and dark hair. He's changing, though—for the first time, his jawline is much more angular than mine. We still have the same combination of thin lips and cupid's bows that we inherited from our paternal grandmother, and the same freckle just over our right eyebrows.

"No. Not at all," I say. "For someone as hippie-dippie 'creative' as you are, I thought you would understand the creative process better."

"I *do* understand the process—on a *very* personal level—and what I'm trying to explain to you is that this is an incredibly complex problem. It's occurred to me today that the conversation doesn't need to be 'fix me so I can do this thing again'—we need to be asking ourselves why it is that you *can't* do this thing anymore.

"I believe wholeheartedly that it feels impossible to you right now. I see you, and I hear you on this. But I think if we understood *why* it is—aside from what we already know, which is that you're depressed, and very anxious, and incredibly worried about the future—we could maybe get an idea of what your artistic purpose might be moving forward."

All I can do is blink at her.

None of this is registering, not at all.

"I think we need to shift the discussion toward the 'Big Why' here—is it because you are afraid of failing? Is it that your interests have shifted and you're afraid of trying something new? You have this opportunity to get your fat out of the fire here, and if we know what the lay of the land is, maybe we can get you back on your feet again artistically—"

It doesn't hit me how much this hurts until concern registers on Griffin's face. Sometimes I feel like I'm witnessing things from outside my own body. I don't actually recognize what's happening to me until I watch people around me react to it.

Griffin's face tells me to be sad.

Just like *that*, I'm registering sadness.

"It sounds a lot like you, my therapist, are telling me the very thing you call toxic in other people."

"No, what I'm saying is that you're putting yourself into a box, and you need to open your mind to other artistic endeavors—"

"I need to go. I honestly thought you'd help me figure this out."

Her smile is soft. "I think you thought I'd give you permission to give up on yourself."

My voice shakes. "I'm not giving up on *myself*."

My tone hits a funny note at the end, too, like Dusk's ukulele. I hear it at the same time Dusk's untamed eyebrows shoot up into her hairline.

"Then what is it you're giving up on, if it's not *you*?"

My finger slams onto the touch pad of my laptop and the chat disconnects, a reflexive action that happens long before my synapses fire and I comprehend what it is I'm actually doing.

I just hung up on my therapist.

I've never just . . . ended a session with her before.

"Glad to see therapy's going well," Griffin says.

He's sprawled onto his stomach to type rapid-fire into a laptop of his own.

"Don't pick on me," I say.

"Oh, come on." He rests his chin on his hands, propped up on his elbows. "Don't take it like that, Rho."

"She is such a shitty therapist." I slap my laptop shut. "Seriously, she's so bad."

"She's really not," he says.

"So what? You're an expert on therapists now just because *you* go to therapy?"

"I'm leaving." Griffin pulls his knees to his chest one at a time, then pushes to stand with his laptop in his arms. "Don't forget that you *asked* me to be here."

"What? No! Don't leave!" I feel like crying again.

Mom always says, "if everyone in the world is an asshole, then maybe you're the problem," and there's a small part of my brain that is nodding to this little bit of mom logic playing itself out in my life right now. But even if a tiny part of my brain confirms I'm the one with the problem, the rest of me just . . . hurts.

It hurts that Dusk is telling me to suck it up and deal with it.

It hurts that Griffin seems fed up with me.

It hurts that Mom is getting what she wants without listening to me.

"You're being *really* shitty right now!" Griffin shoves his laptop into his backpack and dusts the dirt off the back of his khakis. He looks like he's five again, all eyes and flushed cheeks. "And if there's anything *I* learned in therapy, it's that I can't control you being an asshole, but I *can* control whether I stick around to listen to it."

"Griffin!" I feel like *I'm* five again, crying at my own party.

He pauses on his way to the ladder, tall and slender in his tech-track golf shirt and khakis, with his backpack slung over one arm.

"Have you talked to any dance kids since we've been back?" I ask.

I've been meaning to ask for weeks now.

It's a loaded question and a change of subject—one I hope pulls him back close to me.

I need him right now, so, so badly.

He sighs, and the blue of his eyes reflect the wide, November sky stretching over our heads. "Nobody knows what to say to me."

"I get that." No one's known what to say to me, either.

It's a small school. All of us studio and performing arts–track kids are lumped together despite our grade level. Having Griffin begin his junior year in the tech track—which once upon a time existed as an independent school and was absorbed into the Conservatory to escape financial ruin in the nineties—felt every much like the exile my parents intended it to be.

"For the first three periods of our first day back, some jerk had everybody convinced I was dead—"

"I remember you telling me about that," I say. The tug in his voice hurts my heart. "The dance girls were literally crying into each other's leotards until they ran into you in the cafeteria."

He rakes his fingers through his hair, then tucks his hands behind his head. "Then they thought I was a genius for moving out of dance and into tech, which lasted long enough for someone in the sci tech–track to dispute that based on the fact that I'm completely over my head in Physics I."

He frowns at me.

I frown at him.

It's so clear to me right now, how everything we're doing—and not doing—is at the bidding of a woman who is operating more like a dictator than a parent. Neither of us are where we want to be right now, and it's 500 percent her fault.

"Help me . . . ?" My voice is this thin, aching thing. "I don't know what to do."

One hand rakes across his face, lingering to scratch at his eyes. "We're all trying to help, Rho."

"I'm sorry I was mean to you," I say. "Please?"

He draws a long sigh and slips his backpack over his other arm. "Buy me dinner and we'll figure it out."

Denial works like this:

    1) Eating with Griffin at Sylvia's Diner will be *fine*. It's during the week.

    2) Iliana and Sarah have school like we do—of *course* they won't be working tonight. But—

    3) Sarah's car is in the parking lot—maybe it broke down over the weekend. Except—

    4) It's wet on the asphalt under her car, and the hood is still hot when I park in the spot to its left.

"Maybe it's just Sarah." Griffin shoves me toward the front doors of the diner. After our spat earlier, humoring him with his dinner locale choice was the least I could do.

"Yeah, maybe it *is* just Sarah." I snatch the door open first. The bells crash against the glass, and everyone inside the diner jumps in their seats. "They've been fighting, I think."

"Who has been fighting?" Iliana appears like a ghost on my left, cranky and looming with all her curly blond hair stuffed into a net. "Sit wherever you want. *SARAH*."

No answer from the back.

"*SARAH!*" She turns on her heel to march back to the counter, stuffing her ticket book into the front of her apron.

"I can't believe you talked me into eating here." I throw myself into one of the booths like I'm throwing myself off a bridge. "You could have had shitty patty melts back at the caf."

"I can't believe you don't know your roommate's work schedule," Griffin says.

He puts a finger to his mouth and points to the kitchen. The place is so small, we can hear Iliana and Sarah bickering in the back.

"*Your* friends are here. You want the table?" Iliana's voice is predictably shrill. Unmistakable.

"Sylvia's got me doing inventory." Sarah's voice is softer.

I have no idea what I did to upset her again. I don't believe her, and I don't think Iliana believes her, either. Griffin is already gathering himself to leave. I wave him back down into the booth.

"We can't leave now," I hiss.

I want to leave, though.

The last thing I want is to have this conversation with him in front of an audience—but leaving would be giving Iliana what she wants.

There is low-level grumbling in the office, and finally Iliana appears through the kitchen door a second time. She's still in her clothes from school: a frilly top that clashes with the war in her eyes and the kind of tight jeans that cause both Griffin and me to glance a second, then a third, then a fourth time before we remember that she's a harpy and her legs in denim will never fix her craptacular personality.

Griffin and I catch each other looking. We both flush, and simultaneously become Very Interested in the Formica tabletop between us.

The thing about being out to your family that no one ever prepares you for is the specific kind of horror that comes with having the same taste in girls as your little brother. The idea of Griffin as a sex-having person makes me want to vomit.

The idea of him thinking about Iliana and sex in the same line of thought makes me want to vomit—because of *course* that's what he was thinking about; we were both staring at the same ass.

The fact that the thought crossed *my* mind . . . Well, I don't really know what to do with it at all. The way she treats me has always been made worse by the fact that there was a time that I *desperately* wanted her. It feels like a hundred years ago, but every once in a while my body remembers.

Iliana slaps laminated menus down under our noses.

"*Well?*" She's shifted her weight onto one hip, and she waits, poised, with the pen positioned over the pad in her hands.

I glance at her thighs again.

She notices, but she doesn't blush away. Instead, a brow pops up toward her hairline and she can barely bury the wicked smile inching its way across her face.

Great—more ammunition. One more thing to tease me about.

"Oh, uh. Sorry." I glance over the menu. I can't make my eyes focus on anything. "Coffee? And, um, pancakes."

"It's a dollar-twenty-five after the second cup," Iliana says.

"That's a rip-off!" Griff glares up from his menu. "Everyone else does free refills on soda and coffee. It's just, like, law."

"Take it up with the management." She's completely unperturbed. "What do *you* want?"

"Coffee." The sour expression on Griffin's face would make me laugh if I were in a better mood. "Hash browns, scattered. Covered in cheese, with ham. And grits with cheese. And bacon, cooked crispy but not burnt. Are you getting all this? Repeat it back to me." He throws me a conspiratorial glance. I choke down a laugh and cough into my fist instead.

"Hash browns. Scattered, covered, oinked." She reads through her teeth. "Side of grits with cheese and bacon. Crispy but not burnt."

"Okay, but be sure the grits and bacon are *separate*," he says as she's jotting it down. "It sounds like I want bacon in my grits. " He nods and shifts to pretending she isn't standing six inches away.

Once upon a time, he didn't think Iliana was as vile as I do. She reminded him of the bitchy, driven girls he shared a studio with as a dance-track student, and he thought a girl with her kind of focus would be a good fit for me—either as a friend *or* a girlfriend. Today, he wouldn't piss on her if she were on fire.

After a moment, she disappears.

Griffin settles into his seat, collects his thoughts, and picks at a button on his shirt with two fingers. "You know what everyone else is doing right now?" He says, continuing our conversation from the car.

"What?"

"The *Nutcracker*. Every single one of my friends' lives are consumed by it right now." He shakes his head. "Mom just doesn't get it—the Alabama Ballet needs to actually *see me* if I want to get on there. I need stuff like this on my résumé if I want to audition somewhere else. I feel myself getting weaker. I'm *stuck*."

"No, she doesn't get it at all," I say. "She was paying Dusk to convince me to do the Capstone. Can you believe that?"

Iliana appears again with mugs and an oversize coffee carafe. The conversation dwindles as she sets them in front of us, filling each with shaking hands.

Her expression is unruffled, but the coffee splashed onto the table-top says differently.

She wipes it up with the hand towel hanging from her apron and marches away again. A part of me feels bad for Griffin's antics.

A *very, very* small part of me.

Too small to actually say something about it.

It's clear he's getting to her, though.

"I just don't know what I'm going to do," I say. "What are *we* going to do?"

"Well, I'll tell you what *I'm* doing," Griffin says. "I talked to a lady at Dance!Alabama, and she's going to let me come dance with the troupe starting in January, if I teach classes three days a week now. They don't have enough upper-level boys."

"Oh, Griff, that's—" It's amazing.

It's also nearly impossible with his tech-track schedule—exactly the thing my parents were hoping for.

"Be happy for me . . . ?" It isn't typical for him to beg.

"Oh, I am! I just—"

"I know; it's a lot," he says. "But I *have* to do it. Mom and Dad said they won't pay for it, but they didn't say I couldn't dance."

This is how Griffin is paying for that night at the art installation last school year: By being forced into doing the thing Mom and Dad wanted him to do all along.

I always think my life was the one that was irreparably altered—I haven't *really* drawn since Mom shipped us off to rehab last summer—but then I remember the way Mom and Dad clipped Griffin's wings and forced him out of something they were merely humoring until they had the first opportunity to take it away from him.

"You're right. I'm happy for you." I'll be watching closer this time, though. "But now that you've got all the answers, what am *I* going to do?"

"Well, what would you have done a year ago about the Capstone?"

That is an easy answer. I spent three years dreaming about what I'd pitch for my Capstone project. Now, I can't remotely wrap my head around the idea. It's wild to remember a time when things actually sprung forth from my mind, tiny Athenas in full armor splayed out on paper for the world to see.

It was only a year ago, but it feels like a *lifetime*.

"Nudes, of course. A series—lighter than air, soft pastels on dark paper." I ramble the next part off from memory, word for word: "The study would emphasize each person's innate vulnerability while focusing on their shared humanity in spite of their physiological differences."

Griffin golf claps. "Lovely. And then what would you do?"

"Well, I'd draw them. I'd email the figure-drawing professor at Montevallo, tell her I'm a Capstone candidate, and ask to sit in on a few classes."

The look on Griffin's face speaks more than anything he could actually say:

Duh.

You have everything you need, right here in front of you.

What's the problem, then?

Except *ideas* are never the problem. I know what I *would have* said, and what June and the other board members expect of me. I know what kind of brand I've created for myself.

The problem, as in everything else, is the execution.

"Okay, so I propose a series of nudes," I say. "I call Montevallo and line up a few classes. I show up for class—and then what? Nothing *works* anymore. It's like my brain doesn't know how to—"

"Connect your eyes to your hands?" Griffin dumps half a cannister of sugar into his coffee, then stirs it with a tiny brown stirrer.

"No, it's more like . . . I don't know *how* to care anymore. And when I don't care, I don't know how to produce anything." I'm aware of how it sounds—like I'm just not willing. Griffin and Cheshire are the only ones I can tell that it feels like a slow death to try.

Iliana reappears, her arms loaded with plates: one tiny, unimpressive plate of pancakes in front of me and an entire constellation in front of Griffin. "Does that look right to you?"

Griffin studies each plate, snaps a slice of bacon in half, and takes a bite. Iliana's brows hike up into her hairline and she crosses her arms. I don't know why he's testing her like this, when she would absolutely be the type to spit in his food.

Finally, Griffin shrugs with an air of resignation: "It's fine."

"It's *fine?*" Iliana huffs. "That bacon is *perfect*. I fucking put it in the *deep fryer*, for crying out loud—"

"It's fine." Griffin takes another bite. "Fine, fine, fine."

Iliana's face goes red.

With an *UGH!* that rattles the windows, she turns on her heel and directs her attention to a gaggle of older ladies shaking empty mugs at her from two tables away.

"Look," Griffin says, shoving a fork into his hash browns. "All I'm saying is, fake it 'til you make it. You know what you *would* say, so just . . . say it."

"And then what?" With one finger I push a half-melted rectangle of butter around the top of my pancake. The syrup is warm in the bottle, and it soaks into the stack of pancakes as I pour.

"I really think if you take the pressure off yourself to come up with something and start going through the motions, it'll click again." Griffin speaks around the load of hash browns in his mouth. "Sort of like muscle memory, but for your brain."

Maybe Griffin's right.

Maybe *this* is what Dusk was trying to say during our therapy session, what she's been saying about Ocoee all along.

I should quit thinking about not being able to do it and just . . . do it.

Get out of my own way.

"Maybe you're right," I say. "I'm gonna do it."

Griffin lifts his half-empty coffee mug in a toast. I lift mine, and we clink them together with a little-too-loud *Prost!*

I'd forgotten what relief feels like.

I let it wash over me and take a massive celebratory bite of my pancakes.

CHAPTER 9

ILIANA

Username: Curious-in-Cheshire
Last online: 20m ago

All I can do is eat.

Dry toast scratches its way down my throat, followed by chocolate milk straight from the carton. Next, a fistful of the deep-fried, crisp-but-not-burnt bacon that Griffin barely touched.

What does Rhodes think she's about, coming here? Bringing Griffin with her, talking about her Capstone project, fucking *clinking their coffee mugs together*? What kind of after-school specials has she been watching that she thinks this is the way people act in real life?

I couldn't listen like I wanted to.

The only thing good about the old ladies at my other table—the Bridge Club Biddies, as Sylvia has called them since forever—is that they like me enough to tip well, but my *God* do I have to work for it: endless cups of coffee, even though Sylvia started charging after the second cup because of them a *decade* ago. Details about my personal life, how school is going, who I'm dating (a concept that I don't even attempt to broach with them, so the answer has been "focusing on my studies" for the two years I've worked here, in spite of two rela-tionships with girls and one nightmare of a fling with a boy while I was still figuring everything out).

Today, their antics are costing me something far more important: information.

"Slow down. Jesus." Sarah is all eyes and sisterly concern.

She drops the inventory book onto the red-tiled floor and hops up onto the counter to my left. Our legs are short, and they dangle side by side, toes inches from the floor, and she takes the half-consumed carton of chocolate milk from my hands.

"Nudes." I cringe through a large swallow. "*Breathy. Nudes.* It's like she called June Baker herself and asked what she wanted."

"To be fair, she's medaled with stuff like that in the Ocoee Arts Festival for three years. She took the Young Adult Achievement Award for a hand study last year, remember?"

I scoff. "She's dialing it in."

"She's *playing to her audience*," Sarah says, frowning. "There's nothing wrong with that."

"Ugh! Why are you defending her?!" I snatch the carton back from her and pour another three gulps down my throat. "What even is this?! Did you guys make up?"

"What! No? I don't know," Sarah says.

I don't believe a word of it, coming from her.

The slump in her shoulders screams otherwise.

"It's just, like"—her voice is soft—"you can hate her all you want, but there's nothing *wrong* with picking what you know someone else will like."

She pauses for a moment, turns to check her red lipstick in one of the pots hanging around our heads, and makes a face at herself.

"It's smart," she says finally.

"It's cheap! It's dialing it in! It's—"

"A strategy you didn't think of," Sarah says. "Admit it: You're pissed you didn't think of it first."

"And you're not?" I turn the chocolate milk carton up one more time, but it's empty. It flies past the trash can and hits the back door instead.

Sarah shrugs. "I think I'm just . . . I dunno. Going about it differently."

"Strategy," I say.

Sarah nods. "Strategy."

After spending so much of my time at the Conservatory being compared to Rhodes's pristine, well-developed artistic style, it feels like this is one more way something is going to be weighted for Rhodes to win: Her style is everything women like June Baker and the Bridge Club Biddies love. It's art for people who think they love art more than they really do, the kind of stuff people buy prints of and hang in their mahogany-cased studies because it makes them feel smart.

Sarah's phone dings from her back pocket.

She retrieves it and glances at the screen.

"Rhodes wants the check," she says.

My face goes hot. Immediately, everything is so much *worse* than it already is. Everything feels like a test with Rhodes, an opportunity for me to fail and for her to judge my right to be a resident of this planet accordingly.

"What does it say?" I snatch the phone from Sarah's hands.

ring.ram 5:52p: can you ask iliana for our check please

ring.ram 5:52p: Griffin has to get back for AP review

There's nothing *really* to be upset about.

Still, it feels like criticism.

I'll be reading into it for the rest of evening.

"You take it." I thrust the check into Sarah's hands. "You need to go, like, talk to her or something anyway, right?"

"No way. Griffin's been weird with me ever since the art installation." She places it in my hands as if it's made of glass.

"No, he's been weird with you ever since you went all *Swimfan* on him last summer."

Sarah's crush on Griffin last year is just another one of those myriad uncomfortable things we never really talk about.

Griffin was surrounded by ballet girls in their perfect buns, leotards, and frilly little tutu things. It's completely lost on me why Sarah ever thought her shredded, acid-washed denim and oversize flannel would be his type—and apparently, it's lost on Sarah, too, with the way she conveniently forgets she was ever blowing up his phone at all hours of the night or constantly trying to get him alone.

"You can have my tip," I say.

"No." She hops down from the counter and resumes her spot on the floor by boxes of cornstarch lined up like little soldiers. "That'll cost you more than three bucks."

"You can have my tips for the rest of the afternoon," I say.

This one hurts. I need my tips today to pay my phone bill. I still owe Mom for my car insurance, and I used the last of my birthday money on gas last week.

Sarah ponders this for a moment.

She takes up her pen and runs her eyes over the rows of numbers she's already logged. "Nope. You can't afford me."

"She is your *roommate*, Sarah—"

"Negative, Ghost Rider. Pattern's full."

"God. You're lucky I'm literally the only person in the entire school that's seen *Top Gun*." I check my teeth in the microwave door for bacon, clean up my lipstick with two fingers, and fluff my hair through my hairnet.

The scene I walk out to shouldn't piss me off: The Bridge Club Biddies have stopped at Rhodes and Griffin's table, all six of them fawning and tut-tutting over them the way they usually fawn and tut-tut over me.

Rhodes and Griffin remind me of Von Trapps, soaking up all of the attention and sending loaded glances at each other when they think the ladies aren't looking. They're the kind of beautiful, well-groomed children that are used to this sort of thing—Daddy's bosses patting them on the head and Mommy's Daughters of the American Revolution board-member besties asking them out-of-touch questions about their interests.

"These two say they go to the Conservatory, too," the Smallest Old Biddy says to me as I approach. She's grasping a set of keys that belong to a Reagan-era Cadillac parked in a disability access parking spot she doesn't have a permit for. "Do you know each other?"

"Yep." I slap the ticket on the table between Rhodes and Griffin.

The ladies make eyes at each other. "She says she's doing the Capstone scholarship contest, too. Isn't that wonderful, to have a friend in all that competition?"

"It's a dream," I say.

Rhodes's eyes follow from the Smallest Old Biddy back to me, but her expression is completely impassible. Griffin's more interested in his fingernails than anything else, his permanent state since he's been back at school. Rhodes has grasped for eye contact every time I've looked in her direction, and Griffin won't look at me at all.

With a wink, Another Old Biddy in a floral-print sweater set hands me a ten-dollar bill. "This should cover their ticket, right?"

"This is fine." I stuff it into my apron and snatch the ticket out of Rhodes's hands.

The old lady's so pleased with herself, flushed pink and eyeing Rhodes and Griffin like they're a pair of squishy babies instead of asshole teens. I've known this crowd long enough to know that they don't have very much money—and the money they *do* have is tied up in overpriced independent living apartments, and doctor's appointments, and prescriptions for the kind of medication that keeps your heart beating and reminds your lungs to work.

Rhodes opens her mouth, and I cut her the nastiest look I can manage.

Don't be shitty *once,* Rhodes. Say "thank you."

"That—that wasn't necessary—" She stumbles through it.

I can't believe that's the best this spoiled, precious child can do.

"Oh, of course not." The old lady pats Rhodes on the shoulder, oblivious. "Few things in life *are.* Let someone spoil you a little, eh?"

The physical contact causes Rhodes to jump out of her skin.

"They've got plenty of experience with that," I say.

"Mmm?" The women are migrating toward the front door now. "Bye, girls! Hold my change for next time, Iliana. Maybe buy yourself something nice, yeah?"

"Thank you," I say, waving them out the door.

When they're gone, I whirl on Rhodes and claim every inch of my height that I can. But she's now standing behind me—*when did she stand up?*—and there's a single moment where my breasts are pressed against the soft plane of her stomach.

Vanilla cake–scented dry shampoo, coffee, and maple syrup bloom from her hair, her breath, her skin. I don't know what I expected her to smell like, but it wasn't *that.*

I take one sizeable step back.

"Look, I've had it with today," I say. "What the *hell* are you doing here?"

I'm absolutely *vibrating*—my hair, my hands, my words.

It's a violation of my personal space for her to even *be* here, much less standing six inches in front of me.

Rhodes gestures to the table filled with empty plates. "We were hungry. This is a restaurant. You do the math."

"You *know* what you were doing." My face is immediately hot—I regret it the minute I say it.

I can't ever—*ever*—show my cards with her.

It's as if when I let her see what I'm thinking, or how I feel, or what makes me tick, she knows precisely how to weaponize it. Getting upset at all gives Rhodes the upper hand, but I can't slow myself down.

Griffin gently, carefully, moves toward the door and waves Rhodes on to follow. This version of him is such a far cry from the cocky, hubristic jerk who gave me the runaround just less than an hour ago.

Rhodes doesn't move. She stands with squared shoulders, dark hair spilling over them in pretty waves, tall and strong. In an instant, the balance has shifted: Where I was looming over her only moments before, she now claims every extra inch she carries over the top of my head.

"Really? And what's that?" She stares down her nose at me.

"You're messing with me," I say. "Now that you're doing the Capstone, you want to spook me."

The minute I say it, I hear the paranoia in my words.

I want to cram everything I've said back into my mouth and run for the kitchen, but it's too late now.

"Oh, that's it," she says. Her smile is slow, but eventually it spreads to take up her whole face. "You think I came here to intimidate you."

"That's not—"

"Iliana, come *on*," Griffin says, crossing his arms. "Why would *Rhodes* need to come here to mess with *your* head? She medaled at

Ocoee three years in a row. All she's gotta do is show up and they're going to give it to her. You know that."

Rhodes smiles at this. It doesn't reach her eyes, but there's color in her cheeks. She doesn't look like a ghost haunting the place for once.

"*Breathy nudes*? Are you serious?" I thrust my hands onto my hips. "Can you *do* anything else?"

"And what are you turning in?" Rhodes's smile vanishes. "I'd poke a little fun at you, too, except the only consistent thing about you is your *inconsistency*. What is it this week, pottery? Fiberwork? You might actually have a chance if you worked on something for longer than five minutes."

"You *know* that's not true—" I'm angry enough that my vision is crackling at the edges, and I shove shaking hands into the pockets of my apron. Rhodes doesn't miss this, and she playacts perfect concern.

"You're nervous." She steps a little closer and touches my hair through my hairnet. I swat her hand away. "This has to be your first show, right? The first time is really sweet, if you can get past yourself."

I don't know what to make of this.

It's so unlike her.

She knows she has me in a corner, and she's drunk on it.

I step back to put more space between us. "You haven't finished a project in months, Rhodes Ingram. *Months*. You know why I'm not nervous: because you don't threaten me anymore."

"Yeah, this is exactly what not being threatened looks like." Rhodes runs a finger along my cheekbone, then the edge of my jaw, before booping my nose. Her hands aren't as soft as I thought they'd be—even the tips of her fingers bear the mark of a skilled artist.

I feel it in my thighs.

I don't know what to think, where to put my limbs, where to put my body.

"I hate you, Rhodes Ingram."

It's the best I can do, and it falls out of me limp. It's something I've thought forever, held close to my chest and nurtured like first love, but it loses its power the minute I speak it.

"Iliana—" Sarah materializes out of nowhere.

I didn't hear the kitchen doors slap back into their casing behind us, just like I didn't hear the other patrons standing around the counter to watch our conversation unfold as if it's free entertainment. Sarah and Rhodes make awkward half smiles at each other but say nothing otherwise.

"The customers are complaining. Gonna call Sylvia—come on." She's tugging me back toward the kitchen, and I let her pull me away. "Switch with me. You run inventory, and I'll take the next couple of tables . . ."

Griffin and Rhodes haven't said anything to each other or anyone else. They only stand together, tall and dark-haired, flipping between more of the same loaded eye contact and watching us with expressions I don't understand.

"You know what?" I dig my heels into the linoleum and put out an arm for Sarah. Rhodes is waiting, watching, passive. I want to slap a reaction out of her.

"Capstone is the end of the road," I say. "Only the best is going to win, and it's going to be me—I swear to *God*, Rhodes, you're going to regret the day you met me."

"You're wrong," she says, moving for the door. She walks past Griffin, and he follows. "I'm not going to regret the day I met you. I'm going to win the Capstone, and I'm going to Alabama College of Art and Design." She pulls the door open, and her grin is enough to light the entire city. "And I'll forget you ever existed."

And with that, she and Griffin are out the door and into the chilly evening.

It isn't until I'm in the privacy of the kitchen, with Sarah working the diner floor, that I allow myself to splinter into a thousand pieces.

CHAPTER 10

RHODES

Username: I-Kissed-Alice
Last online: 6h ago

Great-Grandma Ingram loved to tell the story of how Griffin's first step wasn't a *step* at all—at just over a year old, he let go of my mother's hand and *twirled*. I don't know which cousin's wedding it was, or where I was at the time (probably hiding under a table, scribbling into a composition notebook), but little Griff shocked everyone by standing on his own and swaying to the music before he could even walk.

It was Great-Grandma who insisted Griff and I attend the Conservatory. She was the one to leave behind the money that would pay for it. She knew my parents well enough to know that holding them hostage with access to a trust fund would be enough to bend them however she wanted—and she wanted Griffin to dance.

And my *God* did he dance—he was six the first year he performed in the *Nutcracker*. *Harlequinade* at nine, *Coppelia* at ten, *A Midsummer Night's Dream* at eleven.

Sleeping Beauty.

Le Corsaire.

Raymonda.

My parents *hated* it.

They hated the practices, and the rehearsals, and the costumes, and the all-consuming vortex of hair spray and rhinestones. When Griffin (and I) were discovered by Conservatory campus police high as kites at the Kwickee Mart installation in May, our parents were *delighted* to force him out of it and into the kind of tech concentration—coding—that would eventually lead him to a career that would feed him physically but starve him spiritually.

My parents didn't anticipate what I know, though: Griffin always finds a way. Just like that first sashay-step he took at my cousin's wedding, he will always find a way to put dance first. Even if it means actively defying the very thing my parents told him that he could no longer do.

In front of me, an entire gaggle of tiny, squealing girls in matching black leotards press around Griffin on the sidewalk, all eye level with his navel and practically climbing over one another to vie for his attention. An older woman with shaggy hair lords over the chaos with a red-and-white megaphone in her hand.

It's my turn to idle at the curb, waiting to pick Griffin up from his first day as an instructor. Dance!Alabama has an absurdly official process, and I hold up a pink card in the shape of a flower that signifies my place in line for the woman with the megaphone. Her voice booms loud enough to rattle through my windows:

"RIDER 153! 153? 153!!!"

Griffin frowns out into the parking lot, unaware until she finally swats him with the back of her clipboard. "153, Griffin!"

He blinks at her for a moment, processing, until recognition falls over him and he pushes past a group of girls watching videos on their iPhones, to open the passenger-side door of my car. He stretches out in the seat next to me, closes the door, and I take off before he can even finish clicking his seat belt.

It's been mere hours since my showdown with Iliana last night.

Not even twenty-four hours since I felt in control of a situation with her for the very first time, since I watched her blink and stammer and paw at her hair through her hairnet with twitchy fingers.

I feel jittery still, and I'm going to need another hour *at least* to recover.

"Is the entire class like that?" I ask, thinking of the girls swarming him on the sidewalk.

Oblivious, Griffin downs at least half of the to-go cup filled with coffee between us in one swig.

"Imagine the whole thing set to Disney tunes being piped through the speakers," Griffin says. "Allllll of those little-bitty kids—pretty much all girls, I heard there's *a* boy that takes class during the week, but I think he's half yeti because no one I've talked to has actually set eyes on him—and not a single soul paying attention."

"Disney tunes *are* my description of hell," I say.

When I swing around to the back of the strip mall and put the car in park, it's as much for me to calm my nerves (and my shaking hands) as it is for Griffin to change out of his leotard.

"*Here?* Really?" Griffin's eyes shift from the passenger-side window, back to me. "You couldn't pick somewhere more secluded?"

"Are you kidding? Look: trees." I point to the right. My hands are still shaking. "Building." I point to the left. *Still* shaking. "No other cars anywhere." I gesture all around. *Still effing shaking.* "Just make it quick, okay?"

"What if there are security cameras?"

"There aren't security cameras."

"You didn't even look!" Griffin is frowning again.

This is the Griffin I know and love, mouthy and anxious in a leotard and compression shorts. I always miss him—until I have to deal with him again.

"*Get out OF THE CARRRR—!*"

"UGH, fine." He snatches a duffel bag from my backseat and leaves the door open as a kind of privacy screen, ducks down under the tinted window, and gets to work.

"You need to hurry," I say. "Mom and Dad are supposed to be at the school to pick us up for lunch in, like, ten minutes."

"Chill! I'm hurrying!"

"Don't tell me to *chill*, Griffin Ingram."

"Don't tell me to hurry—"

"Oh my *God*, put your jeans on."

After a few moments of struggle and a brief glimpse of bare back that I couldn't avoid, Griffin reappears in the passenger side in a mint-green polo shirt and jeans scuffed at the knees. He musses his boyish mop of hair with his fingers, his eyes trained on his reflection in his visor mirror, then drops back into the seat and clicks the seat belt.

We navigate our way out of the parking lot in silence.

It isn't until the front of Dance!Alabama appears behind us again, in all its controlled chaos during pickup line, that I find the words for what I've wondered since Griffin let me in on his little secret.

I wish I understood what this *thing* is that keeps driving him forward, even when the circumstances surrounding doing what he loves are so completely horrible.

"Is all of this worth it?" I ask. "The sneaking around and dancing at that hellhole of a place? You've always had *opinions* about places like Dance!Alabama, but now—"

"I can't *not* dance, Rho." He glares out the window. "I still can't believe they sunk to that level. *You* didn't have to leave the visual arts program."

"Oh, come on," I say. "They've always been supportive of us."

We both know this is a lie. But it feels disloyal if I don't say it.

"No, they've pushed what they want on us. They decided before we could even walk what they wanted us to be: You were some kind of creative prodigy before you could even hold a pencil. I'm supposed to do something 'productive,' as if the performing arts isn't."

I frown into traffic.

I've never articulated it to myself this way, but he's right. If they didn't want me to pursue art, they would have used it as an opportunity to force their wishes on me. All I have is the privilege of being too much of a people pleaser to pursue the things I actually love.

I don't even know what those things are anymore.

There's a truth underneath all of this that's pushing its way up toward the surface, something I'm not quite ready to admit to myself. It's evident now more than ever: The way Griffin throws himself into his art, despite every single challenge that's been thrown in his way. The way Iliana throws herself into her art, staring down any threat to her success with a kind of tenacity that is honestly terrifying.

And then there's me.

"I don't understand why you don't hate me for this," I say. "I got to stay in my program, and I don't deserve to be there anymore. You were living your dream, and it all got taken away from you."

"I do, some days. Then I remember that you're dying inside because they've forced you somewhere you don't want to be, too, and I know that we're *both* in hell right now."

"Well, you aren't wrong," I say. "Every bit of this."

I pick up my phone from the dash and hand it over. Cheshire's direct message is still open on my screen:

Curious-in-Cheshire 11:03a: so, how do you want to do this meeting thing?

The read receipt hangs at the bottom of the DM like some kind of albatross around my neck, and I know it's probably torturing Cheshire, too.

I have no idea what to do anymore.

Griffin sucks his teeth for a moment before he tosses it back onto the dash. "I didn't know y'all were still talking."

"Of course we're still talking," I say. I couldn't imagine not talking to *Cheshire*. "She's going to be in Nashville that weekend, too."

"Rho. We have talked about this a thousand times—don't tell people on the internet where you're going. That is literally the worst idea I've ever—"

"She's going for the Capstone Award, too," I say. "That's why she's going to be in Nashville. We're going to be in the same *room*. A lot over the next few weeks."

Griffin rolls his eyes so hard, it looks like they'll fall out of his head and fly off into the stratosphere. "Anybody can say 'me too' about *anything*. Give me a break."

"No, *she* asked *me* if I was doing it," I say.

"Oh." He squirms in his seat next to me, then shoves a fingernail between his teeth.

I don't want to ask what he's thinking.

I don't have it in me now—not enough bandwidth to deal with the Capstone alone, much less Cheshire's needy clinginess and Griffin's agonizing over my life choices. I've never had a girlfriend or anything remotely close, and the idea of somebody checking up on me when I already need Very Badly to be alone is more than I can handle.

Not to mention, Griffin's got opinions about this—about everything—and I'm extremely not in the mood to have any of them foisted on me . . .

Until that little voice in the back of my head starts to whisper.

What if he's *right*?

What if Griffin is providing a universe-ordained opportunity to save me from this, and by not listening I'm sealing my fate as a future missing persons headline?

What if we find out later that Cheshire is a forty-two-year-old man with a lesbian fetish?

No, I want to scream back to myself. *Cheshire is the realest thing I have right now.*

Cheshire is real. What we have is real.

And yet.

The whispering continues. Anxiety doesn't care about the laws of the universe.

All it takes is one singular seed of fear and all bets are off.

"Just say it." I pull into the Conservatory parking lot, and into the spot next to where our parents idle in their massive SUV. "You're practically choking on it."

"Even if Cheshire *is* real, do you *actually* think this is the right time for you to be doing this? Everything about the Capstone has been a capital-S *Struggle*." He waves to Dad through the passenger window. "Do you really want to be distracted by a girl, for the first time in your entire life, when you've never needed to focus on something more in your life?"

"You don't think I can have both?"

He turns to face me in the seat. "All I'm saying is that you have to make sacrifices for the things you want. You need to decide what you want and be ready to lose something."

"Ugh, you can be such a jerk sometimes." I throw my car in park and pop open the trunk. "I can have both, Griffin. I don't have to choose."

It sounds real when I say it out loud. There's no reason for him to doubt me.

I just hope I believe it before I meet Cheshire, too.

TWO WEEKS UNTIL THE CAPSTONE AWARD

ILIANA

Username: Curious-in-Cheshire
Last online: 20m ago

Curious-in-Cheshire 11:03a: so, how do you want to do this meeting thing?

The message shows as "read" the moment I sent it, but there is no response.

I'm supposed to be helping load the van, but I can't tear my eyes from my phone.

My heart is in my throat.

I flick back over to the email from the Capstone committee and scroll through the names a second time. Twenty-five names in total. My name, Sarah's name, Rhodes's name, and then twenty-two potential Alices—seventeen if I weed out the boys from the list.

Kiersten Keller, a girl from our *actual school*. A real human person that I've probably set eyes on before.

Kiersten Keller, who was supposed to be here fifteen minutes ago to ride with us to Nashville for the Capstone project proposal because her parents can't make it, either.

It's crept up on me, slowly but surely, but Kiersten's absence and my conversation with Alice on Slash/Spot feels related somehow.

"Iliana! Get your shit!" Sarah is a flushed, wide-eyed pixie on the other side of the van, hoisting her own beat-up luggage into the backseat. The van rental place is up the interstate, on the way to Nashville and away from the city, so we all agreed to meet here rather than loop back and load up at the school. My suitcase actually belongs to my brother—a squared-off, hard-shelled thing he bought for a spring break spent in Cancun during college—and I stow my phone in my back pocket to lift it out of Sarah's trunk with both hands.

I imagine these are not the sort of problems Rhodes is having right now.

They're probably staying in their condo and calling it a little family vacation.

Neither my mom nor my dad could even get off work to see my presentation. Sarah's mom is meeting us there for the day and promised to record everything so my mom can watch when her shift at the factory ends. I switch back over to the Slash/Spot direct message platform. I have a message.

> **I-Kissed-Alice** 11:10a: do you want to try to meet at all in Nashville?

Something in me crumbles a little.

Why isn't she more excited about meeting? We've been friends—more than friends, really—since the beginning of the summer. I couldn't imagine getting through losing the Savannah College of Art and Design scholarship, community service, and the fallout with my parents without her. I was there for her, too.

This shouldn't hurt as much as it does.

I reply right away.

> **Curious-in-Cheshire** 11:10a: why wouldn't we? Haven't we always wanted this?

I-Kissed-Alice 11:10a: I just don't want to mess this up by confusing competition with our feelings for each other . . . or vice versa.

My phone disappears from my hands. It takes exactly three seconds for my brain to register that it's gone, and another second to realize it's because Sarah took it from me. She flicks up and down on the chat screen, reading. I snatch it back from her, but it's completely pointless—she's read everything she needs to read.

"'*Do you want to meet at all in Nashville*'?!" Her eyes are wide and bright. "Who *is* this?!"

"I don't want to talk about it!" My face burns all the way into my hairline.

But Sarah is my best friend, and she knows me better than almost anyone.

Almost anyone. Except Alice.

"Well, she's my friend . . . I guess . . . on the internet," I say. Immediately I regret it. I don't want her to know, but the catharsis of sharing this part of my life with someone—*anyone*—is irresistible.

I can't stop once I start.

I tell Sarah everything—how we bonded over fan fiction at the beginning of the summer when I was grounded to my house after my arrest. How we write comics together now, and the role-playing that happens between comic updates, and the way it feels so completely real except that I've never even set my eyes on her before. That Alice is the reason I haven't been with anyone in months, because my heart can't bear the idea of investing itself in someone else. The fact that she's going for the Capstone, too, and she needs it as much as I—as we—do.

By the time I'm finished, I can't look at Sarah anymore.

This is the first time I've ever said any of this out loud.

"*OH MY GOD! YOU HAVE TO MEET HER!!!*" Sarah grabs me around the middle, jumping up and down. Her eyes are wide and glittery, like an anime character's, and she lets go of me to clutch her hands to her chest. "This is ADORABLE, Iliana!"

"You're so embarrassing," I say, but I can't help the excited trill in my chest.

I never wanted to admit how much I want Alice.

I want her in a tangible way: I want to put my hands on her. I want to feel her on my body the way I feel her in my soul. I want to hold her hand and look into her eyes and hear her voice whispering my name as if she's uttering a prayer—

Now that I've imagined it, I don't want to settle for anything else. I don't want to be her *friend* anymore.

I don't want this weird, murky, sort-of-romantic-but-not-really thing—I want to love her openly. I want to be an acknowledged part of her life, and I want her to be an acknowledged part of mine.

"Oh my God, *the list!* The email! Iliana!!" Sarah drags me from my thoughts when she pulls her own phone from her pocket. She claps her hand over her mouth. "What if it's Kiersten? What if Alice has been under your nose the entire time?!"

"I know. It could be Kiersten. The Marianna Walters girl feels like a possibility, too."

"Marianna sounds pretty. Kiersten *is* pretty." Sarah lets out a girly squeak. "And she's riding with us, if she ever fucking shows up."

"Is she?" I pop Kiersten's first and last name into the first social media app I can pull up. Her face appears, and I recognize her immediately.

I've definitely noticed her around campus before. Her hair changes color every week or two, almost as if it's made of magic. She's pretty in an almost cartoonish sort of way, with big eyes and cutesy-femme clothes in wild floral prints.

She's not how I picture my serious, tenderhearted Alice, but looks can be deceiving.

In an instant, my idea of who Alice could be shifts. I want it to be true *so deeply*, almost more than I've ever wanted anything, and I know if I think too hard about it I'll start poking holes in my own hypothesis.

Sarah and I make shell-shocked eye contact.

"We have to figure out if it's her," Sarah says finally. I'm glad I told her. "You need to know what you're dealing with before you go into this."

"I don't think Alice *wants* to meet in Nashville, though, remember? She said she didn't know if it was a good idea."

"That's because she's nervous," Sarah says. "Everyone does that when they're nervous."

Like clockwork, a zippy, expensive car with a Conservatory rider tag pulls into the parking lot. After a moment of shuffling, Kiersten Keller appears out of the passenger side with a bright pink overnight bag tossed over her shoulder and curiosity in her eyes.

I've stayed so caught up in the world of the visual arts track at the Conservatory, I forgot that as someone in the theater track, Kiersten doesn't really know us, either.

"I'm going to go get Dad from the rental office, and then we can hit the road," Sarah says.

She flashes her eyes at me, and a second later, Kiersten and I are alone.

A second later, and I've forgotten that Alice could have been anyone other than Kiersten: Her hair is nearly black at the roots, graduating to periwinkle at the ends, and today she's wearing it in a long braid that hangs messy over one shoulder. Her pink bomber jacket has studs at the neck and pockets that look like lace, her eye makeup is smudgy and dark, and she's sewed patterned patches behind frayed holes in her jeans.

"Hi," she says finally.

I didn't realize I was staring at her.

She's just *so pretty*. I have lost all ability to brain.

"Are . . . you on . . . um. Drugs? Still?" She pops her gum.

My face burns hot enough to ache. Oh my *God*, this is a God-forsaken disaster.

I giggle involuntarily for way too long—*WHO THE HELL AM I?*—before it occurs to me that I can hide it in a series of fake coughs in the inside of my elbow, vampire cough–style.

A half a beat later, it hits me that she thinks I'm on drugs.

"*Still?*" I ask. Where the hell is Sarah? This is terrible. Everything is terrible.

"Didn't you, like, get caught high on campus last year?" Kiersten pops her gum again. "You're the only Iliana at the school—"

"I wasn't *on drugs!*"—*WHERE THE HELL IS SARAH? OH MY GOD!*—"It was just pot. It's not, like, uh, a regular thing—or even, like, a sometimes thing."

Pot's too expensive for anything remotely resembling even occasional use.

I don't really care for how it makes me feel, anyway.

Finally—*fucking finally*—Sarah and her dad emerge from the rental office. He has a genuine smile for all of us—and not much else by way of conversation—and rounds the side of the van to start the engine. Sarah isn't far behind, eyeing my and Kiersten's faces with a level of curiosity that completely mortifies me.

Kiersten's interest moves from Sarah to myself, then to the phone in her hands.

"What the hell *happened*?!" Sarah tries the locked front passenger-side door, then bangs on the glass.

The locks pop, and she hops inside.

"More like, what the hell *took so long*?" I sling open the side door and clamber to the back. Kiersten claims the middle row.

Sarah and I blink out an entire conversation at each other in a Morse code of waggling eyebrows and shrugging shoulders:

> Sarah: Dad's gotta be Dad. I dunno. He always takes forever.
>
> Me: I completely bombed that. She thinks I'm weird and that I use drugs.
>
> Me: SHE THINKS I'M WEIRD NOW. Does she even like girls?
>
> Sarah: Well, you're weird.
>
> Me: But does she like girls?
>
> Sarah: I have no idea if she likes girls, Iliana.
>
> Me: SHE THINKS I'M ON DRUGS. HELP.

Sarah doesn't help. Instead, she puts headphones on and turns to the book in her lap.

It occurs to me that maybe we were having two different conversations.

We have enough room in the back of the passenger van that Kiersten and I have rows to ourselves. I've turned to rest my chin on the back of my seat, and Kiersten rests against the window with her legs stretched out in front of her. Alice has told me before that she's tall, but Kiersten is small like Sarah and me: Her feet—clad in gorgeous, one-of-a-kind floral Doc Martens, because of course she has amazing, one-of-a-kind floral Docs—don't even make it to the end of the row.

She's a theater-track kid, I've learned, but her passion isn't *acting*. She loves costume design.

"It's DIY," Kiersten says, fingering the studded details around the neck of her jacket. "I found my mom's old BeDazzler in our attic and just . . . figured it out myself. Ordered the studs and stuff off the internet and googled the user's manual."

From the front seat, Sarah and I make eye contact in the rearview window.

The internet! She's on the internet!

Of course she is on the internet. Everybody is on the internet.

Still, it feels like a clue of some kind.

"So you're studying costume design," I say, eyeing the sketchbook in her lap. If I could get a glimpse, I'd recognize Alice's unique drawing style immediately. "But you're an artist, too."

Instead of showing her work, Kiersten pulls the spiral-bound book closer to her chest. "Costume design *is* art."

"Fair," I say. "But costumes won't win the Capstone Award. What are you pitching?"

I gesture to the sketchbook. Kiersten doesn't hand it over, though— she pulls her phone from her pocket and flips through a photo album.

I've never seen anything like what's on the screen: fabric collages— silks and cottons and brocades, dyed spectacularly and hand-sewn together, topped with intricate embroidery. Some of her pieces have poetry sewn into them; one is a self-portrait.

"At some point the world decided embroidery—sewing—was women's work," she says. "So it doesn't have value as art. I want to reclaim it."

"This is incredible." I hand her phone back. Her fingernails are painted periwinkle, too.

"You should tell her about *your* project, Iliana," Sarah says from the front seat.

Kiersten waits, smiling. I don't have a sketchbook on me to show her, or pictures on my phone. All I can do is tell her about it, but if she's Alice, that's all it will take. She'll know me immediately.

"It's—" I take a breath. I didn't even know Kiersten five minutes ago, but I want her to be Alice *so* much. For better or for worse, I'm not sure I'm ready to find out what the outcome will be. "It's a paper-cut project. Alice in Wonderland–themed tarot cards, mounted between sheets of glass."

I can feel Sarah watching from the front seat.

My eyes are only for Kiersten.

"I don't think I can picture it," she finally says, smiling. "I don't know much about tarot. It sounds very interesting, though."

I don't know if I'm relieved or disheartened.

It had been so easy to believe it was Kiersten.

I need to guard my heart this weekend.

I turn to Sarah. "Tell us about yours!"

"Oh." Sarah waves her hand. "I'm still marinating on it. You'll find out with everyone else."

Sarah and her dad share *a look* across the center console.

"Don't look at me like that. I know what I'm do—"

One moment, everything's fine. The next—*BANG. BANGBANG-BANGBANG POW.*

The entire passenger van seizes.

Two hours until we're supposed to check in for the Capstone project proposal, and we've blown a tire. *Crap.*

Sarah's dad curses as he swerves hard to the right, and all of us are screaming as we lurch to the kind of stop that tests the functioning of our seat belts. He slings himself out of the car, grumbling about the rental company and the tires and AAA.

Sarah, Kiersten, and I smooth each other's hair and collect each other's strewn cell phones and water bottles from all over the inside of the van.

"We're still, like, two hours away," Kiersten says, frowning out the window.

"I'll text Rhodes." Sarah doesn't wait for us to object before her thumbs fly over her phone's screen. "They left town after we did, so maybe they're close."

It isn't even fifteen minutes later that a lipstick-red SUV pulls onto the shoulder behind us.

In the blink of an eye, everything has gone to hell.

CHAPTER 12

RHODES

Username: I-Kissed-Alice
Online now

"So . . . you want me to wait with Dad," Griffin eyes our dad and Mr. Wade—Sarah's dad—as if they belong to another species.

Truthfully, our dad and Mr. Wade *are* a different species from boys like Griffin. They'll probably love the whole rigamarole of waiting for AAA, having the tire changed by a professional, and then driving up out of earshot from my mother's never-ending string of biting criticism.

"There isn't enough room in the SUV for all of you," Mom says, frowning.

Kiersten Keller shifts from one foot to the other, visibly uncomfortable.

Sarah's used to the rude way my parents talk in front of people as if they aren't standing *right there*, and Iliana glowers into the distance with such force I half expect the mountains on the other side of the interstate to move.

Mom's comments from when we pulled over to pick them up echo in the back of my mind as I take in each of them:

"Why does the purple-haired one look like an extra in a Cyndi Lauper video? What is it with you girls and your Kool-Aid hair? Ugh with the nose rings, already—"

"Do Sarah's parents just give her their old clothes? Why does she always look like she crawled out of a donation bin at the thrift store? You should take her shopping, honey."

"Iliana would be so much prettier if she smiled. Does she smile, ever? No? Well. She'll spend the rest of her life—and all her husband's money—trying to make those frown lines disappear."

A year ago, I would have been whispering the same things back to my mom, judging girls like Iliana and Kiersten for how they dress. But there are things about Iliana I know now that give me pause—even if I can't stand her: that she's stern-looking because she's driven to the degree that she spends her life consumed by her work.

That she probably won't ever take a husband—she won't want or need a man at *all*.

That if she ever settles down at all, it will be with a woman who wants her exactly as she is. As much as I hate Iliana Vrionides, I know she's the kind of bitch that never settles for anything.

Sarah's never talked about what she wants, and she's never been clear on who she is. I don't know Kiersten at all, but knowing Sarah and Iliana the way I do now has completely shifted the way I think over the past year.

It's shifted what I want for myself, too.

It feels like some kind of divine mystery, the way people learn to love themselves like Iliana and Kiersten have. Or, for that matter, to *know* themselves like that.

Coming out was hard enough two years ago. Admitting to myself—and anyone else—how I might have changed over the past year is still harder than I could have ever imagined.

"I can, um"—Kiersten glances at her phone—"call an Uber, I guess—"

"No, you're not," I say. "Mom, you stay with Dad. We'll take the SUV."

"No adult?" Mom's Botox-frozen eyebrows don't move, but her

face does this weird thing where I know they'd hike up into her forehead if they actually worked like they were supposed to. "Five teenagers and no adult?"

I shrug, and gesture for the keys.

This has nothing to do with concern for our safety and *everything* to do with spending the next two hours in solitary confinement with Dad.

"I'm not leaving Griff to listen to Dad grunt and fart at the Triple A guy."

"*Language*—"

"I said *fart*. Give me a break."

Mom and I glare at each other for a solid minute.

"Mom," I finally say. "We only have two hours until we have to be there."

Mom sighs and whirls on Griff. "Put everybody's luggage in the back of their rental van, and there will be room for all five of you in the SUV." She turns back to me. "Dad can wait with Mr. Wade for Triple A. *I'm* still driving. You need an adult."

Behind where Griffin and I sit in the middle row, Sarah, Kiersten, and Iliana are purposely not talking—not in a we-just-fought sort of way but . . .

The energy is *odd*.

"Something happened in the van," I whisper to Griff. "Don't you think?"

The way Iliana *isn't* looking at Kiersten speaks so much louder than anything either girl could say *to* each other. Iliana's earbuds are in, and she hasn't taken her eyes off her phone since we got back on the road. Kiersten is doing the same, sketching with giant candy-colored headphones covering her ears.

I start to ask Sarah what happened, but my phone vibrates in my lap instead.

> **Curious-in-Cheshire** 1:21p: I know you think knowing each other—and doing this irl—will muddy everything up with the competition but like
>
> **Curious-in-Cheshire** 1:22p: we go so much deeper than this
>
> **Curious-in-Cheshire** 1:22p: we both know we deserve the award, we can be supportive of each other. Right?

I wish I could believe she's right.

I steal a glance at Iliana, whose mere presence is a testament to how toxic competition really is.

> **I-Kissed-Alice** 1:22p: I just don't want to mess this up
>
> **I-Kissed-Alice** 1:23p: you're the realest thing I've got going for me right now

The truth of the words blooms somewhere deep. It honestly hurts, telling her no like this. I want so much for the circumstances to be different, for us to have just decided on our own to do this thing like we've talked about a thousand times before. The only difference? We'd *choose* to find each other.

The fact that life is just throwing us together should feel like fate, but instead all I have is an impending sense of doom.

I take a screenshot and text it to Griffin. His phone lights up, then he cuts his eyes to me.

What would you do? I text him.

I didn't know y'all were so serious, he types. Rather than hit send, he just shows me his phone. I cut him *a look*.

He types: *Do you think knowing who she is will change anything? Like if you find out now or later, you're still going to find out eventually.*

I type: *What if we fall head-over-heels in love and have all this head-over-heels sex and don't care about the scholarship anymore?*

Sex. A real-life possibility I had not considered until I typed it out. We've sexted so many times—would Cheshire expect it when we finally meet face-to-face?

I don't even know her first name yet.

It wouldn't be my first time, but I can count the number of times I've had sex with anyone on one hand. I'd need *maybe* two or three fingers. Max.

Would she wait until I was ready?

Griffin scrunches his face.

   1) ew

   2) spare the sex stuff I am a pure, impressionable child

   3) then you can go flip burgers I guess

"Oh, give me a break." I say this out loud. "You've been with more girls than I have."

Griffin puts a finger to his lips and points to our mom in the front seat. She's oblivious, gratefully, absorbed in an audiobook she has faded to the front speakers. Behind us, Iliana has her headphones on and her eyes closed, but I don't think she's sleeping. Sarah is asleep and snoring slightly. Only Kiersten seems to be listening with interest, and I don't care what she does or doesn't know.

If you're so worried about it, tell her you'll meet her after the project proposal. I think it *will* distract you if you wait until after the winner is announced . . .

That's a good idea, I type. *I'll do that. Why are you so smart?*

I'm not, he types. *You're just exceptionally clueless.*

Oh, eff off.

I swipe back over to my Slash/Spot direct messages.

   I-Kissed-Alice 1:47p: let's do it after the proposal

"DO IT?!" Griffin whispers over my shoulder.

"That's not what I meant!" I elbow him in the stomach, but the damage is done. My face throbs with embarrassment.

I-Kissed-Alice 1:47p: MEET I MEAN. LET'S MEET AFTER THE PROPOSAL OMG

Smooth, Griffin texts me.

I turn to give him an earful, but he's already leaned against the far window with his eyes closed, feigning sleep. I punch him in the arm, and he spreads his knee past the seam between our two seats—an old-as-time breach of territory lines. I kick him in the shin, and he pinches me in the ribs, and I poke him in the ear, back and forth until Mom threatens to pull over the car like we're six and eight again.

It isn't enough to distract me from the fact that Cheshire still hasn't messaged me back.

Curious-in-Cheshire 1:41a: okay

I-Kissed-Alice 1:45a: okay what

Curious-in-Cheshire 1:45a: let's meet. After the proposal

I-Kissed-Alice 1:45a: okay

I-Kissed-Alice 1:46a: where

Curious-in-Cheshire 1:46a: I don't know anything about Nashville

I-Kissed-Alice 1:47a: There's a coffee shop around the corner from Frist. It's called Glace. They have ice cream too. And glaces . . . like both.

I-Kissed-Alice 1:47a: Ice cream and coffee together

I-Kissed-Alice 1:48a: well I mean not coffee. Espresso. If you like espresso.

Curious-in-Cheshire 1:48a: so we'll meet at 8, then?

I-Kissed-Alice 1:48a: 8 is good

Curious-in-Cheshire 1:48a: we're really doing this

I-Kissed-Alice 1:48a: we're really doing this

CHAPTER 13
ILIANA

Username: Curious-in-Cheshire
Last online: 20m ago

On paper, the Frist Art Museum didn't sound like a big deal at all. I should have known when Rhodes gave one of her bored shrug-slash-sighs and said Frist was "just, you know, fine."

She didn't call it unoriginal, or boring, or anything else.

It was "*just, you know, fine,*" and that should have told me everything.

The Frist Art Museum is grand in the kind of way that I feel a little too dirty to step inside. It looms over Broadway, granite and angular, as if one of Frank Lloyd Wright's houses and a medieval fort had some kind of strange, glorious love child.

The front is lined with—*what, Doric? Corinthian?*—columns cast through an art deco lens, a pantheon dedicated to the only deities people like Rhodes, Sarah, Kiersten, and I worship: the patron gods of culture.

It seems like I'm the only person here that didn't realize—*really, truly, absorb*—that the project proposal was an actual, bona fide, stand-in-front-of-a-podium *presentation*.

"Randall *literally told us* it was a presentation," Sarah whispered to me as we were queueing up backstage. "He even said, 'Plan

143

for five-to-seven minutes—use the whole time, and bring a slide show—'"

"*I know what he said!*" I hiss.

She laughs at me.

She's told me before she thinks I sound like a goose when I whisper through my teeth like that.

I'm not laughing.

I don't think it's funny.

I don't have a presentation planned. I wasn't planning on a *speech* at all—I know my strengths. I know that if I'd written out what I was going to say, it would sound clunky and robotic. I know that there's a burning in me that fascinates people, and I know that I'm anointed by fire when I get going on something I care about.

I know I will never beat Rhodes at being poised, prepared, and rehearsed—but she'll never match the way I *glow*.

Except I'm not standing in a small room full of old ladies—I'm waiting with the others backstage in a stranger-filled auditorium. This is how I pictured it would go: one of those coffee-and-paper-scented conference rooms people rent on the bottom floors of big libraries with outdated artwork on the walls. The Capstone Award judges would sit at a long table on the far wall like the judges on *The Voice*, each of us finalists entering one at a time to pitch our potential projects to three women who hold the fate of our worlds in their hands.

A feminine, disembodied voice—someone's aunt or mother, probably—whispers my name from deeper within the cavernous backstage area. She butchers it, actually, so much so that she has to say it three times before I realize she's speaking to *me*.

Based on the others who have gone before me, and the thunder of applause for the previous presenter—Marianna Walters, who is exiting stage left—I know that it means I have to go.

I'm not ready. I don't know what I'm going to say anymore.

I wasn't going to beat Rhodes at her own game here, and I'm not going to beat anyone by my own rules, either.

Worse still, I'm damp with sweat. *Everywhere*: My upper lip, the base of my skull under my curls, my armpits, under my breasts, at the small of my back, my ass crack, between my thighs. My pulse thunders away with such force, I can *see* it in the way my peripheral vision throbs in wild, frenetic unison with the beat of my heart.

This is how I die.

Except I don't die—I end up out onstage somehow, but I don't remember marching myself out. Except I know I had to have marched myself out there, because otherwise I would still be standing backstage with the others.

The lights are bright on my face, and I can't see much farther than the table of judges along the front row. Whispers and shuffling echo up from the built-in theater seating, so I know in theory the room is at least moderately full of people—parents, probably, and the myriad people who style themselves as "patrons" who keep art festivals like the Ocoee Arts Festival going.

The heavy wooden podium is too tall for me, so I remove the microphone from its stand and step around it. The screen behind me is empty, because I don't have a PowerPoint presentation.

All I can do is paint a picture with my words instead.

The room settles into silence.

I open my mouth, and I begin to speak.

CHAPTER 14

RHODES

Username: I-Kissed-Alice
Last online: 20m ago

I should have never agreed to meet Cheshire.

This is exactly what I was worried about: That I would be distracted by being nervous about *her*, and I wouldn't put energy into my presentation—which, to be honest, still feels like pissing in the wind.

I have no idea if I'm going to pull this off. Not when I look down the long row of finalists and wonder whose face I've fantasized about kissing.

None of this feels like real life.

A stack of index cards sit in my lap unread, and even with my laptop opened to my PowerPoint presentation in front of me, my attention is transfixed on the stage with everyone else. The cards are professionally printed, and per my coach I'm not allowed to bring them onstage with me.

"It needs to look seamless," he said, adjusting his tie. "Completely poised, like you're just, you know, breathing it out of you."

Onstage, Iliana is pulling off something exactly the opposite. Without the benefit of a slideshow, she's weaving together a story: Feared by some, and disbelieved by most, artistry and tarot carry a long, storied history that most overlook.

"Seventy-eight cards means seventy-eight pieces of individual artwork," Iliana says. "And within those seventy-eight cards are five complete story arcs, worlds inside of worlds, whose symbols relate to our own experiences as humans. The kinds of stories that were relevant five hundred years ago and are just as relevant now."

Rather than stand behind the podium like the rest of us, she paces with the microphone in one hand. The other hand flies around her as she talks, painting pictures with her mind's eye that none of us can see.

Her words fall out of her, hurried and jumbled, a willy-nilly stream of consciousness that doesn't quite make sense, except that it *does*. There's an unvarnished charm to it, almost as if she's opened the front of her skull and allowed us to see the intricate inner workings of her brain.

It's almost like a TED Talk.

It just works.

I thrust a cuticle between my teeth and swallow bile.

"Traditionally, tarot imagery is drawn or painted. But I, um, submit for your approval a series of seventy-eight paper-cut cards in red and black paper, layered between sheets of glass for depth."

There is a long pause before Iliana speaks again.

Her tongue clicks against the roof of her mouth.

"Rather than prepare a slide presentation," she says, "I've made my sketchbooks available to you. The pages with my preliminary sketches are, uh, dog-eared. Or, you know, um, folded down."

Another long round of silence.

Shuffling paper echoes throughout the auditorium.

Pages with my preliminary sketches sounds like a handful at most, but it sounds like the judges are looking at her other work, too.

Iliana's so jittery that her curls shake around her face, but no one can take their eyes off her. Something about her wild, frenetic energy is fascinating, in the same sort of way as watching a captured firefly try to fight its way out of a Mason jar.

There is no poise to her at all, and yet she could very well be the one to take this thing from me. The small audience thunders with applause, and Iliana strides offstage like an electric, malevolent goddess.

ILIANA

Username: Curious-in-Cheshire
Last online: 20m ago

Rhodes, of course, is everything the Capstone Award committee has ever wanted.

She's not sweaty and shaking and babbling about tarot cards.

The stage lights shine on her dark hair, and her sweater falls over her curves in a way that's equal parts flattering and nonthreatening to a battery of crotchety old women. She moves like an automaton: Eye contact with the first judge, eye contact with the second judge, eye contact with the third judge. Glance at the clock. Pan the crowd. Eye contact with the first judge, eye contact with the second judge, eye contact with the third judge. Glance at the clock. Pan the crowd.

Her presentation is canned, a regurgitation from that day in the diner a few weeks ago.

"Breathy nudes," she says, clicking the remote in her hands to move the slides. "A series."

Behind her, one of her trademark "breathy nudes" spreads across the screen, cream-toned pastels swept across paper toned deep claret. Each stroke of pastel is just a whisper, half smudged into the paper. And still, my brain completes each line the way it completes Sarah's sentences: The nip of a waist leads to the curve of a hip. The swell of a breast, that delicate strait that runs from an earlobe down to the crest of a clavicle.

Every piece merely *suggests* the shape of the figure in question, leaving my imagination to fill in the rest.

They're exquisite: Technically perfect. Clearly inspired. Intellectually stimulating. Tantalizing on a very basic, physiological level.

I wish I could find any fault in these at all.

She clicks the remote again.

"Lighter than air, soft pastels on colored paper. The study would emphasize each person's innate vulnerability while focusing on their shared humanity despite their physiological differences."

Her right eyebrow twitches, then the third finger on her left hand.

The judges nod thoughtfully.

"How is this different from last year's Ocoee Art Festival submission?" asks one of the judges—a *Mrs.* June Baker, the woman who visited the school for the interest meeting earlier in the year. She gestures to the work on the screen behind Rhodes, the piece in question.

Rhodes took the Young Artist's Achievement Award for this piece.

"It's—It's true that my work follows a theme," Rhodes's voice quivers, just on the end of each sentence, "but I—I believe an artist's work goes where their interests are."

"So, would you say this is a continuation of your Ocoee Art Festival series, then?"

"Yes." Rhodes's smile is broad. "Do you have any other questions?"

Sarah is down at the other end of the line, but Kiersten is positioned to my right. She's watching Rhodes with the same interest as I am, and her face twists into something that reflects the sick dread that's settled into my gut. Rhodes's brilliant, beatific smile confirms something in my mind so clear, *so* apparently obvious, that I can't believe I didn't see it before this very moment:

"This feels like a setup," I whisper to Kiersten. "They haven't had questions for anyone else."

"I heard y'all's faculty advisor called in a favor," Kiersten whispers. "Apparently, *he* told June Baker that Rhodes's grades weren't good enough, and June waived the GPA requirement so she could enter. Sounds like they're trying to stack the deck."

"How do you know that?" My voice echoes out into the audience, who have all gone quiet between presentations. The audience responds with a titter of soft laughter.

Ah, *yes*. Dramatic teenagers.

Hilarious.

"One of my friends was doing some filing in the office weeks ago. Y'all's drawing guy doesn't realize how loud he is."

"Mr. Randall," I speak over the thrumming pulse in my ears. "So, you actually *heard* him saying all this?"

I want to cry. I want to laugh.

I am *furious*.

"Not *me*, but yeah. He was talking to her mom about it, and she was really excited. It just seems, I don't know—slimy." She frowns. "I almost dropped out after he told me, but I really need this, so—"

Of *course*. There was no way she was getting into the Capstone without some kind of outside help—I've seen firsthand how little she's actually turned in for class. I also have French and AP Euro with her, and I know she barely scrapes by in her core classes, too.

There's no doubt that she's gone from just-okay grades to literally, actually, *failing*.

"It was slimy for Randall to do it," I say, "and slimy for Rhodes to follow through with it."

Rhodes isn't smiling when she steps off the stage. She only galvanizes when our eyes meet, her shoulders going ramrod straight and her jaw freezing into hard angles.

She pauses in front of me just long enough to look me over from the top of my head to the toes of my shoes before she makes her way past the others, in the direction of the stage foyer.

I follow her.

I don't know what I'm going to say when I get where she's going.

The door slams in my face.

Suddenly, *everything* I want to say strains against the inside of my mind, two years of it stretching and pressing and growing and screaming—

I fling the door open behind her.

When she whirls around, her eyes are wide, and her jaw is set.

I close the distance between us. She's got at least six inches on me, and probably a good twenty pounds. She pushes me away from her to create space, and I push back. Harder this time, maybe too hard.

It's an orgasm of its own kind: euphoria followed by an instant break of tension.

I started this fight, and it isn't one I'm going to win fairly.

CHAPTER 16

RHODES

Username: I-Kissed-Alice
Last online: 20m ago

Iliana is a force of nature, practically flying through the door to claim any space between us.

Her voice is thunder, and her eyes are lightning.

Electricity surges in each curl that flies about her face; it crackles and glows over the top of her skin—

Her hands are on me, and her breath is on me, and her hair is on me—

I throw out my arms and push her back.

Disbelief hangs heavy around us.

After everything, this is the first time we've ever actually *touched* each other.

"I fought for my place at the Conservatory." Iliana is first to break the silence. Her chest heaves. "I fought to be here."

"Of *course* you think you're the only one fighting," I say.

Sarah, as ever, is alternately hovering between the two of us and trying to blend in with the wallpaper. Kiersten hovers close, hammering away at the phone in her hands as she watches. I throw a hand out in Sarah's direction as proof.

"Sarah is fighting to be here," I say. "I'm fighting to be here, too."

"Sarah doesn't matter right now!" Iliana is on fire. "This is about *you*."

Sarah clutches her cheek as if she's been slapped, but if Iliana notices she doesn't care. She's the sun, burning bright and brilliant. She's too much to look at like this, a black hole caving in on itself and threatening to subsume me into nothingness.

It takes everything within me not to roll over and show her the soft underside of my belly.

"Your family has given you *everything*," Iliana seethes. "They paid out the ass for you to start the Conservatory in the eighth grade. You know why you've done Ocoee every year and I haven't? *I* can't afford the two-hundred-and-fifty-dollar entry fee."

"That's not fair!" I cry. *She* isn't fair. "I am *so sorry* I've had advantages in life that you didn't have—"

"I know you're only here because June Baker waived the GPA requirements for you."

Heat flies to my face. *"THAT'S NOT—"*

"True?" She rests a hand on her hip. "So why do I know that Randall was the one who talked to her?"

"Iliana—"

No. No. No no no no no.

No one is supposed to know this.

Iliana steps closer. Her eyes are brimming over with tears, and her hands are shaking when she presses one finger into my chest. "I know your secret, Rhodes Ingram. The emperor isn't wearing any clothes, and you're *failing at everything*."

It never hit me *just how bad* everything is until now, or the fact that over the past year I've lost more than Iliana has ever had. She's so new at this—so new at everything.

She'll never understand what it feels like to have nothing left like this.

"You're going to run out of steam one day, too," I say. "You're going to look around yourself and realize everything you're doing makes you feel like you're watching paint dry, and you won't know what to do with yourself anymore."

She isn't a malevolent goddess, or a force of nature, or a dying star in a neighboring solar system. She's completely, unerringly, 100 percent flesh-and-blood *human*.

She doesn't say a word, so I continue.

"You have done an incredible job of fooling *literally* everyone into thinking that you're some kind of prodigy," I say, "because nobody believes in you more than you believe in yourself."

"That's not true," she whispers. "I deserve to be here, just like anyone else."

"You know it's true," I fire back. "No one else sees where this is going, but I do: You're going to blow through all this energy you have, and you're going to piss everyone off, and you're going to end up nowhere. Alone. You don't actually have the talent it takes to make it, and you know it."

Iliana lunges forward, swiping and cursing.

Kiersten grabs her around the waist and pulls her back.

"Are you *stupid*?!" Kiersten's louder than either Iliana or myself. "Everyone in the auditorium can hear you. If someone from the Capstone sees you, you're both done! Like, *done!*"

Iliana's irises are blown out and her stare is black, every part of her in twitching, frenetic recoil.

Another spike of adrenaline.

Meanwhile, something in me starts to spiral. My heart hammers in my ears, but the rest of me is going to stone, and if the world was moving slow enough to count the motes of dust in the air a minute ago, it's fast-forwarding at triple-speed now.

Everything around us comes crashing back into focus—the hall outside the Frist Center for the Visual Arts auditorium, with its broad marble facades and art deco–inspired metalwork. Sarah's wide eyes and liner-smeared cheeks.

Sarah's never coped well when Iliana and I fight.

The fact that she's crying is almost too much for me.

It's like I've suddenly become aware of gravity for the first time—my bones are made of lead. I start to sink to the floor before I catch myself and throw more effort into staying vertical.

"Y'all are fucking crazy," Kiersten says.

She releases Iliana, adjusts her jacket, and smooths her hair.

"You can't call something crazy just because you don't like it," I say.

"Fine." She wrenches the door open and glares back at us. "You're *assholes*, both of you. I hope they kick you out."

Sarah watches the two of us wordlessly. She looks down at the swaths of dark eye makeup smeared on the sleeves of her sweater dress; to Iliana, to me. I don't understand the expression on Sarah's face, but Iliana's reading her like she's been doing it her whole life.

"Sarah—" Iliana reaches for her, but she only takes a step farther away.

"Is that what you think of me?" Sarah's attention shifts between Iliana and myself. "That I don't matter?"

"That's not what I meant—" Iliana says.

"I—" Sarah is careful to dab at her cheeks with the hem of her sleeve, in spite of the mess that's already there, "I need to, I don't know, be alone—"

I don't know how long the three of us stand here, staring at each other. My head is throbbing to the beat of my heart, and I gag on literally nothing—I'd be throwing up right now if I'd had the stomach to eat at all today. Instead, I choke out a painful cough behind my hand that only makes my head pound.

Finally, without a word, Sarah turns back toward the stage door.

"My turn should be coming up soon," she says. "Wish me luck."

There's literally no way to respond to it, nothing I can do to make the situation better. The door slams behind her, and the air falls still until Iliana spins on her heels to march straight out the glass doors and onto the sidewalk.

I-Kissed-Alice 6:18p: I don't know if tonight is going to happen

Curious-in-Cheshire 6:18p: you're joking

I-Kissed-Alice 6:18p: no. I have a splitting headache. Mom and I got into it pretty bad after the presentation today

Curious-in-Cheshire 6:19p: there is no way you had it worse than I did

I-Kissed-Alice 6:19p: So why do you want to meet, then, if everything is terrible

Curious-in-Cheshire 6:19p: because seeing you is the only thing holding this day together

I-Kissed-Alice 6:19p: ugh. Me too. I'm sorry.

Curious-in-Cheshire 6:20p: go take a nap. We still have time.

I-Kissed-Alice 6:20p: 8, still? Do you want real food instead?

Curious-in-Cheshire 6:20p: real food sounds good.

I-Kissed-Alice 6:20p: meet me in front of Frist at 8 and we'll walk until we find something

ILIANA

```
Username: Curious-in-Cheshire
Last online: 5m ago
```

"Stop apologizing." Sarah is a smaller version of herself, hunched forward with her arms crossed in front of her middle as if she's holding her guts in.

It's the fourth time I've apologized tonight, and the third time she's told me to cut it out, but . . . nothing's happening.

She still looks the same—sad. Small. Hesitant.

"I just—" *I want you to pretend it never happened*, I want to say.

I *need* you to pretend it never happened—rather, I need my oldest friend, and I need you to not be angry with me anymore.

I *need* you to be excited with me and be brave when I feel so, so afraid.

But nothing changes. We're walking in lockstep up the hill from our hotel, and even if the Frist Center for the Visual Arts is two city blocks away, I can still see the glow of its lights like a beacon calling us home. Under all that light stands Alice—she's never late to anything—and for all I know, she's scared to death, too.

"You're quiet," Sarah says.

We run out of sidewalk, and the light turns red across the street. I hit the button to cross with a gloved hand and turn back to face Sarah again.

"The traffic light is turning your hair red," I say weakly.

People accumulate behind us, all finding their way wherever the heck it is they're going. Probably somewhere fancy. The light glows red on their faces, reflects off the screens of their smartphones and catches in their hair, too.

"Do you have any idea who she is?" Sarah whispers.

The red hand on the crosswalk sign flips over to a brilliant white stick figure, and we step out into the road. Sarah's hair flips from red to green, too.

"None," I say. "I sort of wonder if she hid herself from me on purpose—know what I mean?"

"That's paranoid." Sarah is careful not to look at me.

Her eyes are on the shop windows, lit from the inside against the dark night. We pass a nail salon and an empty Chinese restaurant with a counter covered in take-out orders. A bookstore next, then a law office that's closed for the day.

"Is it paranoid, though? Really? What if she's as afraid of who I am as I am of her?"

"If you're afraid of each other, why are you meeting?"

She has a point. The edge in Sarah's voice doesn't make it easy to swallow, though.

"Look, you didn't have to come with me—"

"Like hell I'm going to miss this." Sarah's smile is hesitant. She reapplied her makeup hours ago—the project presentation is long over and we've had time to crash at the hotel before dinner, but her eyes still carry a little bit of cry in them. She turns to face me and takes my gloved hands in hers. "I have to know how this ends, all right?"

I nod. "I know."

"Just—quit worrying about it."

"Yeah." *Like hell*, as Sarah says. Until I find my way to Alice, and I know everything is okay, I won't quit worrying about it.

We walk the rest of the way to Frist in silence.

I purposely *don't look* at the person standing alone on Frist's massive front staircase—instead, I drag Sarah to hide behind a car parked on the curb.

"I think she's over there," I say. I can't breathe.

Traffic flies past us, and we press closer to the parked car.

Sarah strains to look up at the stairs through the parked car's windshield. "What did she say she's supposed to be wearing?"

"Um." I pull my phone from my pocket and open the Slash/Spot app. It shows she's online now, of course. Probably staring at her phone, waiting for me—a sign—*something*. I'd be doing the same if it were me waiting for her. I flick over to our direct messages. "A baby blue coat, uh, and a black ribbon in her hair."

Like Alice, she'd said. I didn't tell her what I would be wearing.

The time at the top of my phone screen reads 7:50.

A shiver runs over me, then settles in my hands.

Ten more minutes until Alice is in my arms and the entire universe is turned on its ear.

"Iliana, look! Rhodes!" Sarah thrusts a pointed finger toward the other side of the intersection.

Sure enough, there she is, all gussied up and headed God-knows-where.

Probably to meet her parents for dinner.

Or to meet someone none of us are supposed to know about.

I've never seen her date, and it didn't occur to me until now that maybe she's spoken for. It would not be unlike her to have someone tucked away in her back pocket because she doesn't like her fancy Nashville and lowbrow Birmingham foods to touch.

"Sarah—no!" I grab for Sarah just as she starts to dart across the road through waves of traffic. Before I can clamp my hand over her mouth, she's yelling Rhodes's name and waving with enough enthusiasm to accidentally flag down a cab.

Rhodes Ingram, shrill as she ever was, doesn't wait until we're standing on the same street corner to shriek at us. "What the *hell* are you doing here?"

We're going to make Rhodes wait until we cross the street before we dignify her with a response. Or at least I am—Sarah is practically a dog jerking at the end of her chain trying to get to Rhodes on the other side of the street.

Rhodes is usually the one making *me* feel small because I haven't learned all those tiny social nuances she thinks are so important—those myriad things that make classy people classy and the rest of us seem just a little frayed around the edges. But this time, she's the one that's unraveling too fast to care what anyone around her sees her doing.

"Come on—another break in cars is coming up—" Sarah starts to launch across the intersection again, but I hold her back.

"Wait," I say.

Sarah hangs back, again, but every muscle in her body is coiled tight and ready to launch into the street the moment the light changes. Rhodes watches us between the cars that zip by, expectant.

All three of us know exactly what this is: Earlier today, Rhodes and I drew a line in the sand. There is no more coexistence, and Sarah is facing a choice: She's either Rhodes's friend, or mine.

Choosing one means losing the other, even if it isn't fair. After everything that happened between Sarah, Rhodes, and me today, there's such a thin chance that Sarah would pick me at all—not after what I said about her, and not with the way I went after Rhodes.

And yet, we have history.

She's standing here with *me* now, not Rhodes. That means something.

Across the way, the walk signal beckons us to the other side of the road. I don't expect Sarah to walk close enough for our hips to brush, but she does. A fraction of a second later, traffic is flying behind us again.

Rhodes is headed *somewhere*, by the looks of her. Her hair is curled at the ends, and mascara makes her eyes seem even bigger than they really are. I've never seen her in makeup before. I've never seen her in the little powder blue dress coat she's wearing, with wide lapels and a tied belt at the waist.

She's in tights and pointy-toed black ballet flats.

"When'd you learn how to curse, Ingram?" My fingerless gloves aren't enough for the cold anymore; I shove my hands into my pockets.

"Your mom," Rhodes says, crossing her arms.

The most asinine response any sixth-grade boy *ever* thought of.

Sarah has drifted away from my side to stand between us. She's hovering back and forth like a bleached-out, worried ghost, wringing her gloved hands and staring into the street.

"Can we not do this again?" Her voice cracks.

Neither Rhodes nor I acknowledge it.

"I asked *when* you learned how to curse," I say, "not *who* taught you."

Seriously, Rhodes is terrible at this. I'm not sure if it's the traffic lights casting red across her face or if she's blushing.

"I guess that's what I get for stooping to your level." Rhodes's eyes dart around behind me—literally just a flash of a second—and then her attention turns to my face again. "I really should have known better. I'm sorry."

"Aaaaaaand there she is, the uppity bitch we're all used to," I say.

I give her a generous smile and pet her arm. She's warm. I don't want to think about it. Rhodes jerks away from me and crosses *her* arms this time.

"*That's* how you do it, by the way—you want to pepper it in just enough to give your insults a little flavor." My smile could be the Cheshire Cat's, broad and toothy.

One of those billboard trucks speed by, flashing from an ad for an injury lawyer in a cheap suit to a local information screen. It's forty-two degrees, apparently, with fifteen percent humidity.

7:58 p.m.

Two minutes left.

With Rhodes in my face, at least I'm not thinking about how nervous I am.

She rolls her eyes, then checks her watch. "Listen, this has been fun, but I have to go—"

"Wait, do you have a *date*?" I know she doesn't have a date. There's no way this awkward, uptight little princess meets people to hook up in another state.

Sarah's expression sours.

"*You* have a date," Sarah whispers in my hair. "Do you really want Alice walking up on this—?"

"That's none of your business." Strangely, Rhodes's shoulders *relax*.

Mine do the same.

She isn't here to *meet someone*. As in a mysterious, anonymous sort-of-girlfriend.

Sarah's eyes flash back and forth between Rhodes and me.

"You don't have to leave our zip code to find people who'll put up with you, Rhodes." The game's back on. Getting under her skin is like shooting fish in a barrel. "I'm sure there's *somebody* in Birmingham that hasn't sworn you off yet."

"I'm not here to—"

"Plus, I've heard big-city girls move a lot faster, gotta decide if you're ready for that—"

"*Iliana!* I'm not here to meet . . . girls." She glares out into traffic. "Can you just, like, go away?"

"Sure you're not." I know she's not. But what if she is? I thrust my hands into the pockets of my coat. "Just don't forget protection. Planned Parenthood has dental dams for free."

I might have wanted the last word, and maybe I wanted to mortify her, but there's also a part of me that 100 percent knows she's the type to be too innocent to think about something like that.

She can thank me later.

After a moment of hesitation, Rhodes doesn't move to cross the street, and she doesn't make her way farther up the sidewalk. She slowly, quietly, makes her way to Frist's front steps.

Next, she gathers her coat around her and takes a seat.

All I can do is keep walking. I'll watch for Alice from a distance, I guess.

She said I'd know her when I saw her.

"Iliana— Listen, you really need to think about—" Sarah's eyes are brimming over for probably the five-hundredth time today. She isn't following me anymore, but she *is* watching Rhodes from a distance.

"Not now, Sarah." I loop my arm through Sarah's and pull her along with me.

We round the corner to march up toward the green. The tall,

thorned roses standing in the center of the green seem like the perfect place to wait for Alice, anyway. Where else would she look for me?

I glance at my phone's screen again.

No messages from Alice.

The time is now 8:05.

"No, no, no." Sarah pulls herself loose. She moves to stand in front of me, the only person I know short enough to meet me eye-to-eye. "This isn't like that. Okay? For once in your life, just listen to me—"

The way she's holding my hands, and looking into my eyes, and her voice is quavering—I can't take it. I know what this is.

This is the let-down talk.

She's going to tell me that Alice isn't coming, and the person I've put every ounce of love and hope and energy into hasn't deserved any of it.

"She's coming, Sarah." I'm crying, now. "I mean something to her. She'd never do this to me—"

"Of course you mean something to her," Sarah says. She's crying too. Again.

Traffic flies past us around the curve; we press close.

"Iliana, babe, you haven't figured it out . . . ?" She's watching me as if I'm some kind of fanged beast. She paws at her face in frustration. "Like, come on."

"There's nothing to figure out." I shake my head. My hands shake. My hair shakes. Everything shakes. "She's just running late, or something."

Sarah frowns.

Her voice cracks. "It's Rhodes, Iliana."

Sarah's words don't register at first. It's like she's speaking another language.

"Alice is Rhodes Ingram."

I-Kissed-Alice 8:44p: are you still coming?

I-Kissed-Alice 8:51p: this sucks, Cheshire.

I-Kissed-Alice 9:15p: out of anybody in the world, I would have never expected this of you.

I-Kissed-Alice 9:20p: like, really?

I-Kissed-Alice 9:20p: this is how it's going to be?

I-Kissed-Alice 9:20p: just . . . nothing?

I-Kissed-Alice 11:30p: can you please let me know you're okay?

I-Kissed-Alice 11:30p: we never have to talk again.

CHAPTER 18

RHODES

Username: I-Kissed-Alice
Last Online: 6h ago

Cheshire never showed, and everything I know is a lie.

There are sets of eyes in every bush, every darkened window, every alley.

They peer out and watch.

They wait.

They're poised for attack.

The oversize can of wasp spray I keep in my bag always seemed like overkill, even if it was the one thing I promised Mom when I moved onto campus, but tonight it feels like perfect logic to walk with it clasped to my chest as if it's some kind of life preserver.

By the time mace has been wrestled from its little faux-leather holster, uncapped, and twisted into the spray position, it's already too late. But a can of wasp spray? There's no mistaking what kind of poison sloshes inside the can. No doubt that aerosol will propel it with accuracy wherever the wielder directs it to go.

The condo my family and I are renting is quiet when I tiptoe inside. The entire open-concept living space is dark except for the three pendant lights hanging over the island in the small kitchen; glitter shimmers in the mosaic tile facade that flanks the fireplace. It's at least after midnight now and no one's here, which means Mom, Dad, and Griff went to hear one of the indie upstart country-boy-with-a-guitar types that Nashville is bursting at the seams with.

It's so much easier to fall apart with no one home to witness it.

I kick one shoe across the room, then the other.

Shed the jacket, shed the sweater, shed the jeans.

The first thing I do is close the blinds on either side of the fireplace. Cheshire could be anywhere. She could be anyone, looking in my windows, watching me wander around the great room in my T-shirt and socks without me ever knowing.

I don't let myself cry until I'm washing my face.

It's a habit as old as life, to wait until my face is hidden and already wet to pour my heart down the sink. Nobody is here now to see it, but it doesn't matter. The grapefruit scent of my prescription face wash is a source of comfort, and the water is warm on my cheeks.

My bones galvanize as I dry my face and smooth on moisturizer.

The tears are out of my system. The ache is still there, that feeling that my lungs are full of concrete and my sinuses are on fire, but I can finally look at myself in the mirror and see that old hardness staring back.

Every time I close my eyes, I see an image clear as day: the *Intergalactic Underland*'s hangar bay, the setting for one of the first panels I ever designed with Cheshire over the summer.

Alice sneaking through a spaceship filled with escape pods was the idea—and the conversation—that started it all. What if Alice were set in space? What if she were hiding in a hangar bay instead of the Red Queen's croquet grounds?

What if the hangar bay is where it all ends, too?

With no one here, the island in the kitchen is the perfect place to draw. The surface is wide, with pendant lights hanging low enough for me to bump with my head if I could get close enough.

It comes over me so fast I don't have time to think about it. My oversize sketchbook and pencils are easy enough to grab, but I have to improvise with the rest: A cereal box is a right angle one minute and a straightedge the next. My mom's giant Tennessee-shaped novelty hard eraser is actually getting put to use. I outline with a ballpoint pen from the bottom of the junk drawer.

In a matter of minutes, I have three panoramic panels on the paper in front of me. *This* was a deliberate choice—I love the drama of it.

I love the warmth spreading through my chest, the ecstasy of seeing the thing in my mind's eye sprawled out on paper in front of me.

The wide, sweeping shots give a sense of size and space that smaller panels don't. I want this panel to be the goodbye I won't ever give Cheshire—not just relationship closure, but an ending to this thing we've spent the past six months toiling over together.

Time is subjective: I don't know if I've been sitting here for minutes or hours.

My hand moves, graphite scratches against paper, and slowly each panel becomes a window into another world.

God knows how much time has gone by when the hair on the back of my neck stands on end. It's a weird feeling, to sense that you're no longer the only human in the room. The condo is quiet, though— there are no other steps on the polished concrete floors. The room hums with silence, only cut on occasion by the sound of sirens.

"Why aren't you wearing pants?" Griffin's voice is a jolt of electricity down my spine.

A shudder ripples through my torso and out through my limbs; a sound leaves my body somewhere between a shriek and a sob. Even if a part of my brain knows it's just Griffin, Anxiety Brain screams *DANGER!*

My pencil goes flying.

I think the eraser hits Griffin in the face, but I don't see it happen because one minute it's in my other hand, and the next it's on the other side of the room and Griffin is holding his eye.

"You look . . . uh, terrible," Griffin says, frowning.

"I'm not wearing pants because I thought I was here alone."

We frown at each other. I tug the hem of my T-shirt down around my hips to cover my underwear.

"God, attitude much? What happened?"

I'm not answering that. "Where's Mom and Dad?"

"Meeting with Bob and June at the country club." His tone is thick with significance: Bob and June *Baker.* The forefather and foremother of the Ocoee Arts Festival. He stares at me carefully. "I'm serious, you look *horrible*."

"She didn't show, okay?"

"I had a feeling something like that would happen," he says.

Griffin glances past me, and his eyes fall on my sketchbook. I throw myself across the paper, but it's too late. He swipes it from under me and holds it close to his nose.

"Whoa, this is—wow. What was all this crap about not being able to draw?!" He runs his finger down to the third panel, where the Red Queen and Alice are talking one last time. There are only empty speech bubbles on either side of them—I don't fill the speech bubbles with text until I've scanned the panels into my design software. "What are they going to say?"

"I—" I swallow. Griffin's never seen my comics. He barely knows how much Alice in Wonderland means to me.

"I think the Red Queen"—I point to the Red Queen, a smaller, curvier silhouette than Alice's tall frame—"is asking Alice if Alice thinks she can just . . . leave. And Alice"—I point to Alice—"is telling the Red Queen that Alice can't be . . . part of her world anymore."

My throat is a vice around those last words.

My eyes sting, and my lungs begin to burn again.

"Oh, so it's sort of like *Through the Looking-Glass*—"

I nod. Griffin is consciously Not Looking At Me, which is good because I'm definitely crying again. I cough away the frog in my throat before I speak again. "It's, uh, fan art. A web comic—alternate universe fan fiction, basically. Alice in Wonderland, set in a different place."

"This says number fifty at the top. There are forty-nine others?"

I nod.

This is how I end up telling Griffin *everything* about tonight, how she never showed and now I don't know what I'm supposed to do with six months of daily conversations and sometimes biweekly comic updates and a story that lives and breathes because of the two of us. The worst part about this is that there's no part of my life I can retreat to and hide from how I feel—Cheshire's handprints are everywhere.

"What I don't understand," Griffin says, "is why you aren't turning something like *this* in for your scholarship award. Don't you see it—you're *evolving*, Rhodes. 'Breathy nudes, lighter than air,' isn't *you* anymore."

"I did what you told me to do," I say. My voice shakes. "I phoned it in and pitched what I know will work."

"You can't blame this on me!" He throws his hands up. "I had no idea this was going on. Just turn in a few of these—the Jabberwock ones are SO GOOD. I can guarantee they've never seen anything like it."

"I have to submit what I pitch." I pick up my sketchbook off the counter and tuck it under my arm. God only knows how late it is, and Mom and Dad should be home any minute. "I pitched breathy nudes, so they're getting breathy nudes."

"Why don't you just call June—?"

"NO. I've already called in enough favors. I have to do this like everybody else."

We both dart our eyes to the doorknob jiggling in the front door's frame. Griffin rakes his fingers through his hair.

"Well, we won't be *nude*, but if you insist on trying to make the nude drawing thing happen, you can always come to mine and Sierra's rehearsal on Monday night. I'm helping her with her recital solo. You can sketch."

It's not a bad idea.

Different is fun. Different is good.

Maybe Griffin is right: The Same Old Thing is the problem, not me.

"I can probably wiggle a little bit on the nude thing." I could do some quick sketches and focus the pieces on sense of movement..." It's hard for me to see right now, but in an academic sort of way I understand that *this* is the next logical step: to focus attention away from the figure, and to point the viewer's eye to the model *in medias res*.

It won't take technical skill in a literal sense, just clever compositional choices.

Yes. I can do this.

I *have* to do this.

"I'll bring dinner," I say. "Is Sylvia's okay?"

Mom's and Dad's voices filter low through the cracks in the frame, moments before a key rattles in the lock. Griffin and I make eye contact one more time. We gather up my mess and bolt to our bedrooms.

He doesn't want to deal with our parents, either.

I flick off the lights in my room a fraction of a second before I hear the door open. And I'm in bed with my blankets over my head before the door to my room opens and *somebody*—Mom?—peeks inside. With my blankets over my head, I stare at my direct messages with Cheshire on my phone screen for what feels like forever. I don't know what I'm expecting, but it only feels natural to be here, waiting to tell her good night.

I lapse out of consciousness like this, in that weird place between sleep and the waking world where my dreams feel like real life and the reality of my relationship with Cheshire being over could simply be fabricated by my imagination.

When my phone lights up again, it's a phone call, and Sarah's name is spelled out across the screen. I send it to voice mail and fall back asleep.

6 comments // 45 kudos // 67 reading now

USER COMMENT

Curious-in-Cheshire

I can't believe you'd submit something without letting me see it first

—

USER COMMENT

I-Kissed-Alice

are you effing serious right now

What, I have to get your permission now? Hearts & Spades is mine. It's yours. It's also *ours* together. I don't have to ask your ~permission~ on anything

—

USER COMMENT

Hearts-n-Spades-Fan-01

omg our moms are fighting, guys

—

USER COMMENT

Curious-in-Cheshire

Whoa. Settle down killer, I just thought we always ran things by each other first

—

USER COMMENT

Stay_curiouser1

Popcorn emoji x 10000000

—

USER COMMENT

I-Kissed-Alice

Don't tell me to settle down, Cheshire. Ever.

CHAPTER 19

ILIANA

Username: Curious-in-Cheshire
Online now

Rhodes's—Alice's—last *Hearts & Spades* update sits open on my laptop screen, staring back at me. I'm at home, and in bed, and everyone else in the house is asleep.

I got home from Nashville yesterday.

Which means it's been two days since Alice—*Rhodes*—and I were supposed to meet, and we haven't spoken since—either online or in real life.

Until now, I never missed living on campus—I've always understood that finances would never allow it, and at the end of the day, I needed the space. But I would give anything to be physically close to where Rhodes is right now.

I want to know what she's doing, and if she's okay.

I want to know if Sarah and Rhodes are talking, and if Sarah is Team Iliana or Team Rhodes right now, and if she's going to spill the beans to Rhodes about who I am before I get the chance to do it myself.

In a cerebral sort of way, I know it's my fault, but I can't feel guilty about it. Months of drama between Rhodes and me has tossed around my mind ever since, searching (and ultimately connecting) with events I remember hearing about when I was *Cheshire* and Rhodes was *Alice*.

The "School Bitch" Alice always complained about is me.

I talked about Rhodes to Alice more than I talked about anyone else—not just about our fighting, but about the myriad character deficiencies I have always perceived in Rhodes. Character deficiencies I never saw in Alice.

This is the thing that keeps me up at night: Perception is 75 percent of reality, and now I have no idea how much of Rhodes is some kind of monster I've created in my mind because of the way she ruined my life, and how much of the things I believed about her actually exist in reality.

That night at Sylvia's won't leave me alone, standing with Sarah by the dishwashers.

You can't blame Rhodes for your problems forever, she'd said. *Her parents paid the school off for you. Are they supposed to pay for your college, too?*

What *was* Rhodes supposed to do?

There's no way Rhodes can really make this right.

It's been so long since that night. It's hard to remember much aside from sitting in the head of school's office at one o'clock in the morning, higher than a kite and terrified. I never told Alice what happened that night—I was too embarrassed—but Alice told me *everything*.

I open my DMs with Alice—Rhodes, I'll never get used to calling her by her real name—and scroll back as far as I can go. The time stamps read November, then October, then September, then August.

July.

June.

It feels like it was an entire lifetime ago.

I-Kissed-Alice 6:51p: One day I'm going to write a book called

178

"The Seven People You Meet in Rehab."

Curious-in-Cheshire 6:51p: lol

I-Kissed-Alice 6:52p: It's family weekend. This lady brought her baby, and they've been feeding it Dr Pepper and Moon Pies since they got here four hours ago.

I-Kissed-Alice 6:52p: these people are why stereotypes about the South exist

I keep scrolling. My heart bottoms out.

I-Kissed-Alice 10:09a: what do you do when you know you hurt somebody, and they were just, like, collateral damage?

I-Kissed-Alice 10:10a: this entire thing is a frigging mess, and I found out today that I probably ruined somebody's life

I-Kissed-Alice 10:10a: I don't know how to live with myself anymore

I remember this conversation now.

I was convinced she was being *Dramatique*™ at the time—how can a teenager ruin somebody's life in any real, tangible way? Particularly someone as kind and noble-hearted and wonderful as Alice? It's so easy to say third-period French, or your curfew, or even the bitch in Drawing III who doesn't know how to leave you alone is "ruining your life." Never in a million years did I believe that Alice ruined someone's life in a literal sense.

But Alice is Rhodes, and now I know differently.

Alice—*Rhodes*—was talking about me.

Curious-in-Cheshire 10:10a: you didn't ruin somebody's life

I-Kissed-Alice 10:10a: no, I really did

Curious-in-Cheshire 10:11a: well, I mean. You just have to do your best to make it right.

Curious-in-Cheshire 10:11a: And give them space—don't hurt them and then ask them how to fix it.

The time stamp is June 23. On June 26, my brother called home to tell me that Rhodes's parents had paid off the school to handle things in-house rather than press charges. Nicky spoke up on my behalf with the school, and rather than being expelled, I spent the summer cuddling with kittens and scooping dog poop from stalls at the Greater Birmingham Humane Society.

The only thing I would never get back was my Savannah College of Art and Design scholarship. She did the very thing I'd told her to do, and irony of ironies, that very thing is the one reason I've always hated her.

I honestly believed that she was too spoiled to face any real consequences on her own—which, to be realistic, her money and social status *does* give her a level of power I'll never have—when at the end of the day, she had done exactly what someone in her position should do: She used her privilege in a way that ensured we were all treated by the school equally.

It wouldn't have happened that way if her parents had only looked out for her and Griffin—neither my family nor Sarah's could afford the palm-greasing necessary to make drug use on campus go away.

And now, after that night, we're all still suffering.

Neither Rhodes nor myself know what our futures look like anymore—me, because of the scholarship I lost, and Rhodes, because of the way the past several months have affected her ability to create art—and yet all we've done is continue to fight each other.

I can't help but recognize that so much of what Rhodes is experiencing might actually be my fault. She's suffering *now* because of my behavior as Cheshire.

Things could have been so different right now if I'd just told her who I was the night we were supposed to meet.

I close my laptop.

The house is quiet. I slip my arms into my sister-in-law Whitney's old housecoat and pad out of my room, down the carpeted stairs, and into the hall. Mom is already sitting at the kitchen table, staring out the window and smoking a cigarette.

I jump at the sight of her, and she jolts at the sight of me.

We stare at each other for a moment, clutching at our chests, mirror images: wild frizz scraped into half-assed piles on top of our heads that still manage to somehow hang over our ears. Big dark eyes (hers flanked with heavy crow's-feet, mine still edged with the liquid liner I didn't wash off before bed) and dramatically dark brows. Overly large mouths, and left incisors that tilt slightly toward the right.

Finally, I walk past her and open the fridge for the jug of milk.

"It's out on the counter, baby." Mom taps ashes from her cigarette out the open window.

I grab a clean bowl from the dishwasher and pour a bowl of cereal, then cross the room to drop into the chair on Mom's left.

"Why are you awake?" I ask.

The only light sources in the room are the glowing embers on the end of mom's cigarette and the streetlamps shining through the window. I fumble to get a spoonful of cereal into my mouth and dribble milk onto the front of my T-shirt.

"I'd ask you the same." Her tone is warm. "When you get old, you stop sleepin'."

She's been getting up for first shift at the pipe factory as long as I've been alive. Four thirty a.m. alarms every day eventually rewire your brain.

"You're not old, Mom," I say, laughing.

"Sixty-two and counting," she says. "Feels more like eighty-two most days, honestly. Why you up?"

"I—" I sigh. I don't even know where to start.

"Got somethin' to do with that hang in your shoulders?" I don't have to actually *see* Mom to know the way her own face is twisted into an amused smirk. "When you gonna tell me what happened?"

"Rhodes and I got into a really bad fight," I say. "I know Sarah's dad probably told you."

"He didn't tell me nothin'—he *did* ask me why his baby girl cried the whole way home. He thought I'd be the one to know." She pauses. "You used to tell me things, Iliana Grace."

"I found out Rhodes called in a favor for the scholarship, and I just . . . snapped."

"The straw that broke the camel's back," Mom says. "I guess I can say I saw it coming after all the carrying on you've done with her."

Mom doesn't say anything else.

She doesn't have to. I know what this silence means: *Continue.*

"What if I've been wrong about her? This whole time?"

"Who, Rhodes?" Mom looks like a dragon, with smoke pouring from her nostrils. She tilts her head to the side and blows it out the window.

"Yeah."

"She's been awful to you," Mom says.

"I've been awful to her, too," I say. "Like, Super-Saiyan-bitch-mode *awful*."

"I don't know what any of that means, but I think I gotcha." Mom pauses for a moment to collect her thoughts. "There are always two sides to every story, honey."

"I *know*." I turn up the bowl to drink the sweet cereal milk and set it back on the table. "But have you ever, like . . . only seen *your* side? And then finally you realize they have a reason to hate you, too?"

"'Course. That's being human."

"So what did you do?" I ask.

Mom's vision isn't great without her glasses.

I hate it when she can see me cry, and I can only hope I'm too blurry for her to notice. I don't know whether she's willfully ignoring it or legitimately can't see past the end of her own nose, but for once she doesn't acknowledge the tears I'm catching on my cheeks with the hem of my housecoat sleeve.

She flicks the butt of her cigarette out the window with two fingers and closes the window.

"I made a promise to myself: From that moment forward, I would treat that person with the respect they deserved. Not only that, but I'd do everything in my power to make it *right*. Help them, push them forward, support them however they needed to get our relationship back on two feet again."

"Did it work?"

Mom chuckles. "You ask like I only had to do that once. Most of the time it didn't—a few times it did. The thing about it is, you gotta do it whether they forgive you or not. Do what you can, then what *they* do with your change of heart is up to them."

There's a long pause. I know this expression in front of me—Mom is sorting through a hundred different ways to say something in order to find the one version that won't send me off into one of my usual Mom-proclaimed "Iliana moments."

"I don't think Rhodes is the only person you need to be worried about, honey," she says. "Mr. Wade sent me the video from the presentation—Sarah. She isn't okay."

"Sarah? I mean, I think she's probably fine now—what made you think she isn't?"

She's always fine. She knows how Rhodes and I are.

"Mmm." Mom swills from her coffee mug. "Remember that time it had been raining for what felt like weeks, and the creek out back was swollen? And the two of you had decided to build every manner of boat to see which ones would actually stay on top of the water, and then which ones would actually carry things downstream?"

"I asked to use Sarah's Barbie doll," I said, "the one in the bathing suit."

"The one she'd just gotten for her seventh birthday," Mom adds. "Do you remember what happened?"

"The little boat we made carried away her doll so fast that we weren't able to catch it. It went into the drain, and we never saw it again."

"I remember seeing her on our back porch after," Mom says. "She wasn't going to tell me what you did, loyal little thing, but she was so *pitiful*. Her shoulders were all hunched over, and her hair hung in her face, and she was working so damned hard not to cry. I finally got it out of her—"

"And I had to use some of my leftover Christmas money to buy her a new one," I say.

"She looked the same in that video. She was every bit of seven, crying because she just watched something she'd wanted more than anything in the world fall down a drain and disappear forever."

Mom and I find each other's eyes in the waning dark.

"She isn't fine," Mom says.

"Look," I say, throwing up a hand. "She isn't seven anymore, and the world is going to eat her alive if she doesn't learn to stand up for herself."

"That might be true, but the person who chews her up and spits her out is *usually you*."

Mom stands from where she sits at the table and bends to press a kiss into my hairline.

"Cut that girl some slack, all right? Take care of her. She's been in love with you for as long as I can remember, and you know it."

She disappears around the corner, then the door to the master bedroom shuts behind her. For the first time since everything began, I sit quietly and give myself the space to think about what it is I really want.

Nighttime makes me sentimental. I have spent every night since the failed meet-up waxing poetic about the person Alice is, but being back in Randall's class for makerspace only reminds me of everything Rhodes *isn't*. Even if Alice was always noble and good, Rhodes is still the person who has devoted so much of her energy to making me feel small.

And yet, Alice and Rhodes are two sides of the same coin.

Knowing Alice for who she is, I have to wonder how much of Rhodes's antagonism was something I created in my own mind because I have always been so unbelievably, unrelentingly threatened by her.

It's such a knee-jerk reaction to hate the girl sitting across from me now, with her dark hair hanging soft around her shoulders.

I catch myself lapsing into it, and then I remember who she *really* is again.

The only person I have to hate right now is myself.

With absolutely zero preamble, the list for the final round of the scholarship appears in our inboxes on our first day back to school after the project proposal.

Rhodes's name on the list is a big fat *of course*, of course, but Kiersten's name makes my stomach twist.

I can't think about her anymore without wanting to crawl into a hole.

I placed so much hope in her. She saw so much ugliness in me.

There are three others: Marianna Walters, Chelsea Leath, and, rounding out the hat trick, *me*.

"It's fine." Sarah frowns into her fingernails.

It isn't fine.

Three Conservatory students are Capstone finalists: two art-track students and one from the theater track.

Sarah isn't one of them.

Rhodes glances up from the giant clipboard across her knees, but she says nothing.

Our eyes meet for a fraction of a second.

My heart scatters into a thousand pieces.

Her eyes drop back to her paper, and for once in her fucking life she's actually working.

"It's okay to say you're upset about the Capstone," I say to Sarah.

My eyes re-center on the empty paper in my lap, but Sarah's tense frame is easy to perceive in my peripheral vision. She isn't working at all: Her paper sits empty in front of her, too, and she hasn't even bothered to pull a pencil from the Hello Kitty pouch she keeps in her book bag.

My conversation with Mom echoes forward from the recesses of my mind:

She wasn't going to tell me what you did, loyal little thing, but she was so pitiful. *Her shoulders were all hunched over, and her hair hung in her face, and she was working so damned hard not to cry.*

Also, most important:

The person who chews her up and spits her out is usually you.

"It's *fine*, Iliana." She frowns back down at her hands.

I don't know what to say to her. Do I *really* bear some kind of responsibility for what happened with her presentation? Sarah knew, and I knew, that she didn't *really* have anything planned for the presentation, either, and was hoping when she arrived at the presentation that she'd be inspired. She doesn't think on her feet like I do, and she doesn't prepare like Rhodes.

She isn't the kind of person who could cobble together a slideshow presentation in the car on the way to the project proposal itself, and yet that's exactly what she tried to do.

Mom's right: Sarah is loyal and forgiving to a fault.

She is also weak-spirited, and manipulative, and spent the past several weeks waiting on either Rhodes or myself to develop a project for her to present. I assumed Rhodes would help her, and there's a solid chance that Rhodes assumed the same of me—but in the end, it was blatantly clear that she presented something neither of us would have played any role in whatsoever: a three-dimensional, low-relief installation of trash found around Birmingham, attached onto large planks of plywood and spray-painted into one of Roy Lichtenstein's crying comic strip girls.

The idea itself *could* have worked if Sarah had taken any time to figure it out on her own.

It was blatantly obvious that if she didn't know the medium well, she didn't know her audience at *all*.

But if Rhodes had told her to help the Capstone judges connect by utilizing trash polluting the nearby Ocoee River, or if I had encouraged her to study the work of modern artists such as Francesca Pasquali or Tim Hobbelman before she pitched *anything*, she would have spent the next couple of weeks depending on us to hold her hand through actually executing it. If she somehow won the Capstone Award, it would have belonged just as much to Rhodes and myself as it would have to her.

I don't know where Sarah's fault ends and mine begins.

I don't know how to apologize if I'm not even sure how much my behavior affected the situation to begin with.

My eyes drift back to Rhodes, and for the ten thousandth time I wish I knew what to say to her. Watching her now is like rereading a novel a second—or third, or fifth—time. So many plot points and fine details, all of them bringing the story into a kind of context that simply wasn't there the first time around.

Everything about Rhodes, everything about Alice, all of it makes sense in a way it didn't before. They aren't two different people, two opposing forces in my life.

They're layers of the same story.

I can't take it anymore. I stand from my seat and edge the corner of the room to stand over Rhodes's shoulder.

"Not today, Iliana." Rhodes doesn't glance up from her paper.

Her tablet is open in her lap, paused on a pair of dancers in motion. I don't know the girl, but I recognize Griffin's dark hair and soft eyes.

"I, um." I lick my lips.

She's working on her Capstone project: A single piece of deep plum paper is clipped to her board, and she's laying down whisper-light preliminary sketches with a white pencil. Her paper features a progression: A pair of dancers, moving through some kind of complicated turn-leap in perfect unison. In the sketch on the left, they're coiled like springs, preparing to leap. In the center frame, they're flying. The third frame is still just a few lines that simply orient Rhodes's use of space.

I get what she's trying to accomplish, but I have literally zero idea how she's going to be able to pull it off. The fact that she's creating anything at all is monumental.

I can't help but wonder if the problem was her focus on our comic strip all along.

What if *I* had been the thing that kept her away from her work?

"*What?*" She whirls to face me, scowling. "What, Iliana? What. What, what, *what*."

"Congratulations," I say.

Heat creeps up into my face. This was a *terrible* idea.

Rhodes waits, blinking.

"Can you please get whatever this is out of your system?" She twirls her pencil between two fingers.

Randall appears between us, wide-eyed, with a pack of empty detention slips already tucked in the front pocket of his blazer. "Ladies—?"

Rhodes huffs. "Iliana is—"

"The scholarship finalists were announced earlier," I say. "I was congratulating Rhodes."

"Oh." Randall blinks. "Just . . . congratulating her?"

"Is that allowed?" I raise my brows.

I hate this man.

He smells like birthday cake–flavored vape and a lifetime of bad decisions.

"Well, I mean, yes." Randall turns to Rhodes. "This is the part where you say 'thank you.'"

"Thank you." Rhodes mimics Randall's inflections with perfect accuracy.

"Take a seat, Vrionides," Randall says.

I take a seat. To my right, Sarah is still glaring at empty paper. I lean forward with my eyes fixed on Sarah's face in search of eye contact, but she never rises to the occasion. Barely anything has changed since we've been back to school, but *everything* feels different.

CHAPTER 20

RHODES

Username: I-Kissed-Alice
Last online: 4d ago

Light from one of the Conservatory dance studios pours brilliant into the night.

The scent of coffee from Sylvia's still clings to my hair and the fibers of my jacket; bacon-scented steam blooms from the bags of takeout in my arms.

My residential access card gets me into the building, then the rest of the way is a fumbling maze of dark foyers and back hallways. I can hear the music from the studio before I make it through the door: It's an instrumental percussion—heavy with a strings section that pulls at the edges of the stuff that knits me together. Probably from the score of some fantasy movie, the kind with people from our world who fall through portals and find themselves on the other side of time.

When I step through the door, Griffin is throwing his former dance partner, Sierra, into the air like a sack of flour.

Mom and Dad don't know he's practicing with her like this, and I would never tell either of them. Sierra and Griffin have danced together since *ever*, and tonight they're preparing for the school's Winter Showcase—even though Griffin isn't *technically* in the dance track anymore—and since he isn't in the performing arts track anymore, our parents won't even be present to find out it ever happened.

It's a duet slot Sierra's parents paid for, and the dance-track teachers are understanding enough of Griffin's situation to let this one slide. As much as the Conservatory frustrates me at times, I would be remiss not to admit that we *are* surrounded by people—students *and* adults—who love us. I can't imagine something like this happening anywhere else.

Sierra twirls and a breath later she's cradled in his arms, one leg stretched high over their heads and the other tucked underneath. One bare foot hits the floor, then the other, and Sierra takes off in a series of leaps and twirls as effortless as flying.

"Dinner," I say.

It's all I *know* how to say. I wish I knew what it is to sail through the air like that.

"One more," Griffin says.

Sierra nods, Griffin starts the music from the beginning, and I set my phone up to record.

The overhead lights scatter on Sierra's deep brown skin, and rather than her usual bun, her natural curls fly free around her face. Griffin, on the other hand, *looks* like he's been working his ass off. The studio is probably sixty-five degrees, cold enough for me to keep my jacket on, but sweat drips down his face and he's cast off his shirt, dancing only in a pair of compression shorts.

The toll of the past year has never been more apparent to me than it is right now, watching him move.

Anyone else watching Griffin dance would think that he's a sixteen-year-old at the top of his game: He moves like someone who's devoted their life to it, working through choreography like it's as easy as breathing. Strong, conditioned muscles flinch and relax through each lift, a contrast to soft hands and a relaxed face.

It's a wonder to me that Mom and Dad aren't prouder of him.

I could burst with the pride I feel right now.

I've spent my life watching him toil at this thing, seeing him reach a kind of personal zenith his second year in the Conservatory's dance program as a particularly prodigious tenth grader.

I've also witnessed how the summer paired with his first fall in the tech program has forced him to regress: There's a pause now every time he prepares to do one of his complicated leap-turns. His hands fumble through a narrow catch that could have landed Sierra in a crumpled heap on the floor. Sierra sees the struggle, too, with the way she nods him through moments of insecurity and the kind of mistakes he would have made years ago.

Even still, they glide through the choreography with near complete ease.

I sit with my oversize sketchbook across my knees and sketch what I see with a piece of charcoal between my fingers—angles.

Angles that can be fleshed out and turned into a pair of people.

With Griffin's and Sierra's constant movements, I can't stop and think too hard about what I'm doing—I can't even look at the page, not really. It's the closest thing to the intuitive kind of work I've been incapable of creating in months, and I almost don't know what to do with it.

I just keep drawing, on and on until the music ends.

The piece is only three and a half minutes long, and it's over as soon as it began.

Before long, we've arranged ourselves next to the window with our bags of food between us, Sierra and Griffin sprawled into splits and stretches with Styrofoam boxes open in front of them. They're sweaty, mopping at their faces with discarded cover-ups and chug-ging water from aluminum reusable bottles, but I'm *exhausted*.

I haven't drawn like this in months. The memory of earlier days, when this was something I loved and wanted, only leaves me feeling haggard.

There was a time when this would have been effortless for all of us.

I lean against the cold window and tear off a piece of syrup-loaded pancake with my fingers. My sketchbook lays off to the side, closed and out of sight.

"Did you get anything you think you can use?" Sierra asks from over the top of a patty melt.

"Oh yeah," I say, because how else am I going to respond?

I have no idea if I'll be able to use any of this, and it's not for Sierra and Griffin's lack of trying. Watching old videos on my phone over the weekend, I thought the problem was with the method of delivery—I needed to see them *live* to experience the full essence of their art. Sit-ting here tonight, though, I realize that the problem isn't the method of delivery at all.

Still, there were moments of intimacy between Sierra and Griffin that spoke to me: Sierra, cradled in Griffin's arms, with her fingertips brushing against his cheek. Griffin, holding Sierra by the ankle as she strains out toward the night. So many frames where they're pulling and touching and clashing and holding, and I wonder if the exercise is one step closer to whatever my art is evolving into.

"I wish I could move like that," I say. "You're both so talented."

"You could have, if you'd stuck with ballet," Griffin says, and Sierra laughs.

"You don't know how good you have it," I say. "I wish I could just . . . turn off my brain and move like that."

Griffin rolls his eyes, but Sierra chokes out a laugh around the straw stuck in the corner of her mouth. "You think we turn off our brains for this? Guess I could take that as a compliment."

"That's not what I mean, just—" I sigh. "It's effortless, the way you move. Just, like, instincts and your body."

"No," Sierra says, "it's not just *instincts*. It's supposed to *look* like that. Have you ever seen my feet after I've been at ballet rehearsal all day?"

I don't have to imagine: Her toes are buddy-bandaged now, with the nails clipped down short and a delicate Hello Kitty bandage wrapped around one big toe.

"Try dancing through that, knowing how much your feet hurt. Having to remember the choreography to four different parts, and God forbid if you're paired off for a *pas de deux* at some point and have to depend on some new transfer because your old partner got moved to the tech department—"

"*Sierra*—" Griffin frowns.

"Look, I'm *sorry*—" Sierra isn't actually sorry.

I laugh, despite everything else.

"What she's saying," Griffin says, "is that the artistry is in looking like it's effortless. We're having to constantly think three steps ahead, though."

"That's *literally* what I just said," Sierra says. "Thanks, mansplainer."

Griffin makes a face at her, and she flicks a piece of cheese onto his chest.

"You have to love it, though," Sierra goes on. "It'll never look easy if it's something you have to force yourself through."

We descend into silence, stuffing our faces and watching the interstate traffic fly by on the other side of the glass. Before long, Sierra and Griffin lose themselves in an entire semester's worth of dance-track gossip, names I've never heard before and stories that don't pertain to me. It's just as well, though, because Sierra's words won't leave me alone:

You have *to love it.*

It'll never look easy if it's something you force yourself through.

Sketches of Griffin and Sierra stare back at me from where my sketchbook lays on the floor, one abandoned almost-drawing after the next. I smooth my hands over each one, pick up the piece of charcoal from where it rests on a napkin, and search for some way to turn them into something complete.

I don't love what I'm doing anymore, and everything looks like *effort*.

Admitting that I don't love this anymore is a relief.

The problem is that I just don't know what it is I'll do if I don't do this.

It's just after eleven when my phone's ringer startles me out of sleep.

For a long moment, I'm stunned by the screaming white against the total darkness of my dorm room. My first thought is Sarah in the bed across from me, but my phone's flashlight feature tells me that she either isn't back yet or is sleeping somewhere else. A month ago this would have worried me; lately the only way I even know she's darkened our doorstep is by a steadily rotating pile of dirty clothes in her hamper and a sometimes-damp towel that hangs from a pants hanger next to her closet.

Mom's picture stares back at me on the caller ID.

My stomach twists into a knot, and I answer the phone just before it goes to voice mail.

"Is Griffin—"

"He's fine, honey." Mom's voice is tense. "No one is bleeding, on fire, or dead."

Of course he's fine.

I was with him four hours ago, and he was the picture of health.

"Isn't it past your bedtime?" It's *definitely* past mine.

"I've been on the phone for four hours with June Baker," Mom says. "She was forced to resign from Ocoee today."

"What? Why?"

Mom's sigh rattles the speaker. "Somehow they found out that, ah—I—we—had a little bit to do with June, er, working around your grades when you entered the scholarship contest."

"What do you *mean* 'we had a little bit to do' with the Capstone?" I can't feel my face.

I thought crappy grades and a dead muse were my worst nightmare.

I was wrong. *This* is my worst nightmare.

"People like June don't do things out of the goodness of their hearts, all right?" Mom's tone is loud and fast. "Pulling strings costs money, Rhodes. I thought we were on the same page about that."

"We have never been on the same page about any of this," I snap.

"Well, I guess it's good you don't want it, then," Mom said. "Bootsie Prudhomme, the old bitch, is the interim chairwoman now."

My heart sinks. Bootsie hasn't had a problem with *me*, per se, but she's always hated June—which means this won't be the first time I've been caught in the blast zone between the two of them.

"So they're kicking me out," I say.

"I have a call with Bootsie tomorrow," Mom says. "She wants to schedule a meeting to 'sort this ol' thing out,' whatever that means."

"*So they're kicking me out,*" I say again.

"Don't jump to conclusions," Mom snaps. "You're always so quick to think the worst of things."

"What's going to happen to Randall?" I ask. This doesn't affect just me.

Just *how* involved was he in all of this? Is Randall complicit?

If Randall had no idea, then he could be another body in my mother's blast zone. She's taken down so many people around her who haven't deserved it.

I think of Griffin, in his tech-track uniform with the light lost in his eyes.

I think of Dusk, tempted week after week with Mom's money to manipulate me into doing something I didn't want to do anymore.

As much as I can't stand the guy for harping on me at school in perpetuity, I don't want him to lose everything because my mother is a horrible human.

"What do you mean, *what's going to happen to Randall?*"

"Well? Is he going to lose his job because you're a conniving bitch?"

"Rhodes Anne Ingram! Don't you dare—"

"Oh, you're going to try to talk to *me* about values?" I scoff at her. Her character has never been more apparent to me than it is now, and I don't think I've ever been more disappointed in the kind of human she actually is. "*What's going to happen to him?*"

There's a long pause on the other end of the line.

I half expect mom to throw back her usual favorite response: *I don't owe you an explanation.*

Instead, her tone is measured.

Rage seeps between the edges of each word, given one at a time, but she never loses control of her emotions.

"Well, I've been getting your progress reports. I knew you wouldn't hit the GPA requirement months ago."

"And . . . ?"

"Let's just say, Mr. Randall has more than enough deniability. He'll be as surprised as everyone else."

"You mean, you went to June behind his back."

"I told June to call him and check up on you, yes."

"If this somehow comes back to him, if he somehow catches the blow because of you—"

"Don't you dare threaten me, not after everything your father and I have done for you—"

This is the point where things are going to fall apart. I hear the tears in her voice now—everything is drenched in the kind of emotional volatility that will result in the horrifying crap show of watching an adult throw a very age-inappropriate temper tantrum.

I know her well enough to know when it's time to pull the emergency brake.

"I'm sorry, Mom." I'm not sorry.

But she's a child, and I'm not, and this is the thing that will smooth her feathers.

I hear sniffling through the line.

She says nothing, so I go on.

"Just let me know where to be when you meet with Bootsie, I guess."

"I wasn't planning on you being there."

"You're not meeting Bootsie without me," I say. "I've had enough of you throwing wads of cash at people to get what you want."

More sniffling.

I'm still pushing it with her, but she doesn't push back.

She knows, and she knows I know, that she's finally screwed things up past the point of reconciliation.

"We'll see," she finally says. "Bye, Rhodes."

"Love you too, Mom—"

"Oh, you know I love you. Don't start in on that—"

"Bye." I hang up the phone before she can say another word.

It isn't hard to drift back to sleep.

I'm almost there when Iliana's voice floats up from my subconscious, a clear-as-day memory from our fight at the library: *"I know you're only here because June Baker waived the GPA requirements for you."*

It would be a low move, but this is the first time I've ever been the only thing that's stood directly between Iliana and something she wants.

All pretenses of sleep evaporate.

I throw off my covers, and the tile floors are cold under my feet.

When I click on the lamp, the room is cavernous, empty without Sarah in the bed against the far wall.

The rest of the night goes with me pacing, and finishing a new *Hearts & Spades* panel, and chewing my fingernails.

My life is going to hell.

Cheshire is inexplicably gone, and the scholarship is evaporating into thin air in front of me. My grades are abysmal. There is no way to know what my future is going to look like.

There's only one thing left in my life I can control.

It's not something I think all the way through, but at four o'clock in the morning, it feels *right*. I open my laptop, and in a matter of a few clicks my Slash/Spot account is gone. My last breath on the website is one final *Hearts & Spades* update, a symbolic *goodbye* to everyone who has ever loved this thing Cheshire and I created together.

It's a goodbye to Cheshire, too.

I finally fall asleep when sunrise casts purple-gray through the windows.

Curious-in-Cheshire 12:47p: I haven't known how to say this
User I-Kissed-Alice is no longer found in our system.

Curious-in-Cheshire 12:47p: It didn't occur to me until today that I need to just say it
User I-Kissed-Alice is no longer found in our system.

Curious-in-Cheshire 12:47p: I love you and I'm sorry
User I-Kissed-Alice is no longer found in our system.

Curious-in-Cheshire 12:47p: I want to try to meet again. I'll be there this time. I promise
User I-Kissed-Alice is no longer found in our system.
Curious-in-Cheshire has logged out of the system.
Curious-in-Cheshire has logged into the system.

Curious-in-Cheshire 1:12p: seriously?
User I-Kissed-Alice is no longer found in our system.
Curious-in-Cheshire has logged out of the system.
Curious-in-Cheshire has logged into the system.

Curious-in-Cheshire 1:20p: test
User I-Kissed-Alice is no longer found in our system.

Curious-in-Cheshire 1:20p: test
User I-Kissed-Alice is no longer found in our system.

Curious-in-Cheshire 1:20p: test
User I-Kissed-Alice is no longer found in our system.

2 comments // 21 kudos // 237 reading now

USER COMMENT

WAMH-Fan-01

Does . . . that mean it's over?

—

USER COMMENT

Stay_curiouser1

What the heck just happened

TWO DAYS UNTIL THE CAPSTONE AWARD

ILIANA

Username: Curious-in-Cheshire
Last online: 2d ago

When I walk into Sylvia's, Kiersten is behind the counter with a large frilly bib apron tied over a pair of BeDazzled shortalls and a flannel shirt. I walk past her to stow my coat and bag behind the counter, then pull my time card from the caddy and slam it into the ancient punch clock.

I haven't slept well in days.

Not since the Slash/Spot notification that delivered *two* blows: Alice's—Rhodes's—final *Hearts & Spades* update and the realization that she took the ultimate step in severing contact with me forever by deleting her account.

This is it: This is the sign I needed.

Alice, and Rhodes, are finished with me forever.

I don't even know how to be devastated yet. I remember feeling like this the day I learned I lost my Savannah College of Art and Design scholarship—grief hit me hard and fast in the days after, when I had to look at the rest of my life head-on and try to figure out what the hell it was even going to remotely look like.

That first day, like today, there was *nothingness*.

It reminds me of playing *Mortal Kombat* with my brother on his old Nintendo, when he'd almost beat me, down to one more critical hit until the match would be over. My character (Sonia Blade, *always* Sonia Blade) would wobble back and forth on weak knees, and Shao Kahn would declare, "*Finish her!*"

Nicky, my oldest brother, would deal some kind of overkill level of complicated power move, my character would be put out of her misery, and I would spend the rest of the afternoon watching him gloat.

I feel like Sonia Blade right now. I'm wobbling on weak knees, and in this little exercise of the imagination, it's the voice of the Red Queen declaring, "*Finish her!*"

I simply don't have any fight left in me.

Today is Kiersten's first day on the job, and Sylvia has given her the decidedly unglamorous task of loading and unloading the dishwasher *ad nauseum.*

"Everybody's gotta start somewhere," Sylvia says, bringing me back to reality between counting the ones and fives to balance the drawer. "She wasn't too interested in learning the menu, so she can unload the dishwasher."

Kiersten's vibrant teal, rhinestone-encrusted nails are a sharp contrast next to the simple white of the ancient restaurant-quality dinnerware in her hands. She plunks one mug after the next onto the counter, visibly fuming.

"You don't get tips unloading the dishwasher," Kiersten says, too low for Sylvia to hear.

"Tip sharing, sweetheart." I shake the repurposed jam jar on the counter at her, stuffed with ones. "Everybody on the floor owes the tip jar fifteen percent at the end of their shift."

Kiersten says nothing. Instead, she pulls the industrial dishwasher closed and turns to the sink for another load.

"Nope, don't put your coat up," Sylvia says a beat before I hang my coat on the rack by the back door. She turns to hand me a vinyl bank envelope and her keys. "Breakfast is slowing down. I need you to deposit this so I can watch Sarah train Miss Congeniality."

Kiersten stops to glare over her shoulder. Sylvia glares back.

"What's with the fresh meat?" I put my coat back on and accept the load in Sylvia's hands.

Sarah cuts her eyes from where she takes an order on the other side of the room.

It's the first time I've seen her outside of school since the Capstone project presentation. At school, she's been the last person to walk into our classes and the first person to leave—a grimacing, silent ghost I haven't spoken with in ages.

The room is small enough—and I'm loud enough—that it isn't hard for her to listen to our conversation and her customer at the same time. Our eyes meet, *finally*, and then she turns to face the table.

When Sarah turns, something glittery on her hip catches in the old lights that hang over our heads. Mr. Wade's cassette player hangs from the waist of her jeans like it always does, but now it's completely, inexplicably crusted in crystals.

"Today's Sarah's last day," Sylvia says. "Didn't give me any notice. I told her I wouldn't dock her pay if she brought her replacement in with her for her last shift."

I gawk at the back of Sarah's head. Sylvia is making no attempt to keep this a secret—nor is she sparing anyone's feelings—and Sarah's shoulders hike up around her reddening ears.

"Did she say why?"

Sylvia drops her voice to a whisper, frowning. "No. I felt it coming, though—something's been going on with that girl, and I've been on this Earth long enough to sense when somebody's gonna snap."

"You're not wrong," I say. "This isn't like her."

"I know you two are close," Sylvia says, shuttling me past the bar. "I want you to keep an eye on her for me, all right?"

"Mmm." I pass empty tables loaded with plates.

We *were* close. Now she doesn't even tell me when she makes big decisions like *quitting her job*.

The door to the diner jingles when I push it open with my hip, and I catch the full brunt of December cold to the face.

I make a mental note to mention holiday decorations to Sylvia as I step into the chilly sunshine, but a hand on my arm catches me just before I unlock Sylvia's old barge of a Buick. I don't know what I expect when I turn around, but it isn't good.

It's Sarah and Kiersten.

They're duplicates of each other, their arms crossed in defense against the cold, backs ramrod straight.

"Did Sylvia need something?" I ask.

Kiersten raises her brows to Sarah. She nods once, a gesture of solidarity.

Sarah sets her jaw and stands a little straighter.

"You need to tell Rhodes who you are." Sarah cuts her eyes to Kiersten, who nods her on. "I bombed my project presentation because of you, and now you need to get what you deserve with her. I needed that scholarship, too, Iliana."

"You told *Kiersten*?!" My voice ricochets off the side of the building and echoes into the parking lot. "Sarah! You're my best friend—when I tell you things, I expect you to keep them to yourself."

"Really? She's your best friend." Kiersten snorts. Sarah snorts. "What's going on in her life right now, Iliana? Why is she afraid? Why is she lonely? Do you even give a shit about her, or do you expect her to follow you around because you're a God-forsaken narcissist, and narcissists cease to exist when they don't have a sycophant telling them how wonderful they are?"

I'm disoriented—like I've been slapped.

My vision crackles around the edges.

I dig my heels into the pavement as if I'm going to fall over. I wish Kiersten had just slapped me instead; this *hurts worse*.

I loathe the day I ever set eyes on Kiersten, and I loathe Sarah for being the kind of person who absorbs the worst qualities of the people around her—and I wonder which parts of her I used to love were actually ugly reflections of what other people see in me.

I could blast off at Kiersten about how she doesn't know the lifetime of history Sarah and I share, or everything we've been through together, or how she *really doesn't understand* how complicated things have become between Rhodes, Sarah, and myself.

I could blast off at Sarah for breaking the one sacred thing we had together—trust—and giving away a fifteen-year friendship because someone new is providing her with the constant attention she so desperately craves.

My conversation with Mom over a week ago hangs over my head, an entire childhood of Sarah standing too close to the blast zone while I pack dynamite into the crevices of each wall that has stood in the way of getting what I want.

She has always been in the position to lose something where I've stood to gain.

My face burns, but there's no going back now.

"Are you not going to say *anything* to this?" Sarah is a tearful, choking mess.

I'm supposed to say "I'm sorry" right now, but I want Sarah to apologize for breaking my trust, for putting me in the position for all of this to be *so much fucking worse*. Every bone in my body aches with loss—losing Alice, losing Rhodes, and losing Sarah.

I don't know how to apologize, how to take responsibility for my role in what happened to Sarah without taking responsibility for the *entire* rotten mess.

"You know what? This is the worst. You're the worst." Kiersten throws off her apron and shoves it into my chest. "I'm leaving. Iliana, if you don't tell Rhodes, we will."

"Why the hell do you care about Rhodes, anyway?" My voice leaves me so fragile.

I've never heard it like this before.

I don't think I've ever been so desperately fractured in my life.

Kiersten sneers.

"I don't care about Rhodes. But Sarah does."

"You deserve for this to blow up in your face," Sarah says. "She loves whoever she thinks you are, this online person you pretend to be with her, and she needs to know what she's really dealing with."

The meanness in her face, the cross of her arms, her voice—none of it is remotely recognizable to me. I know every square inch of her face. I've *seen* her earn every single scar and pockmark on her body, and yet this person is a complete stranger.

I miss my friend.

"So that's what this is—you lost something, and now you want me to lose something too?"

"Yeeeep." Kiersten wears her awfulness like a badge of honor. "I think you should be thanking us for giving you time to figure it out on your own first, though."

Kiersten's self-ascribed role as judge, jury, and executioner would throw me into a fury if I had any fire left.

Finish me.

"I'm outta here," Kiersten finally says. She stares at me like I'm some kind of beast she's never laid eyes on before. "Sorry, Sarah. Iliana, I'm serious: You have forty-eight hours."

My stomach feels like it's going to fall out of my ass.

I need time.

Weeks.

Months.

It takes knowing I've lost Rhodes forever to realize she's what I want. I will never, ever, ever make this happen in forty-eight hours.

"How will you know?" I ask.

Sarah's eyes drop to the sidewalk under our feet, and Kiersten nudges her with one elbow.

"We all have our way of finding things out," Kiersten says. She walks past Sarah and me without another word, a girl who struck a match and doesn't wait around to watch the entire world catch fire.

Sarah doesn't hang around, either.

She takes Kiersten's apron in her hands and turns to step back inside the diner.

Sarah is gone. Alice is gone.

For the first time in my entire life, I'm alone, and I absolutely did this to myself.

CHAPTER 22

RHODES

```
Username: n/a
```

Dusk's connection is terrible; half her face is pixelated.

Still, her office is easy to make out behind her: walls covered in concert posters, bookshelves, and paintings from her clients with the signatures masked over for confidentiality purposes. She sits back in her chair, distancing herself from her laptop camera.

"Why did you let my mom pay you off if you told me what she was doing?" I'm not pulling punches anymore.

"I applied it to your balance," she says. "Your mom keeps me on a retainer, so she didn't notice until she called to ream me out for telling you after our last face-to-face meeting."

"That still doesn't tell me why," I say.

The second-floor gallery gardens are *freezing* this morning. The vegetation has been pulled out for the winter: Gone are the brown, very, very dead vestiges of what used to be plots and plots and plots of verdant green. Everything is stark, barren until spring sends another round of sci-tech students up to try Mendel's theories for themselves. Still, it's the best place to hide for impromptu web conference therapy sessions.

"Because—" Dusk clears her throat. "Permission to be frank?"

I nod.

"You spend *a lot* of time in flux between the adults in your life—your mother. Me. Your faculty advisor. This odious June woman. I wanted you to be aware that this was something your mother was doing, because I wanted to be here to support you in exploring how it makes you feel—exploring your options. You won't be in your mother's shelter forever, you know? Either you can take the steps to solve this problem *now*, with people around you that support you, or it can be something you deal with when you have no safety net and a mother that is very much used to manipulating everyone around you with her money."

"You let her think you were doing it, though," I say.

Dusk shrugs. "You're my client, but she's my customer."

I frown. "I think you should be honest with both of us from now on."

"Aaaaaand there it is." Dusk jots something into her notebook. "Good work, Rhodes. Now, I want you to take what just happened with me and apply it to the other areas of your life, too."

I nod. An email blinks at the top of my phone screen: It's from Bootsie Prudhomme.

I've been waiting for this.

For the first time in God even knows how long, motivation is the wind in my sails. I have something I want, and I'm ready to do what I need to get it.

I consider telling Dusk this, but the email from Bootsie is time-sensitive, and I can't spend the next thirty minutes picking apart the how or why behind why I actually feel like accomplishing something. Or why that *something* is circumventing my mother.

"Hey—thanks for meeting with me. I need to answer this email. Can I text you later?"

"Of course. Keep me posted on how things go with your art and this *Cheshire* girl, okay?"

"It's not," I say. My voice tugs. "She never DMed me again after we didn't meet, so I deleted my account."

"Good on you. Bye, dear."

I don't want to hear that it's good, or that I made the right choice, or that I'm better off without her. I don't want to think about it at all.

The line disconnects, and I flip over to my email app.

—

From: b.prudhomme@ocoeeartsfes . . .

To: raingram318@alconserv.k12.jefco . . .

Subject: Meeting with Valerie Ingram

Rhodes,

Mrs. Prudhomme agreed that 4pm would be fine. Please inform your mother of the change in meeting time.

Best Wishes,

Everly Eames

Executive Assistant, Prudhomme Estate

—

I take a breath.

Dusk told me to take what happened with her and apply it to every other area of my life, and I'm going to start here.

It's eleven forty now. In four hours, I'll make my way to the Conservatory conference rooms, and Bootsie will be waiting for me.

Except I don't call my mother.

I want to have this conversation by myself, without her throwing wads of cash at someone to get what she wants.

I pocket my phone and prepare to face down Bootsie Prudhomme alone.

Bootsie is early.

She must have left her house as soon as she got the email. She might have even been here waiting on me when I was emailing her assistant, or even when I was talking to Dusk on the gallery roof. Her tall, thin shape is easy to make out through the frosted-glass conference walls. Her ever-present fire-engine-red heels are visible, too, even if the rest of her is just a darkened blur.

This will be the first time anyone from Ocoee has ever seen me like this: with my hair up in a snarled knot and dark rings under my eyes. My leggings have a hole in one knee, and my hoodie will probably horrify her most of all: a silhouette of the white house, framed by the *Alice in Wonderland* quote that started it all—"Curiouser & Curiouser"—in oversize, whimsical lettering.

I could have made Bootsie wait another fifteen minutes and run upstairs to change my clothes and throw on a little makeup—but no.

I'm tired of playing dress up.

I don't want to be a version of myself I don't recognize in order to make everyone else happy.

Instead, I straighten my spine and pull the door to the conference room open.

Sure enough, Bootsie is in full-blown Southern Grandma Costume: pearls, and red lipstick, and curled hair, and giant door-knocker earrings that hearken back to the nineties, and a chunky white sweater bearing three different antique brooches, and two-hundred-dollar jeans in an unflattering cut.

She takes one look at me, from head to toe, and sniffs behind two fingers as if she can smell me. "Miss Ingram."

A self-conscious sniff-check tells me I showered *and* applied deodorant this morning.

"Ms. Prudhomme." I hide my nose behind my fingers, too.

I can *definitely* smell her—Chanel No. 5, and entirely too much of it.

We frown across the room at each other.

"I suppose you heard about June," she says. "Unfortunate."

"I did." I drop my bag onto the floor and take a seat. "I heard my mother played a role in it."

"Well, er—" Bootsie adjusts her glasses. "To put it indelicately, yes. 'A role' would be an understatement."

"I'd like you to know that I didn't know money changed hands." My pulse rings in my ears. There's a part of me that still wants this. But there's a bigger part that knows this is no longer my path. That part of me knows that my mother's way of fixing problems would only make this worse.

Another long pause hangs in the air.

"Even if that's the case, honey, we have the integrity of the scholarship—the entire art festival—to consider. We can't do this with dirty hands, you understand." Bootsie is careful to stare into the massive diamond on her left hand rather than look at me. "We have to disqualify you."

My pride pops and withers like a deflated balloon.

Bootsie did not come to negotiate.

"I appreciate you meeting me here today," Bootsie says. "I did not look forward to the dilemma of turning away your mother's checkbook."

"My mother is exhausting when she isn't getting what she wants," I say.

"I see no reason to dawdle." Bootsie stands. "I hate that this happened, sweetheart. I always enjoyed your work."

I stand too. Bootsie crosses the table, and she presses her fingertips to her nose again.

Bootsie's tall, but so am I. I stand a little straighter and meet her eye-to-eye.

"Tell me one thing," I say. "A finalist told you, didn't they?"

Bootsie brushes past me.

She throws the strap of her pocketbook over her shoulder and grabs for the door. "Yes."

"Who was it?"

"You know I'm not gonna tell you that," she says. "I don't want somebody finding that poor girl in a ditch."

"Nobody's killing anybody," I say.

Bootsie doesn't respond. Instead, she holds the door for me, and I follow her out into the foyer. Without a word, she leaves for the parking lot.

I make out Iliana's dad's beat-up Honda just behind Bootsie's massive Cadillac and march my way up to the only place she could be: the art wing for open studio.

I may not be killing anyone in *literal* terms, but somebody is about to *figuratively* scrape Iliana off the Studio B floor.

CHAPTER 23

ILIANA

Username: Curious-in-Cheshire
Last online: 2d ago

The Conservatory is a graveyard on the weekends.

Most of the residential students crash on a local's couch as soon as the last bell rings on Fridays, and with only a few days left in the semester, everyone would rather be curled up next to warm hearths rather than in drafty cinder-block dorms. The sky is gray, the wind is cold, and when I pulled in, the parking lot was empty, save for a thirty-year-old Cadillac parked with one tire hiked up onto the front curb.

The chill that's settled into my bones has nothing to do with the weather.

Kiersten and Sarah. *Cheshire*.

Three people, three problems.

The numbers don't multiply, though—they divide against each other, three separate girls and three separate problems.

One Big Fucking Crisis.

Somehow, Kiersten and Sarah have bonded over their mutual hatred of me—a given, since I can't imagine what else they have in common—Kiersten looks like the kind of jewel-studded artsy-fartsy dream girl a creative writing–track boy in a fedora hallucinates into

217

existence for his characters to objectify. I only know three things about her: she loves glitter, being angry, and enjoying her privilege.

Meanwhile, Sarah is malleable. She reminds me of Harry Potter's boggarts: No one knows her true form, because she takes a different shape with everyone she meets. She was still in her performing arts school form the last time I saw her at Sylvia's, flannels and ancient band shirts and frayed denim shorts worn over patterned tights in thirty-two-degree weather.

So much of the same, but the BeDazzled cassette player is the first step in what I predict will be an abrupt change.

It's such a small change, but I feel like I already don't know her anymore.

Everything is escalated to stage-3 *fucking crisis* by Rhodes— Alice—deleting her Slash/Spot account. I have no way to make this right. It will never happen with Rhodes, never. Kiersten and Sarah have given me forty-eight hours, but at this moment Rhodes hates me, so it's practically over before it even starts.

The only grace I have going for me is my Capstone project. I haven't touched it in days, but the knowledge that it's in my work locker waiting for me is the only thing I have left.

I'm loaded down for a long night in the studio: I have bags over one shoulder, loaded with Tupperware full of whatever Mom packed because I can't afford to order in tonight. Bags over the other shoulder loaded with everything from a first aid kit (X-Acto knives are sharp), to changes of clothes (studios are messy, and sometimes too hot, and sometimes too cold, and never predictable), to every kind of technology I could cram into a backpack: laptops, and drawing tablets, and chargers, and external batteries, and point-and-shoot digital cameras, and a handful of cords from the junk drawer in the kitchen because it seemed like a good idea at the time.

The hallways are eerie in their silence. A fluorescent light flickers over my head in the east stairwell, and hard, deliberate footsteps from deep within the school make my hair stand on end. If my life were a movie, this would be the precise moment Kiersten (or Sarah, or Kiersten and Sarah) would show up behind me to take a hatchet to the back of my skull.

But Studio B is bright, and warm, and *empty*. The gray skies are giving way to rain through the expansive windows on the south and east walls, and the residual scent of rubber cement in the air feels like a welcome home. My stuff takes up an entire table in the back of the room, but it doesn't matter because I'm *alone*.

It's not scary anymore, with the door shut behind me.

It's tempting to go straight to the work lockers in the back of the studio, to pull out my work and throw myself in headfirst. After everything with Kiersten and Sarah, though, I need to center myself.

My tarot cards are in the front of my messenger bag, where they always are.

Their silk bag feels like a comfort blanket. The way they curve to fit my hands when I shuffle, the cards are familiar, like an old friend.

I separate the cards into three piles, restack them, then draw the first card off the top.

A knight carries her helmet under her arm, and she wears a wreath in her hair. Her horse has flowers woven into her mane, and there are flowers hanging from the banners behind her, too—six banners, to be specific, because in tarot the number of things always matters.

Six of Wands.

Traditionally, this card represents success: the valiant knight, riding in from war to celebrate victory. It's not just any old victory, either, because other cards carry the same meaning, too: It's a *public* victory. The banners, the flowers in the knight's hair, all of it was set in place by other people. It would be easy to try to assume the universe is whispering the secrets of the future in my ear, but I know better.

The Six of Wands card isn't a promise that I'll win the scholarship.

It's Harry Potter's Mirror of Erised: It's showing me what I want—the thing I'm bleeding myself dry for. I've been so distracted by my personal life, and this little ritual only confirms what a part of me has recognized all along: It's time to be who I'm meant to be, do what I'm supposed to do, and take what the world is offering to get where I need to go.

I shake myself free of thoughts of Rhodes and Alice and Sarah.

Everything else and every*one* else are just distractions.

I'm ready.

The Capstone Award show is in two days, and I'm going to finish my project tonight.

Under normal circumstances, I would shuffle my cards back together and tuck them back into my bag. Tonight feels different, though—I want the knight's protection, and even if I know it's just a tiny piece of mass-printed cardstock, leaving the Six of Wands card out while I work feels significant.

The studio is chilly. It's hard to tug on fingerless gloves with half-numb hands, but it's even harder to operate an X-Acto knife when you can barely feel the tips of your fingers. I flip on the space heater en route to the locker wall, and even though the room fills with the scent of gas, it'll be another hour at least before it's warm enough to take my gloves back off again.

The studio door flies open with enough force that drywall crumbles against the brunt of the doorknob. The *SLAM-SMASH-CRUNCH* rattles the windows, reverberates through my bones, and stops my heart.

First thought: Sarah and Kiersten are here.

They have a hatchet, and it has a standing date with the back of my head.

I KNEW IT.

Second thought: If it's Sarah and Kiersten, they're literally the worst murderers in modern history. They didn't even bother to sneak up on me, and I'm in the back of a room filled with chairs, sharp objects, and heavy projectiles. Even as inexperienced in murder as they are, they both have the basic intelligence to sneak up on someone first.

I don't remember clutching my chest, but my sweatshirt is crumpled when I let go to rake my hair out of my face. There are no approaching steps ringing off the linoleum floors.

Slowly, very slowly, I turn to face the door.

I know the silhouette standing in the door, even if I can't make out her face. I'd know her willowy limbs, her sloping shoulders, and her giant, messy topknot anywhere.

First thought: A flower is blooming in my chest.

Or maybe my ribs are a birdcage, and my spirit is made of robins.

Second thought: *Oh.*

Shit.

She knows and it's over.

"I just left a meeting with Bootsie Prudhomme." Rhodes's hands are shaking when she reaches out for the door to slam it back into the casing behind her. "And judging by the confused look on your face, you have no idea who that is. The new chairwoman for the Capstone Award, Iliana."

She crosses her arms, glaring at me as if this is supposed to mean something.

This was my worst nightmare.

Not Sarah and Kiersten with a hatchet, but even worse: That Rhodes would figure out that I'm Cheshire before I've had a chance to tell her myself. But that doesn't seem like that's what this is at all, and I can't wrap my head around it.

"What happened to the other lady?"

Impatience flickers across Rhodes's features, then her face pinches into an ugly scowl.

"You are such a *bitch*, Iliana Vrionides!" Her voice rings out against the windows. "I don't understand why you're constantly trying to ruin my life!"

"*Excuse* me?" I don't need the space heater anymore. I snatch off one glove at a time and stuff them into the pocket of my hoodie. "You think *I'm* trying to ruin your life? *You* were the one that cost me my scholarship—"

The words are hollow.

I've been thinking like this for so long, it flies from me unchecked. I regret it the moment it flies out of my mouth—instead of bringing Rhodes closer, I know I'm only pushing her further away.

Rhodes recoils, clutching her chest.

"That wasn't my—I didn't *mean*—Jesus God, Iliana, all of this is because of the ACAD scholarship?" Her laugh lacks humor. "You can't just take away *my* opportunities because you lost one of yours. This scholarship is a zero-sum game, but life isn't—and this is super effing shitty, even for you."

One word at a time, I process what she's saying.

You. Can't. Take. Away. My. Opportunities.

The other Capstone Award lady is gone, and she's been replaced.

Something happened, and Rhodes thinks it's because of me.

"What are you *talking* about?"

"Are you really going to make me give you the play-by-play?" Rhodes presses the heel of her palm against one eye, and her chin quivers. Alice—Rhodes—hates it when people see her cry, but I can't look away. "Isn't it enough for you to know I'm out?"

"I have no idea what you're talking about."

Rhodes watches me in silence.

She closes the distance between us in a handful of long, sweeping strides—one moment she's standing in the doorway and the next, her breath ruffles my hair.

I flinch.

She doesn't hit me, though: She simply lifts my chin so I have no other choice but to look her in the eyes. Her skin against mine, even in this small way, stands my arm hair on end.

Everything in her is burning: her eyes, her face, her spirit.

I have no idea what she sees when she's looking at me. I don't know what she's looking for, but she's showing me things I know she'd never want anyone to witness: the way she pants through each breath, the shake in her hands, the intensity of her gaze—all of it tells me that Rhodes—Alice—is vulnerable. *Afraid*.

Something shifts; there's a crackle in the air and everything feels different.

I reach up between us—for what purpose, I have no idea—and Rhodes's eyes widen, just a little. She lets go and takes two giant steps backward.

"Why do we keep doing this to each other?" I ask.

Rhodes shakes her head.

She turns her back to me. Her reflection in the window reveals her hands bunched back up against her face, presumably to catch more tears she doesn't want me to see.

"I don't know why anyone else would have ratted on me—or my mom, I guess—to the board," she says. "It seemed so, I don't know. Neat. Tidy. Like poetic justice or something."

I'm glad my back is to her—I don't want her to see my face right now, all screwed up and screaming concern.

I feel sick even considering the fact that someone was working very hard to sabotage her—even if a few short months ago, that person could have easily been me.

I want to ask a thousand questions—what was said in the meeting? What was Bootsie's phrasing? What exactly did her mom *do*? But I'm afraid that something even as simple as seeking out details could be the thing that sends her scurrying away.

I want her to be close to me, so I choose my next words carefully.

"Life is rarely ever poetic," I say. "No, I wanted to beat you fair and square—I won't ever know I'm the best if I'm not up against you."

Rhodes watches me for a long moment before she speaks again. "Thanks, I think."

"I wouldn't have ever done that to you, not in a million years. Honest." It's easier to fumble with the padlock in front of me, long forgotten in whatever this moment is evolving into. No matter how many times I punch my number into the mechanical dials, I can't get it to unlock. "I've . . . lost everything. I, er, don't mean to say that, uh, like a jab, but—"

"No, I get it." Rhodes's voice is soft. "That night was horrible for all of us."

"I know it wasn't your fault," I say. "I've been really unfair."

Behind me, a chair screeches against the linoleum. One shoe sole, then another, squeaks on the surface of one of the tables. "My dad called SCAD for you, when it happened."

Another pang of guilt. I turn to face her, finally.

Mom's words the other night ring in my ear: "You do everything you can to make things right."

I now know through Alice that she'd done everything she could to make things right with me. This is so much more than even she ever disclosed to me.

"No one ever told me that."

"It went pretty much how our lawyer told us it would: That the school wouldn't talk to us about what happened that night for, like, five different reasons. That they'd already informed the runner-up for the scholarship and there was nothing they could do."

"Rules are rules," I say, echoing the words of my own lawyer— my older brother. "So, what are you going to do now, about the Capstone?"

She shrugs. "I don't know. I guess I have to rethink some things."

"That's not always a bad thing."

I've had to rethink some things, too.

"What are *you* doing here? We don't have anything due until next week."

"I haven't touched my Capstone project since we returned from Nashville." Now is as good a time as any to drag everything back out. I turn and fiddle with the padlock to my work locker again, slap the side a few times, then punch the number in for what feels like the thousandth time.

With another jiggle and a smack, it finally springs free.

There is resistance when I pull the locker door open.

A *POP* and a *splatter-gush* rings in my ears, and my eyes burn with *something* that washes the world in painful, burning black.

"Oh—" Rhodes's voice is behind me.

I don't know if she's inches or miles away.

A fresh wave of nausea spills over with each beat of my heart.

Gentle hands rest on my shoulders, then the small of my back.

"Oh, oh, oh—" Her tone is completely piteous. "Iliana, this is bad—"

"This *burns!* Help!" I swipe at my face with my hands, but whatever it is only spreads.

"Oh! Right! I'm sorry—"

I'm being shuttled *somewhere.*

"Uh—I'm reading the directions on the eyewash station—" Rhodes's breath is quick in my ear, and she smells like fabric softener and warm skin. She bends me forward with splayed fingers between my shoulder blades, and before long, cool eye solution splashes into my hot, aching eyes.

I should be worried about whether I'll ever see again, but—like a love-sick puppy—I can't think further than the warm, bare hand caressing the back of my neck.

CHAPTER 24

RHODES

Username: n/a

The studio is a disaster.

It takes thirty minutes to wash the printmaking ink from Iliana's eyes, and another hour to get it out of her hair and off her skin. No less than fifty tiny paper rectangles are strewn about, crinkled and fragile, across the top of the wide studio tables. The ink completely soaked them, warping the delicate paper-cuts into a thousand organic, three-dimensional shapes. She's been cutting them in both red and black paper, and the effect from where I stand reminds me of autumn leaves on a sidewalk: One gust of wind, or even a breath of air, could send them scattering everywhere.

Iliana sits on the other side of the table from me, with her bottom perched up on the back of the chair and her feet in the seat. Her cheeks are freckled from eighteen Alabama summers, and her toenails are painted a shade of navy blue so dark it could almost be called black.

She hasn't cried yet. I've wanted to cry for the past hour and a half, and it didn't even happen to me.

Iliana's Capstone project is *destroyed*.

I don't like the idea of using the word *sabotaged*—at the end of the day it seems indecent to automatically assume this wasn't an accident somehow—but *sabotage* is *exactly* what this is.

Someone knows Iliana's mettle.

It's something I've known since day one—and realistically, it's something I've hated about her—that clearly someone else is becoming savvy to: Iliana Vrionides is a force to be reckoned with.

She'll be the one to beat at the Capstone Award in two days, and clearly somebody is trying to cut a path for themselves early.

The thought sickens me.

I don't know if I've ever actually seen Iliana cry before, now that I think about it. Instead, she sits with her elbows resting on her knees and her chin in her palms, and she stares at the table in a sort of complete and utter silence I've only ever wished from her.

It's like looking at a snail without its shell—

No.

I've had these kinds of thoughts about Iliana for so long, they've rutted paths into my mind.

I lapse into them, and I don't know how to stop anymore. She doesn't deserve this, now that she stands to lose everything for a second time.

"What are you going to do?" It's a simple question, but it's a start.

"You know," Iliana says after a long moment, with her eyes dropped to the front of my shirt, "most people see Lewis Carroll's work as being silly, but a lot of it is also political satire."

All I can do is stare at her. "That's what you're thinking about right now? My sweatshirt?"

"Your sweatshirt." She shrugs. "My tarot cards. It all comes back to Alice."

As far as she knows, I've fallen victim to Alice in Wonderland's whimsy like everyone else. Bunnies with monocles are universally cute, as are girls in pinafores next to teetering stacks of teacups, but this is usually as far as people's fascination with the stories go.

"I've never been interested in discourse, though," I say. "Like, okay. Carroll never actually said it was political himself, so all we can really do is accept it at face value and enjoy it for what it is: stories he told his boss's daughter about a fictional little girl named Alice." I drop into the chair next to her and crack my knuckles one at a time. "There are other theories, too—that they, like, satirize mathematical society drama in the late nineteenth century because Carroll was a mathematician. That it was—I don't know—word vomit from Carroll's subconscious after his dad died. Just because a bunch of literary snobs came up with all of this doesn't mean it isn't just fan theory."

"When *isn't* art political, though?" Iliana nudges one of the cards on the table with a bare toe. "When isn't it puked up from our subconscious? Even if he hadn't intended it as a criticism of the British government, or the math nerds where he taught at Christ Church, or whatever, that doesn't mean those things weren't on his mind when he was writing them."

"What's Carroll's real name?" I ask, entirely out of the blue. I want to settle this with myself, once and for all—I want to know whether Iliana cares about Alice as much as she wants people to believe she does.

"Really? Is this some kind of fandom litmus test?" She drops her nasally, pitchy tone almost an entire octave to mimic mine. "'You're a real fan? Name five of their albums.'"

"I don't sound like that. Maybe."

She pulls a face. I laugh.

This is a version of Iliana that I don't know: Quiet. Pensive. We've never been this close before, and before now, I've never actually just *looked* at her. Tonight, with the glow of the lights from the parking lot through the windows as the sun is setting, she could be Gentileschi's Judith, or Bathsheba, or maybe Esther: Her mouth is soft, her face round. Her hair begs for freedom from the tie that binds it in place.

She's turned her attention to the mess in front of us, and I don't think she's going to answer my question at first—or maybe she doesn't know the answer at all. Maybe she's not even thinking about Alice anymore. Should she be?

With a puff of air, I could blow her away.

"I don't *really* have any options anymore, do I?" She shakes her head.

"You . . ." I swallow. She's hurting, but I feel this in the depths of my soul. "You always have options."

"Well, you aren't *technically* wrong. I can only think of two: Either start over on the cards or withdraw from the Capstone."

"I could help you." It falls out of me, too fast to catch. "Let me help you, Iliana."

She looks at me for a moment. "I don't understand why you suddenly care about my problems."

"I know what the Capstone ladies like. Maybe—" I don't have the answer myself. Not really. "Maybe I just . . . You already lost out once. *Somebody* wants us out of the running, and you still have a chance. I don't."

"You think this is all the same person? The same thing?"

"I haven't really thought about it before now," I say, "but it makes sense, right? If you didn't rat *me* out, and *I* didn't break into your locker, who would have done this to us?"

A shadow darkens her features—creases her brows, worries her jaw—and she turns her head to look out the window.

"I don't know," she finally says.

I don't believe her.

People like Iliana have enemies in spades.

It just doesn't make any sense who would have any problem with the two of us.

CHAPTER 25
ILIANA

Username: Curious-in-Cheshire
Last online: 3d ago

This is the first stage of Rhodes's plan: We're heading up to Nashville for the Capstone Award early, one day ahead of my family, the other contenders—and the night that could make or break the next four years of my life. Rhodes and Griffin are both flushed with sleep, Rhodes with pillow creases on her right cheek and Griffin with a piece of leftover toast tucked into the front pocket of his shirt for later. We've packed our bags as well as we can, and coordinated with our parents, and fifty-seven fragile, paper-cut tarot cards are packed in boxes loaded with Styrofoam peanuts in the back of Rhodes's SUV.

The interstate is still dark with sunrise, the trees skeletal silhouettes against a burgeoning sky. Streetlights flicker off two at a time just ahead of us, the radio is shut off, and no one has spoken since we left the Conservatory parking lot.

I wouldn't be lying if I said I wasn't more than a little relieved that we'd be hours away from Kiersten and Sarah. They'll have no way to know what Rhodes does or doesn't know about my identity—and even if they *do* figure it out, they'll be too far away to screw it all up.

Kiersten's words loomed in the back of my mind all night, every time one of our phones dinged with notifications, any time we heard steps in the hall. I was poised, waiting for the other shoe to drop—but it never came. My fear of telling Rhodes who I am shifted at some point during the night: before, I was afraid to tell her because I knew I'd never have a chance with her, not with the state of our relationship as it was. Last night, it occurred to me that she might believe I didn't tell her because I didn't want to take advantage of her kindness.

The truth of the matter is that I have been afraid to tell her because I love her.

Hearts are fickle things. Hate is complicated.

Her face has been etched on the surface of my heart for as long as I've known her, and I don't think I'm ever going to know where hate ended and want began—because is there really that much of a difference? Does it matter what I call the way I feel about her, as long as I know she's flavored most of my thoughts?

I judged Sarah's preoccupation with her so harshly, but looking into Rhodes's eyes last night, it occurred to me that I wasn't *judging* her at all.

I was jealous.

"Your gas light has been on for, like, thirty minutes," Griffin tells Rhodes from the front passenger seat.

"Stop micromanaging me! It's fine."

"It's not fine," Griffin says. "You're going to run out of gas."

"I'm sorry, have you seen an actual exit with an actual gas station in the last *hour*?"

"I just saw a billboard for a Love's in five miles." Griffin tilts back his head and turns up his cup for the last drop of coffee from the Styrofoam Milo's cup in his hand. "That was two miles ago."

Rhodes shoots him a glare across the console, then turns her attention to me from the rearview mirror.

"*Iliana*"—Griffin curses Rhodes under his breath, and Rhodes swats the top of his arm—"when Bootsie asks you why your entry doesn't look like how you pitched it, don't tell her about the ink."

Rhodes flicks on her turn signal and merges into another lane to pass an eighteen-wheeler with its hazards flashing.

"Come up with something froufrou about your vision shifting," Griffin says.

"You don't think I should tell her someone tried to sabotage me?" I'm sprawled out across her spacious backseat with my messenger bag stuck under my head. My tarot cards nudge just behind my right ear, and I reach inside to pull them free. "I'd think they'd want to know that."

Rhodes frowns. "They're not like you—"

"Hey!"

It stings. I know that better than anyone.

I still don't particularly enjoy hearing it.

"No, not like that! I mean, they don't handle *anything* up front." She sits back in her seat. "To women like Bootsie, drama is the necessary, unsavory underbelly of society. If you can't avoid it, you have to at least act like it isn't affecting you."

"That's not how the women I grew up around are at all," I say. "My mom and grandma and all my aunts just . . . fight. It's a huge blowup, and then it's over and we all move on. They don't believe in leaving things on to simmer."

"I can't imagine," Rhodes says.

"Mom and Aunt Gina just go weeks without talking to each other," Griffin says. "We didn't see Grandma for three Christmases in a row once, because Grandma said something at Easter dinner about Mom needing to get her lips done."

Now it's my turn to balk.

I can't fathom a world where our family would all give up on each other every time we disagreed about something. Our love for each other runs so much deeper than whatever absurd thing we're fighting about.

And yet this is the only way Rhodes and Griffin know how to live.

It seems more apparent now than ever that there is no version of reality where Rhodes will be able to find a way to love me.

The exit appears out of nowhere, and the Love's station is a brightly lit oasis surrounded by cattle fields in the near distance. Rhodes pulls up to a gas stall and turns off the engine. "Look—if we're going to make it there in time to get over to Frist before it closes, we can only be here for *ten* minutes, got it?"

Griffin rolls his eyes "I've just gotta pee. I can be out in, like, ninety seconds."

Rhodes gives him *a look* that suggests otherwise. She grabs her wallet from the console and steps out to pump the gas, and Griffin and I wander inside.

Inside, everything is bathed in red and orange, with wall-to-wall, backlit refrigerator cases filled with everything from bottled water to cartons of eggs. I have to stop and take it all in: tables of cellophane-wrapped baked goods with a sign begging us to BUY LOCAL, and aisle after aisle after aisle of metal shelves stocked with shaving cream, and bulk-sized bags of trail mix, and little nefarious-looking glass tubes with silk roses suspended inside.

"It's like a Walmart and a gas station had a baby," I say.

"Not too different from the last gas station we stood in together." Griffin watches my face, waiting for a response.

The blood rushes to my head so fast, my ears burn and my lips tingle. He's right: The old gas station turned art installation was probably one of these once. It's like imagining Tim Burton's Underland: The floors here are pristine, shining gray and orange under the overhead lights. The art installation's floors were warped and stained every shade of brown. Rain poured through the hole in the roof, and there was an inch of standing water anywhere there was a low spot in the floors. I'd worked hard to forget that night, but everything rushes back, making me realize that I never actually got rid of it.

Griffin and I both lost things that night. Rhodes did, too, in her own way.

We all chose to be there, at the art installation that night. No one made us go. We can't change the way it ended, and I can't blame either of them for the way it happened.

"What's going on with you and Rhodes?" Griffin pulls me back to the here and now.

Straight up. No pussyfooting around, just fucking *asks*.

"What happened to not asking things and avoiding conflict?" I ask.

Answering a question with another question seems safe.

"What happened to not leaving things on to simmer?" Griffin crosses his arms and raises his brows. "Come *on* with it. I saw the way you looked at her when we got in the car. We're not friends and you don't owe me anything, but she's my sister and she's been *through* it."

He raises his eyebrows and shrugs again, international body language for "*Well?!*"

"Rhodes is just helping me," I say, stunned. There's no way he knows the truth of things—who I am, who she is. "You already know what happened: Someone ratted her out to the Capstone board for paying that June lady off, and someone tried to destroy my Capstone Award project. I'm trying not to assume *why* she's helping me, because assuming *anything* is how Rhodes and I even got here to begin with."

Griffin grabs me by the shoulders and stares into my eyes. His are blue, like Rhodes's, with the same little gray flecks at the center.

Blue like Alice's dress in the Tim Burton film, just like *my* Alice always told me.

I *have* to tell Rhodes who I am, and *soon*.

"You have to help me." It fumbles out of me before I can cram it back in.

For the first time since this all started, I feel myself on the verge of tears.

Griffin drops his hands and steps closer. For a moment, he wears the distinct expression of someone with the proverbial hamster running in its wheel between his ears.

A lightbulb clicks on over his head, and I start to cry.

"You're Cheshire, aren't you?" Griffin whispers it, thankfully, small enough for just the two of us.

I don't have the chance to respond, though: Rhodes appears on the other side of the automatic sliding doors with her shoulders bunched around her ears, red-faced and practically shaking with irritation.

"Griffin! I *know* you haven't used the bathroom yet, and I swear to God, if I have to spend the rest of this trip listening to you complain—"

Without a word, Griffin turns on his heel and makes his way to the restrooms on the other side of the store.

Rhodes whirls on me, and for a second I wonder if she heard Griffin after all.

All she's worried about is getting to Nashville on time.

"What's wrong with *you*?!" She throws out a pointed finger across the gas station. "Go to the bathroom, for Christ's sake!"

I go to the bathroom.

I lock the door behind me and pray Griffin has the good grace not to tell Rhodes first.

Grif.ingram 8:40a: so why did you stand her up

i.vrionides 8:40a: I didn't *stand her up*

i.vrionides 8:40a: when I realized who she was, I had to process, too

i.vrionides 8:41a: I was in love with Alice—that was her name, Alice—and I know how much Rhodes hated me, too

Grif.ingram 8:41a: she never hated you

Grif.ingram 8:41a: she hated the way you treated her

Grif.ingram 8:42a: so why didn't you tell her later then

Grif.ingram 8:44a: how do I know you're not taking advantage of her?

i.vrionides 8:44a: how do I know you won't show her these texts?

Grif.ingram 8:47a: who knows, I might

i.vrionides 8:47a: don't be a dick

i.vrionides 8:47a: I just wanted a chance with her

i.vrionides 8:49a: please believe me

i.vrionides 9:15a: please

CHAPTER 26
ILIANA

Username: Curious-in-Cheshire
Last online: 3d ago

Three people know about my identity as Cheshire, and not one of them are Rhodes.

Griffin and I texted back and forth in silence during the rest of the trip, with Rhodes's eyes trained on the road—and, hopefully, oblivious. We made it to Frist with an hour to spare, just like Rhodes planned—"If I didn't tell you jerks we only had ten minutes at the gas station, you would have taken an hour"—and between the three of us, it only took two trips to unload the trunk.

"No one else is supposed to be here until tomorrow," Rhodes says while hefting a big box. "They didn't *say* we couldn't come before tomorrow, so this will give you the chance to pick the best spot in the room."

"Do you know what room it's in?" Griffin walks between Rhodes and me with my messenger bag over his shoulder. He flips through my *Sacred Feminine* tarot deck, one card at a time. "How do you know any of this with June gone?"

When Rhodes turns to face us, her smile is a little wicked. "Because I called June while we were at the gas station. She doesn't think Bootsie and them would have changed the plans for the weekend—

why would they? I'm not a threat. June isn't going to show up and cause a stink. She told me everything."

"I guess we'd better hope you're right," I say. I struggle under the weight of another box, and my giant art supply case hangs from its cross-body strap, slamming against the backs of my thighs every time I take a step.

"It's going to be okay, Iliana," Rhodes says. Her eyes are so wide, soft and blue. "It won't be like last time. You have a really good chance, even June thinks so."

"Let's read our cards," I say. I want any reason to keep on staring into them. "I always read my cards before something big. I'll read yours, too."

Rhodes gives me *a look*. "You know how I feel about that."

"Do me! Do me!" Griffin drops my bag to the ground.

Carefully, we make a switch, until I'm holding my cards and Griffin is holding the box I was carrying only moments ago.

"Ugh, fine." Rhodes points to a spot on the floor. "Is here okay?"

"Yeah, anywhere is fine." I pull the dyed silk mat I sewed from an old scarf out of my bag and stretch it out on the ground. Blues, purples, and pinks dyed to look like a galaxy shimmer under the florescent lights over our heads.

"Griffin first," I say.

Griffin kneels down next to me. We go through the motions: I shuffle the cards until he says "stop."

He cuts and restacks the deck, then draws the top card.

A Woman-King stares back at us, with soft eyes and a strong jaw. Her hair falls over her shoulders like water, and she grips chalices in each hand that sit on the arms of her throne. Instead of legs, she boasts a mermaid tail. Instead of a traditional chair-style throne, she is seated on a throne of coral.

"The King of Cups," he reads from the bottom of the card.

"This card is telling you to be completely in charge of your feelings," I say. "It says to listen to your heart and trust your intuitions as fact."

Griffin nods with this. He pulls his phone from his pocket to snap a picture of the card, then gestures for Rhodes to sit down next to us.

She sighs and drops to one knee. Griffin takes the box from her arms, and I guide her through the motions of shuffling then cutting the deck.

She places a single card, faceup, onto the mat.

Justitia is blindfolded, as she always is, and she extends a scale in her right arm. She's dressed in a billowing, white toga, and golden curls hang around her cheeks. On one side of the scale is a heart—on the other, a feather.

The Justice card.

My heart forgets how to beat, then scrambles ahead in double time.

"This card means you'll have a decision to make," I say, "and whatever you decide now will affect the people around you in the future."

"Isn't that always true?" Rhodes asks, a taste of the old, snotty girl I used to hate. "Every decision we make affects the people around us."

"This is more than that, though," I say. "It's kind of cause and effect: If you've done harm to someone, that harm is coming back to you. If you've been kind, the same."

"Or if harm has been done to me," she says, running one finger down the card. It isn't hard to guess who she's thinking about. "Who do you think did this to us?"

"I don't know for sure, but I have a few ideas—"

Realistically, I know exactly who did it: Sarah and Kiersten.

Of course, I don't *know* for sure, but it aligns with the only interaction I've had with the two of them since the Capstone project proposal.

Kiersten is still in the running, with her embroidery and dyed silks.

The fact that it's Sarah and Kiersten—two out of the only three people in the world who actually know my secret about my identity—means there is literally *nothing* I can do about it. One shake of the hornet's nest, and every bit of this will fall around my shoulders.

But I know from my days with Alice that Rhodes wants so much to believe in the good of people. It would horrify her for me to admit these suspicions to her if all I have to go on is a hunch. To Rhodes, at the end of the day, everyone is redeemable.

Rhodes picks up the card from the mat.

The tip of her finger grazes the insides of mine when she places the card in my upturned hand. A careful glance suggests that Griffin's eyes are glued to his phone, likely sharing "his" card to every manner of social media. It was a small enough gesture of Rhodes's that there's no way he could have seen it for himself, but I feel it down to my toes.

She's touched me to push me away, to offer first aid, to help me—but never just for the sake of touching.

Our eyes meet again, and this time neither of us looks away.

"Rhodes—" I lick my lips. *Now*. I have to do it now. "I, I just want to say—"

Rhodes's face goes red. I wonder what we look like to Griffin, or the rest of the world, kneeling together.

She's close enough to kiss. I could reach out and touch her if I wanted to.

If I knew she wanted it, too.

"Don't worry about it," she says. "Honestly. This year has been hell for all of us."

"No," I say. "I mean, thank you, I'm glad, but, that's not what I mean."

We hear high, loud voices on the other end of the hall well before we lay eyes on the people they belong to. Rhodes and I both know one of the voices almost as well as we know our own, the person who at one point was the source of at least half of our problems—Sarah Wade. It hasn't been lost on me that removing Sarah from the equation has also put a stop to 99 percent of mine and Rhodes's issues.

I wonder if Rhodes realizes the same thing.

"She was disqualified," Rhodes whispers. "I don't know why she's here—"

"Kiersten," I say.

As if on cue, Sarah and Kiersten round the corner and come into view, pushing a cart loaded with several wide, flat boxes stacked on their sides. There's something performative about the way they cling to each other's arms, throw their heads back, and laugh. Who knows if there was ever even a joke, as much as a conscious choice to make us feel as though we missed something important.

Sarah loves this trick.

God knows how many times we pulled it with Rhodes, on the days Sarah and Rhodes weren't getting along.

"Well, darn." Kiersten pushes the cart to stop only inches away from where Griffin, Rhodes, and I sit on the floor. "I figured we'd be the only ones to think of getting here early like this."

"You overestimate your own basic intelligence, *Kiersten*," I say.

Sarah flusters, but Kiersten only feigns injury.

"I'm surprised y'all are even here," Sarah says. Kiersten shoots her a warning look, but Sarah keeps going. "The board sent out an email. Everyone knows about you, Rhodes. I'd think you'd be embarrassed."

"You make no sense, Sarah." Rhodes twists her hands into the hem of her sweater. "Why are you acting like I did something to you?"

Kiersten shoots Sarah another careful look.

"Well, girls, let us know if we can help y'all with anything." Kiersten's eyes drift to me, for just a moment, and she remembers to smile. "Let's grab dinner later, yeah?"

Rhodes doesn't say anything. I don't say anything.

Kiersten and Sarah push past us without another word, through the double doors behind us, and out onto the terrace. When Sarah turns back to glance at us over her shoulder, her expression isn't haughty anymore. She looks small, and tired, and sad, and it occurs to me that maybe Rhodes is right to believe in the goodness of people.

I'm glad I never told Rhodes my theory about Sarah, because everything in her now tells me that I would have been wrong. She's been angry with me hundreds of times before, but never in her life has she done anything to try to actually *hurt* me.

"I think we know who screwed us over," Rhodes says.

"Kiersten," I say.

Griffin stows his phone in his back pocket, stands, and picks up a box. I push my fingers through my hair and stuff my tarot cards back into my bag.

Our saboteur could have never been anyone else.

The second phase of Rhodes's plan is, of course, brilliant.

"They're still your tarot cards," she whispers from the base of a nine-foot ladder. "They can't disqualify you for not displaying what you pitched. They might be wrinkled up and covered in ink, but they're still *beautiful*."

"I can't believe you thought of this," I say. I'm at the other end of the ladder, straining as high as I can go to hook humble paper clips into the metal framework over our heads, a part of the wide tent pitched in Frist's sprawling courtyard. We've laced thin metal wire through the clips as if we've laced a pair of shoes, and from here the tarot cards will hang to move with the breeze.

My corner of the tent is small, and placed unceremoniously between sweeping, technically difficult paintings of the Tennessee Valley, but it's *perfect*. A corner was exactly what I needed for this to work.

"I got the idea after the ink on the paper-cut cards had finally dried. They were scattered across the studio table like autumn leaves, all crunchy-looking and fragile. It wasn't hard to imagine them falling in showers from the trees."

I climb down from the ladder, one rung at a time. Rhodes is there when I finally reach the bottom, with her hand pressed against the small of my back to steady my balance. I can still feel the warmth there, even after her touch falls away.

"It's genius," I say. "If I somehow win this because of your idea—"

"I'm not just doing this for you—this is for me, too." Rhodes glares across the tent, where Kiersten unpacks a series of canvas frames mounted in hand-dyed oranges and pinks. "She did this—I know it. You *have* to beat her, for the both of us."

"I'm going to do everything I can," I whisper. "It's all I have left, too."

CHAPTER 27

RHODES

Username: n/a

One of these days, it won't take my life to be dumped over like a basket to figure out what it is I want. Every change in my life has come with so much upheaval, it's almost like I've only ever had to take myself apart and put myself back together because I was broken, not because of anything I ever wanted to achieve.

Everything I had six months ago is gone now: my relationship with the Ocoee Arts Festival.

My relationship with Cheshire.

My friendship with Sarah.

The fallout doesn't stop there, though: I haven't known how to even speak to my mother since June was let go from the arts festival and I was disqualified. Her meddling is what has brought me here, and her meddling is what took it away from me. It feels abusive, to have something forced into your hands and then have it snatched from you.

The condo is quiet. Griffin is asleep, and Iliana is—I don't know—taking a shower, or texting her friends, or reading her tarot cards.

I step outside onto the balcony and find where Iliana has been all along.

I've always associated her with motion—if her curls aren't vibrating with frenetic energy, she's pacing. She's moving and talking and bitching and stretching, and she never sits still, ever.

But tonight, she's curled up tight into the corner of a wicker couch. She's perfectly still, and awe glows warm in some kind of aura around her.

The Gulch stretches below our balcony, wild with activity: Christmas is only a few days away, and thousands of people mill around the sidewalks like a colony of ants.

The air is dense with ideas, the thoughts of thousands of people blooming up like steam from the streets below.

This feels closer to where I'm meant to be than I've been in months.

Maybe Griffin was right: Sweet, simple, and socially acceptable isn't where I am anymore.

"This place is wild," Iliana says. She's bundled under coats and sweatshirts and jeans over leggings, but she's still shivering with cold. "Is this, like, your parents' vacation place?"

"Mom works in Nashville during the week." Iliana holds out the seven-layer blanket situation across her lap, and I take a seat next to her on the couch. "It was cheaper—and safer—for Mom and Dad to get a second place than for Mom to commute from Birmingham every day."

"Is your mom, like, a businessperson?"

"Investment banking," I say.

The barely functional drinking is only the tip of the iceberg with Mom. There's also a rich boyfriend that Dad doesn't know about, and a cover side-hustle writing code, to explain where the money for the condo the boyfriend's funding is coming from, and more than likely more debt than Satan himself.

Even if it's beginning to feel like Iliana and I have been friends for years, I don't know if I'm ready to say any of this out loud.

I told Cheshire once. Ultimately, I couldn't trust her, either.

"Ah." She says nothing else.

I have no idea what she thinks about me.

Iliana's hair is an unholy mess, and she isn't wearing any makeup. She watches the world fly by with the same kind of quiet awe that I only felt moments before.

Everything about her demeanor is a version of Iliana I only knew existed because Sarah swore it did: Her body language is casual, if a little nervy-twitchy, and her shoulders are relaxed back into the couch cushions. It never occurred to me that nervy-twitchy might be baseline for her, that she might worry about *anything*.

Maybe this—the lights and the sounds and the hustle—is what Iliana wants too.

"I don't want to be a fine artist anymore. I want to be an illustrator," I whisper. "I want to be a comic artist."

Never in a hundred million years would I have thought Iliana would be the first person with whom I'd tell that piece of truth.

That's its own kind of coming out, admitting something big and scary to myself out loud.

I'm relieved.

I ache with the honesty of it, and I fear for what it will mean for my future.

Iliana has no poker face. She brightens, for a moment, eyes wide and shining, and then she pulls it all back in again. The expression she seems to be going for is "blank but interested," but with the way her brows are furrowed together, she only looks confused.

"That would be a . . . departure," she finally says.

"Yeah." I stare out into the night. It's not hard to picture the street like I would illustrate it, lines and angles and splashes of neon against indigo.

This could be one of the worlds Cheshire and I never explored in the *Hearts & Spades* universe, an entire planet overrun with steel and concrete.

"A lot would change, actually," I say. "I'd need to change a few things with Randall on my schedule—I'd need to take another illustration technology class and drop Drawing III. I've gotta figure out how to get my grades back up."

"You can do it, though." Iliana shifts a little closer. "My brother bombed his last year of high school, then went to junior college for a year before he transferred to University of Alabama. It took a little longer, but he's a lawyer now."

"I know. It'll be harder, though—Mom *hates* the idea of me doing something like graphic design or illustration."

"What? Why?"

"She says if I'm going to be poor, I might as well do something that people will celebrate after I die." I shrug. "If I'm doing apprenticeships in Paris and Italy, and fellowships at galleries here, maybe I will make a name for myself and the money won't matter."

"Wow . . ." Iliana balks for a moment. "There's so much wrong with that. She only cares if you're poor as long as she can be proud of you."

"I think she just wants to make sure I can take care of myself," I say. "I think she thinks I don't understand how the world works, or that living costs money."

"Says the woman who's paid hand over fist to break every rule in the way of you doing what she wants." Iliana frowns. "My family is broke. Like, flat broke. My brother was the first person in our family to go to college, then the first person to go to grad school, now the first person to work in an office for a living. People who are born poor are more likely to die poor. So much of having money or being poor is about who your parents are, and their parents, and *their* parents, all the way back as far as it can go."

It's like a lightbulb clicks on over my head, and guilt tugs at the smallest corner of my heart.

I've misunderstood so much about Iliana—and Sarah, too.

Sarah grew up three houses down from Iliana, and I've always been acutely aware of how much *less* was available to her, compared to Iliana's family. I've never tried to understand, only judged.

I've been so unfair.

"I want to show you something," I say. My hands are shaking.

I've never shown anyone this, other than Griffin. It feels right, though.

If anyone will understand, I'm realizing that it will be Iliana Vrionides.

I lean forward to grab my tablet from the glass coffee table in front of us, and arctic cold hits my back. I don't have my Slash/Spot account anymore, but I archived the original files for my *Hearts & Spades* panels in my cloud storage. I tap open the most recent panel, my best work.

Iliana's eyes soften. She shakes her head a little, pinching and dragging the screen with her fingers to study the image more closely.

"You *should* be a comic artist," she says. "I can't believe you learned how to do all of this yourself."

"When you're passionate about something, all of that research and practice doesn't matter."

Iliana looks up from the screen in her hands. She leans back against the couch and rests her elbow between our heads. For a moment, I think she's going to reach between us to caress my cheek.

I've never considered what it would feel like for Iliana to touch me like this.

"Ever since the argument"—she pauses to swallow—"I've regretted everything."

She's right there, close enough to touch.

I could touch her.

I could *kiss* her.

It never occurred to me before now, but Iliana has controlled every interaction we've ever had up to this point: She has initiated, and I've reacted, over and over again. She could have touched me just now. She was thinking about it. For whatever reason, she chose to do otherwise.

I reach between us the way Iliana did only moments before, but I don't hesitate. I run the tips of my fingers along the constellation of freckles that sweep over the bridge of her nose and along her cheeks, then thumb one pierced earlobe

Iliana's lashes flutter. Her mouth forms a perfect O, and she goes deathly still, as if I am some kind of rare butterfly landing on her shoulder.

If she doesn't move, I won't fly away.

Her skin is softer than I imagined, if a little blemished. There are scars, and pockmarks, and freckles, and a hundred other things I've never noticed before tonight, because I've never just *looked* at her.

"It felt good arguing with you like that," I whisper. "I mean, it was always going to come to that, right? From the first day we met, I knew it would come to that one day."

I expect indignation when I meet her eyes. The expression I find doesn't have a name.

"It didn't have to." Iliana's eyes redden. She doesn't cry, but she looks like she could. "Sarah was completely infatuated with you. From the first time y'all met, I didn't know if she wanted to be you, or sleep with you, or follow you to the ends of the Earth."

"You're her best friend." *Was* her best friend? Past tense? I don't even know anymore. "You were little girls together. What makes you think I'd ever hold a candle to that?"

"Because you're everything." She pulls her bottom lip through her teeth. "When she met you, she looked at me and said, 'You wouldn't believe her. She's, like, a real artist,' and that sounds so absurd but, like—what am I? You have everything in the world at the tips of your fingers. You have access to things that I'd never be able to give her."

I can't believe what I'm about to say.

I believe it with every fiber of my being, and maybe I always have.

The night is weird. The lights are dim.

I push a gingery-blond lock of hair out of Iliana's face.

"You were enough," I say. "You *are* enough."

Iliana's small, round palm cups my throat. Her fingers splay into my hair, and her thumb grazes the curve of my ear.

My pulse is a fractious thing, and now Iliana knows it. It's like the world has gone from black and white to color all of a sudden, like the inside of my brain is nothing but prisms and refracted light. When I touch her again, I know it's the wave of a white flag.

"Rhodes, I, uh, wanted to tell you—"

I fumble forward. It's awkward, but somehow I don't think to be embarrassed.

We bump foreheads; our noses brush. I laugh a little. We inhale.

I pull her closer by the cheeks, by fistfuls of hair, and I finally find out what it takes to make Iliana Vrionides stop talking.

She kisses just like she speaks, honestly and earnestly. But if this is the case—if she kisses the way she does everything else—then there are parts of Iliana I've never even seen before. I've found a part of her who knows how to be slow, careful around the parts of me that are still sore and broken. A part of her that might be shy about getting what she wants.

I want her to know me, too.

I pull her close under the blanket. I'm the one to deepen our kisses, to let my hands wander, to pull her bun loose and let her hair fall wild around her shoulders. She pushes me backward until my head pops against wicker. Iliana's laugh is soft and deep, and she runs a hand through my hair to cradle my head against the hard side of the couch.

I thought I would be afraid.

I'm not afraid.

Around us, the entire world breaks into a million pieces and comes back together into something entirely different.

Grif.ingram 12:17a: well

i.vrionides 12:17a: well what

Grif.ingram 12:17a: did you tell her

i.vrionides 12:18a: what do you mean 'did I tell her'

Grif.ingram 12:18a: did. you. tell. her.

i.vrionides 12:18a: I didn't really have the chance.

Grif.ingram 12:19a: are you kidding me? I've been hiding in my room all night to give y'all ~space~. Why the eff do you think I disappeared?

i.vrionides 12:19a: I tried.

Grif.ingram 12:19a: How do you just 'try'? literally it's maybe three sentences strung together.

i.vrionides 12:19a: I'm going to tell her

Grif.ingram 12:19a: You can't keep going like this. I think she's really starting to like you.

Grif.ingram 12:20a: how could you start something with someone with that kind of secret hanging between you? Jesus

i.vrionides 12:20a: wow condescending much

Grif.ingram 12:21a: this is serious, ok? I didn't want to be like this, but she's my sister so I'm more worried about her than I am you.

Grif.ingram 12:21a: you need to tell her tomorrow, or I will.

Grif.ingram 12:21a: if she finds out I knew and she didn't, she'll never speak to me again

Grif.ingram 12:21a: neither of us want this, ok?

THREE HOURS UNTIL THE CAPSTONE AWARD

ILIANA

Username: Curious-in-Cheshire
Last online: 4d ago

Almost three years ago, as a freshman, I handed an Alabama Conservatory for the Arts and Sciences pamphlet to my parents across the dinner table. It was an invitation to the graduating art track's senior show, carefully scheduled two weeks before the school's portfolio deadlines to audition for the visual arts program the following school year.

They humored me, because they knew that saying no would boil down to the kind of obsession I'd never shake for the rest of my life. I'd never forgive them, and it wasn't worth the drama.

We went, a week later. I didn't know a soul, and I'd never met the teachers that would eventually become inimitable figureheads in the growth of my craft as an artist. I wandered the cavernous second-floor gallery with my dad trailing behind me, but I wasn't there to see the art—not really.

I was there to see the artists. Beautiful, mature seniors in solid black, standing beside their senior projects and answering questions like professionals:

"Yes, the Conservatory has been an excellent way to explore my artistic journey."

And

"I believe that fiber arts are a manner of reinventing the wheel. Each new impression tells a story all its own, and the act of spinning, shuttling, and weaving all tells its own tale."

And

"No, the imperfection of art is an expression of the humanity that inspires it."

At fourteen, I was scattered. I was sloppy and unsure as a freshman, driven and achingly precocious. The mere sight of the Conservatory's eloquent, well-spoken graduating class was the nudge I needed to complete my portfolio and throw myself into the ring as a visual arts–track candidate. The unlikelihood of being accepted as a late transfer didn't matter to me then. *Impossibility* was a word I refused to incorporate into my lexicon, and tonight is no different.

It paid off then, but will it pay off now?

I'd never been to the Frist Center for the Visual Arts before the Capstone Award's project presentation, and I'm just as awed now as I was on the day of the project presentation. Standing here now is more than I could have ever imagined three years ago: It felt like a pipe dream to imagine myself as a student at the Conservatory at all. But with Frist's gorgeous art deco aesthetic and gleaming marble floors, this is the first time I've ever felt like a *real* artist.

We aren't escorted through the delivery entrance this time.

Rhodes reaches between us to hold my hand. We stand at the base of the concrete stairs that run the length of Frist's entrance, and Broadway is nothing but noise and color behind us. The Frist Art Museum stands at attention over us, glowing from the inside with welcome, bearing its standards in banners of every color and anticipating war.

Here we are, again.

Two weeks ago, we were ripping each other's hearts to shreds and we had no idea.

Last night, we held each other's hearts in our hands.

This morning, too, with clasped hands under a blanket on the great room couch while we sipped coffee and took in a part of the local news. With her breath on the back of my neck while she helped me with my hair before we left the condo.

With a kiss for luck just before we stepped off the otherwise-empty elevator and into the vestibule that opened onto the street.

Dense clouds obscure the sky over our heads, and the air smells like rain.

"Let me read your cards," Rhodes whispers. Her hair is up in a high, soft bun and Frist's warm light reflects off her pale skin. "We didn't read your card yesterday when we were unloading the car."

"What?" I force my attention away from the dip at the base of her throat and meet her eyes instead. "You don't believe in it."

"You do, though. It makes you feel better, right?" She extends her hand, palm up, and waits. "Give me your deck."

"How do you know I need to feel better?"

"Going off the looks of you, I can't tell if you're going to pass out or barf on my shoes."

I give her *a look*. She returns it.

"Fine." I reach into my bag, pull the deck out from the front pocket, and place it in Rhodes's hand.

She shuffles the deck like I did yesterday, cuts it, then lets me put it back together.

"Let's do three cards," I say. "A card for me, a challenge card, and an outcome card."

"This sounds complicated."

"Just draw three cards."

She draws the first and places it in my upturned palm. Justice, again.

"What does it mean when you keep drawing the same card over and over?" Rhodes asks.

"It means it's particularly meaningful in your life," I say. "The fact that I drew it for you and drew it for me—well."

The cards are telling me what I already know: Tonight is a reckoning. We can't keep going on like this, like Griffin said, and it's time for me to restore balance in the universe. Apparently, there might not be a timeline where Rhodes doesn't hate me.

She places the second card in my hand, my challenge card: the Four of Pentacles. In this illustration, a vine tightens around a young woman's neck, and four flowers bloom with pentacles in the center.

"That looks . . . bleak." Rhodes frowns into my hand.

"It means I feel like I'm being held down by my money—or lack thereof. It isn't wrong."

Rhodes nods, and places the third card in my hand. "The outcome card."

A woman sits in a chair overcome with all manner of vegetation. Butterflies perch in her hair and on her shoulders, and cocoons hang over her head. Bones are scattered at her feet, and she holds a bull skull—complete with horns—in front of her face.

"Death," I whisper.

"Why is this comforting to you, again?" Rhodes picks up the card and observes it closely. "This illustration makes no sense to me."

"It means death in the sense that something has to die for something else to live. See the cocoons and the butterflies? The flowers in the background? Flowers come from seeds, which come from dead flowers. Caterpillars die to their identity as caterpillars to metamorphose into butterflies."

"Rebirth," Rhodes says. She says it again, for herself this time: "Rebirth."

A beat of silence hangs between us. The wind rattles bare tree branches together like old bones, and police sirens wail past us on the street.

I have to tell her.

"I wonder if Kiersten is as scared as I am?" I ask instead.

"More," Rhodes says after a moment of thought. "Confident people don't cheat. Everything she's done so far tells me she doesn't think she has a chance."

If only that were true.

"Every bit of this has been because Kiersten hates us," I say. "Because Kiersten hates *me*."

Rhodes makes a face. "Kiersten is a toad."

"Yeah, but one of those dangerous ones people use to poison darts." I can't help but frown, and for some reason this makes Rhodes laugh.

I reach between us to take her hand, and she pulls me in for a swift kiss.

I don't have a photographic memory, but God knows I try my damnedest to take a snapshot of this moment and keep it forever.

I want to remember how she feels, she smells, she tastes.

By this time tomorrow, I will want to come back to this and remember what it felt like to have everything I wanted.

Frist's courtyard is a small, contained space that sits between the museum and a large parking lot. I've only seen it in daylight, with its wide swaths of manicured grass bordered by pergolas and seating areas, but night has transformed it into something different. The gossamer tent stands tall over our heads, thin enough to see silhouettes of the tree branches that arch toward the sky. It's thirty-seven degrees out, but you'd never know it—tall, lantern-style heat lamps paired with other bodies in close proximity have prompted nearly all of the attendees to shed their coats by the entrance.

The tent is lit by large, white paper lanterns, and the table arrangements in the center of the space are comprised mostly of tea lights and mirrored objects, sleight of hand to project tiny sources of light into larger spaces. Everything is black, white, and cream, and over-the-top jewelry glitters in the muted light. The only splash of color are violently red roses in the table arrangements, on the buffet, and tucked into the waitstaff's jacket coats.

"Do you think this will be a little bit of what heaven is like?" Rhodes glitters, too. Her knee-length, robin's-egg blue dress is scattered with tiny iridescent beads that catch in the light. It hangs straight from her shoulders, obscuring her shape, and it's accented with a white Peter Pan collar.

She reminds me of Alice, skirting the edge of the Queen of Heart's croquet game.

"What do you mean?" I'm in red, of course—a red sweater, a black leather skirt, black tights, and flats.

There weren't attire suggestions in the email from the Capstone committee, and I'm too short for anything Rhodes could have loaned me from her suitcase.

I cross my arms tighter over my chest. Maybe if I act like it doesn't bother me, people will think I *chose* to underdress.

"Everything is, like, glowing and white. There are all these people we know, and everyone looks happy." She smiles a little.

"Are there people *we* know?" All I see are people's backs.

"Sure. Your parents are over"—she scans the space for a minute, then points over peoples' heads to a table toward the center—"there. Oh, ugh, they're talking to Bootsie, God help us all, and Griffin is waiting in line for something to drink. Kiersten is looking at somebody's Capstone entry—Marianna Walters's? Was that her name?"

"I don't believe in heaven," I say. "I think what Oscar Wilde said works better for this: 'We are each our own devil, and we make this world our hell.'"

"God, you're in a dark mood." Rhodes makes a face.

"But am I wrong?"

Every time our eyes meet, it feels like it will be the last time.

"I guess it just depends on how you look at it," she says.

Mom and Dad swoop in, all kisses and cigarette-scented hugs. I don't have a chance to tell Rhodes I'll come back for her as soon as Mom and Dad head to the buffet line. I don't even get a chance to tell her goodbye.

I'm ushered over to stand by my installation, and almost immediately I'm subsumed with adults asking the kind of questions about my work I've spent my life dreaming of answering—what was my original vision for my work? *I didn't have a set-in-stone vision,* I say. *I only wanted to see where my original idea would take me.* Are the fragile, ink-stained paper-cuts a product of careful planning, or can I thank some kind of happy accident? *It was a happy accident, actually—a run-in with a printmaking student in my school's makerspace.*

It's easier to lie than I thought it would be.

With my shaking hands stuffed in the pockets of my skirt it isn't as hard to push through the Capstone nerves as I imagined—answer the questions. Smile for photos.

Let the twist in my stomach push me forward.

Laugh when I need to blow off steam.

Ask questions when I'm tired of coming up with answers on my own.

In spite of all this, I can't shake the notion that today is a day for endings.

Sarah is lost to me, and the worst part is that I don't know if I ever want her to come back; Rhodes will be over as soon as it began. Alice is a figment of my imagination.

It feels very brave to admit these things to myself.

It's very grown and mature and part of being a woman to look loss in the face and keep moving forward. But I am my own devil. I created this hellscape for myself, and now I don't know if I have the courage to rip off the bandage to set Rhodes free.

CHAPTER 29

RHODES

Username: n/a

Griffin finds me by Kiersten's entry, the first just past the entrance on the right.

Everything about Kiersten's entry screams *I WANT THIS*. Her section of wall is wild with color: Hand-dyed silk is stretched over wooden frames as if they're canvases, each of them embroidered with intricate beadwork.

One is a self-portrait of Kiersten, seated in a chair and staring off into the middle distance as if she's some sort of historical figure. Another is a collage of patterned silks sewn together in the visage of a dark, inviting path through the woods. She's been working on this for months, long before the Capstone Award essays were due.

I want very much to not care right now.

The Capstone Award was never my goal—those breathy nudes were never meant to be. Dusk always asks me how old I feel when my feelings threaten to pull me under, and right now I feel like I'm six: I was on the verge of tears when I was offered something I didn't want, and now I'm on the verge of tears because that thing has been passed on to someone else and my hands are now empty.

It would be very grown-up of me to simply feel joy for the success of people who deserve it, but I'm not entirely sure I have it in me today.

"This is how it was supposed to be," I tell Griffin.

It sounds right, but I don't believe it.

He's handsome in a narrow-cut navy suit. A cherry-red tie stands out vibrantly against the crisp white of his shirt.

"How *what* was supposed to be?" Griffin cocks his head to the side to observe Kiersten's work on his own.

"Tonight. I was never supposed to be a finalist tonight—Mom tried to defy the laws of nature by forcing it into being, and my being disqualified only set us back to the way things are supposed to be."

Griffin follows my attention across the tent. Like the rest of the Capstone Award finalists, Kiersten stands on the other side of a whole army of cameras. Adelaide Lyu and Chelsea Leath stand on either side of her, flushed with pride in their pretty cocktail dresses and chattering between photos; Marianna Walters's smile is brilliant, while an entire battery of flashes illuminates her dark skin. There are a few boys, whose names I never learned, shoved to the back and wearing ill-fitting suits.

Iliana stands to the left of everyone, barely smiling at all.

Her eyes dart between the cameras and Griffin at my side.

Something passes between Iliana and Griffin, and it isn't until he shakes his head that she's even able to turn her attention to the journalists standing in front of her.

Griffin and I meander to the next entry, submitted by a boy named Brian Maguire (based off the nameplate), whose entry is a series of scientific illustrations of native Tennessean river fish using pointillism—entire pieces of art comprised of millions of tiny dots.

The dots are larger in some places and as tiny as the sharp end of a pin in others, dense to the point of black in some places and completely absent in others to suggest light.

This guy knows how his bread is buttered: Because of the simplicity of his work, he clearly sank money into creamy, thick, hand-pressed paper. Based on the microscopic dots on the page, his pens would have had to have been special ordered from somewhere like Japan. Or Germany. Nothing you'd even be able to find in a specialty shop on the internet.

Kiersten's shimmering silk, Brian's paper and pens.

My very British spring break figure-drawing intensives at the Royal College of Art, my connections, my loaded, culture-snobby parents who are very willing to do whatever it takes to thrust my career as an artist into existence.

Iliana has been so many things: Brutally honest. Achingly correct.

Bitter.

Jealous.

But last night, she was something I've never seen in her before: *vulnerable*.

It never occurred to me before how much these things actually *cost*: Parental support. Money for supplies. Money for entry fees. Money for travel. The benefit of knowing the right people since birth. I don't doubt that I got into the festival all these years because I deserved it, but Iliana and Sarah have deserved it, too—they just didn't have the same resources to get here.

I can't stop myself from turning again to check on her. She gestures to her entry as she speaks into a tape recorder that has been thrust into her face. Kiersten stands next to her now, all smiles and polite nods. Her pink-and-purple cotton-candy hair is swept back into a respectable knot, and a simple black sheath dress hangs just past her knees. Sarah stands cast to the side, wearing Kiersten's hallmark crystal-studded, pink leather jacket.

Every time Kiersten opens her mouth to speak, Iliana flinches as if she's been slapped.

"I've never seen Iliana like this," I say.

"She's not herself tonight, that's for sure," Griffin says. "Have y'all had a chance to talk today?"

I shrug. "Some. I've realized that being nervous is just about the only thing that shuts her up."

"Mmmm." Griffin polishes the face of his watch on the front of his coat. "I guess a common enemy can solve just about every kind of conflict."

"Common enemy?" I blink at him.

I have no idea what he's talking about.

"Whoever ratted you out and tried to destroy her Capstone entry." Griffin crosses his arms and continues: "*Somebody* here wanted you out of the running, and you know it wasn't Iliana. So . . ."

He isn't wrong.

Caught up in the moment, it had been so easy to put it to the back of my mind. I pan the line of semifinalists one more time, pausing on each face. The nervous twitch in each set of hands. Who didn't want us here?

Iliana had been so sure it was Kiersten. Was she right?

Iliana's here now, does it even matter?

Iliana's crumpled, fragile paper-cuts sway over our heads like a cascade of autumn leaves. Iliana's entry is the only one that moves, and it swings and shudders against each wave of people. It's beautiful as a whole, but each individual card stands alone as a piece of work: fifty-two ink-dyed paper rectangles, warped and curled and delicate like lace.

It's not the whole deck like she intended, but it's close.

A small crowd has formed around me, their eyes moving with each sway of the paper moving over our heads. The patrons are as captivated as I am, maybe even more—they didn't watch Iliana's installation push into existence like I did.

They're coming upon Iliana's work fully formed, and it's taking their breath away.

I catch one in my hand and turn it this way and that.

I knew they were tarot cards, but I never gave it much further thought. The card in my hand would be the size of my palm if it laid flat, and the image cut into the paper is imagery I'd recognize anywhere: a white rabbit with a timepiece peeking from behind shrubbery trimmed to the Queen of Heart's likeness, offset against scared-looking frogs dressed in livery.

Another card reveals tea cups and silly men in top hats, framed by flowers and leaves; yet another, the Jabberwock. Axes and croquet sets. A silhouette of a cat bearing a wicked smile.

I knew Iliana liked Alice in Wonderland, but this?

This is the magnum opus of someone who knows the story like she knows herself. I think about her hands, always covered in bandages, the tiny cuts all over her fingers and palms, scabbing over and healing in fresh air. It always seemed crass to me, for her to spend so much time bandaged and bloody, but each of these little cards whisper truth to me that speaks the opposite: What I believed harsh at best and disturbing at worst was actually a testament of Iliana's dedication to her craft.

I look up and find Griffin studying my face, frowning.

Something is off.

Iliana and Griffin have watched me the entire night as if I'd blow away with a puff of air.

I'd thought it was concern for me being here, at first. Maybe they were afraid of how I'd cope with facing my loss head-on, or maybe they wondered if it would be shameful to appear at all after basically being sent off in disgrace less than two weeks before the final art show.

"You look like you could use this, babe." Kiersten appears on my right with two flutes of—*surely it's not champagne*—and thrusts one into my hands. I lift the flute to my face, and my nose confirms my worst suspicions. "You look like you're about to throw up."

"Uh." I glance at Griffin, and he shrugs in agreement. "Thanks?"

"I just had to come talk to you." Her red lipstick leaves little crescent moon imprints on the edge of her glass between sips. "You're really, just, amazing."

Iliana's eyes grow wider from where she stands between her parents, watching us. Her mother pokes her, and she turns to the camera and smiles.

"You're kind," I say. It doesn't feel kind.

Kiersten places her hand on my arm. Red fingernails, red lips. Sharp teeth.

"We figured you'd go into hiding after your, uh—" Kiersten takes another sip and cuts her eyes to someone standing behind me. A reflection of a bedazzled jacket in Kiersten's champagne flute confirms the only logical candidate: Sarah. "Unfortunate, um, removal from the scholarship award. We were really worried about you."

"It's been a blessing in disguise," I say. I turn to widen our circle and include Sarah in the conversation. There's something about her behind me that sets my teeth on edge. "Sometimes it takes losing something to realize you didn't want it to begin with."

I don't know who I'm supposed to trust anymore.

Sarah's hair has gone from bleached peroxide-blond to cotton-candy pink. It hangs around her face in sheets, and Kiersten's red lipstick is too harsh on Sarah's fair features. Sarah averts her eyes and takes a too-big swallow of champagne, then cringes.

"Aw, that's nice." Kiersten smiles. "It's really seemed to bring you and Iliana together, too."

"She's representing the Conservatory's visual arts track tonight." I pump my fist in the air, but my face burns. "Go Bobcats."

From across the room, Iliana looks like she's going to vomit.

She's an oasis in the sea of what I now think of as my old life: old ladies in fur coats and gentlemen clutching half-smoked cigars like flotation devices.

Bootsie Prudhomme is one such lady, lush in white ermine with opera gloves the color of cranberry. She pushes her way to the center of the tent, where tables have been scooted here and there to make room for a small platform.

A man in all black quietly tests a microphone, and the quiet confidence in Kiersten's face begins to crack.

"You know," Kiersten says, hurried, "after everything's come to the surface, it really says a lot about you as a person that you've come to stand by her anyway."

Griffin blanches on my right.

The night around me is a giant, blinking arrow: The red roses on the tables. The squat, toad-like wealthy men in their waistcoats, and Iliana's Capstone Award entry displaying an almost obsessive love for something I only thought I shared with one other person.

Cheshire.

Iliana and I meet eyes again, from a hundred feet away, and her expression tells me everything.

She knows. I know.

She knows I know.

Raindrops plod against the tent surface here, then there, before the sky opens up into a steady spatter that covers the entire expanse over our heads. It shakes in the trees and echoes off the pavement, but it doesn't matter.

Griffin grabs for my arm, but I slither away and dart backward toward the crowd.

"Rhodes, don't do anything you're going to regret later—"

Kiersten is barely suppressing a grin behind her champagne flute, and Sarah looks as if the weight of the world rests on her small, round shoulders.

Sarah knows. Kiersten knows.

Griffin knows.

Somehow, everyone in this whole fucking world knew that Iliana was Cheshire but me, when—*GOD*. I can't even think anymore. The room is pressing in on me, all roses and froggy men in their livery, and suddenly I'm Alice.

Drink me, whispers the champagne flute in my hand.

I open my throat and down the entire thing in one long, painful gulp. Little birds and silly men in top hats float around my head, and I'm shrinking, shrinking, shrinking. I'd be small enough to disappear through a tiny door in the baseboards, if this tent had baseboards. But I start to cry, and if I were very, very big, I could flood the place with teardrops the size of dinner plates.

I push past women in their minks and men sipping their scotch, grab my coat from the rack, and disappear out into the rain.

I'd meant to be alone, out here.

I thought the rain would be enough to keep anyone sensible inside, especially if the person I want to be far from most has a real, honest-to-God chance of leaving tonight as the newest recipient of the Capstone Award.

It isn't, though.

Iliana's voice echoes out into the night behind me.

My heart eases into the sound of my name on her lips, like a hot bath. I scald myself and retreat farther away. Her footsteps ring out behind me, louder and louder until I know she's close by the warmth of her hand clasping mine.

She catches me and turns me around to face her, thrusting a wide, black umbrella over my head. She stares up at me with matching streaks of mascara down her cheeks, and her hair has grown three times in size from the moisture in the air.

This is Cheshire.

I knew it when I looked up that night standing in front of Frist and saw her staring at me from across the street. She was looking at me like I was a ghost, all wide-eyed and hollowed out. That night I chose not to see the fear, the disappointment, or anything else other than her anger, but it showed up in my dreams.

It's nagged at the base of my brain ever since: When we were talking. When we were working together in the gallery. When she was kissing me, every time she gazed at me—so full of hope and warmth and lovesickness and eight thousand other emotions without a name.

I didn't know, I chose not to believe, but I *knew*.

"You had so many chances to say something," I hiss. "You told everyone else, but you didn't tell me?"

"I didn't tell everyone else," Iliana cries. "Sarah was with me that night, remember? She knew what I was doing before I knew you were *you*. *She* told Kiersten, because of course she did."

"Griffin?"

I wish so much to be brave. I envisioned this conversation with Cheshire eight thousand times, and in each little dream I was strong, and had courage in my convictions, and I didn't cry.

"Griffin figured it out somehow. He's really smart."

"Yeah, he is." I palm at my cheeks, and my fingers come away black with makeup. "You—Cheshire, I mean—were my best friend. Why didn't *you* tell me?"

Speaking it out loud settles like lead in my bones.

You, Iliana, were my best friend.

Iliana Vrionides was the dream girl who once only lived inside my computer.

"Because we were horrible to each other," Iliana says. "*I* was horrible to *you*. I was so angry with you about last summer, and it was so unfair. But I knew Alice's heart, and I knew from my relationship with Alice that she—*you*—did everything in her—*your*—power to make things right. When I realized that you and Alice were the same person, I wanted time to prove that I'm worth loving, too."

"Oh, Iliana—" I can only shake my head.

What an ugly, ugly mess.

"Tell me," she says, punctuated with a sob, "if I'd shown up that night and told you who I was, would you have given me a chance in hell?"

I don't have to answer that, because she's right.

Iliana reaches up to touch my cheek. Our eyes meet, and all I want is to melt into her.

But it's all so much to reconcile. Even if I see the way Cheshire and Iliana puzzle together, my mind flip-flops in protest and I can't get my thoughts all the way around it.

"I—I don't know—"

"Iliana!" Iliana's mother's voice is a throatier version of her own. I'd know it anywhere. "Baby, come on! They're calling for you."

Iliana's eyes grow wide like saucepans, the color of honey.

"It's you, baby," her mother calls out to us—no, to *Iliana*. This isn't meant for me. "You *won*! What's *wrong*, sweetheart? Ah, come inside—"

I burst into tears. Again.

Here we are, at the end of this, and it's all come down to Iliana after all.

"You need to go," I say.

I'll give myself this: It feels like I've lost something tonight, seeing the Capstone going to her. I'll be happy for her tomorrow, I hope, but tonight the grief is real in more ways than one.

"But—we need—" Iliana glances back at her mom. Applause thunders from inside the tent, and people are peeking out into the courtyard, grinning.

"I need *time*," I whisper. "Go. You've worked so hard for this."

Iliana rocks forward to kiss me on the cheek. "Thank you," she whispers. "For everything."

With that, she leaves the umbrella in my hand and darts back toward the tent.

Applause hits a crescendo, and I turn to the sidewalk to walk two blocks back to the condo with Iliana's umbrella over my head.

For, you see, so many out-of-the-way things had
happened lately,
that Alice had begun to think that very few things
indeed were really impossible.

—Lewis Carroll,
Alice in Wonderland

CHAPTER 30
ILIANA

Username: Curious-in-Cheshire
Last online: 2w ago

I thought my first night back at Sylvia's since the scholarship award would have entailed a hero's welcome. My entire world flipped on its ear in Nashville, but being back here in Birmingham, strung up in one of Sylvia's frilly aprons, feels like some modicum of my normal life.

Plus, I was right: Telling Rhodes the truth put the universe back in balance.

Except it isn't in balance at *all*, because this level of security is something I've never actually experienced before. For the first time, maybe ever, I feel like I can think past what will happen to me in a week. A month. A year. Five years.

I've burned bridges and broken hearts, but now everything is paying off—I know where I'm going to college, and I know how I'm going to pay for it. The Capstone Award women have shifted from horrifying, Argonaut-esque harpies into women who champion for me in every area—Bootsie Prudhomme asked her friends to help pay for my freshman year art supplies. In spite of June Baker's fallout with the organization, her daughter-in-law asked their junior league chapter to help me buy a new computer.

The thing is, I don't really know if I can call it "paying off" at all—maybe a year ago, I would have been okay with the way all of my relationships became collateral damage in my fight for all this.

But so much has changed since then, and there is this chilly, impenetrable silence that has been draped over my life like some kind of burial shroud—there is no one around me to share in my joy. My parents are thrilled for me, sure, but I have no friends who care about me enough to really be *happy* for me.

I'm lonely. I ache for what I don't have anymore.

It's been two weeks since the Capstone Award finals, and I haven't spoken to Rhodes since. Lord knows I've tried—I texted her a week after finals. I tried to call her in a moment of weakness a few days after that, even though I knew that if she wanted contact with me, she would have texted me back in the first place. Then I emailed her.

I eventually accepted that I had come on too strong.

It's what I do when there's something in front of me that I want—and it's the trait that got me into this whole mess to begin with. This time, though, I didn't push forward.

I gave her what she needed—space—and I turned my heart toward the very specific pain of getting used to the idea of what life will look like now without the person who filled it with color.

There was never going to be a timeline where Rhodes and I would even be friends, much less anything else. I wish I could say I've resigned myself to the truth of this. The only thing that keeps distance between us is that we both know I deserve it.

Sylvia stands at the counter with her old-fashioned reconciliation book opened wide in front of her. Sammy Davis Jr. croons over our heads, and Sylvia hums along as she counts tiny pots filled with margarine under her breath.

Sleigh bells crash against the glass door.

Kiersten Keller appears in the threshold, bringing the cold in with her.

There's nothing to be afraid of with Kiersten. I heard through the grapevine that she was the one to break the truth to Rhodes; I heard it was sneaky and calloused and expertly sandwiched into a barrage of lovely, well-executed platitudes.

A bitch slap followed by the stroke of a cheek.

No, I'm not afraid of Kiersten anymore.

I don't even hate her.

All I see is a fun-house version of myself that I'm growing out of, cutthroat and desperate, and I'm sad for her.

"You gonna make me get that?" I ask Sylvia, already grabbing for a menu.

I still have no desire to talk to her.

"You work here?" Sylvia licks her thumb, then flips the page.

"Fair enough." I step around the Formica-topped counter and meet Kiersten by the door.

Kiersten's face goes red, and she squares her shoulders. Nothing about her has *really* changed since the Capstone finals—she still has the same pink-to-purple hair, the same violently red lips, the same look of bored defiance in her eyes. But she's foregone her usual BeDazzled leather jacket in lieu of a sensible black peacoat. The only true essence of Kiersten is in the hand-dyed silk scarf at her neck, embroidered in such a way that I know it's something she's created for herself.

Her shoulders tug just a little farther toward the ground.

"Just one today?" I glance behind me. "All the tables are taken. There's only room for one at the counter."

"I'm not here to eat." She might as well have spit the words onto my feet.

I raise my eyebrows and wait.

"I—" She swallows. "I'm here to ask for my job back."

After she rage-quit, I'm amazed she has the guts to show her face in here at all.

"You really think Sylvia's gonna give you another chance?" I tuck the menu into the back of my apron. "Her niece just started after the holiday."

"My parents are making me, okay?" Kiersten's features twist into a snarl. "It's nice for *you* that your college is paid for, but some of us still have to work."

"I'll have to work until the day I die like everybody else," I say, "so cut that shit out. You know, you wouldn't be in this situation at all if you took five minutes to think about the way your shitty behavior affects people. You may not have won the scholarship, but you'd still have a job."

"Oh, like you have any room to talk, Iliana Vrionides." Kiersten tries to push past me, but I step in her way.

I don't know when I'm going to have the chance to say this again.

"You know what? I learned some things. And even at my worst, I would have never—ever—*ever*—destroyed someone else's chances at the scholarship. Even if you'd have been the best entry there, you still wouldn't have deserved it because you're a damn snake and karma is a bitch."

"Wait—*what*?" Kiersten takes a step back. "What are *you* talking about?"

"You're trying to tell me that you weren't the one to tell the Capstone board about Rhodes's mom buying her way in? Or the one behind the ink balloon in my locker?"

Kiersten's eyes widen. "I had no idea that's what happened with yours. It all seemed very . . . intentional. Like you'd planned it that way."

"That's because Rhodes is a genius," I say. "She helped me because we wanted to beat whoever was responsible for this. You."

Kiersten's features soften. "Look, I was pissed about the fight at the project presentation, and I felt bad for Sarah because she seemed kinda caught up between y'all, but I swear to God I never would have tried to sabotage you or anyone else." She shrugs. "I wanted to screw things up between you and Rhodes because I felt like you deserved it, but I wanted to beat you both the old-fashioned way."

We regard each other.

For better or worse, it's easy to see that we're both cut from the same cloth.

If it had been anyone else, I'm not sure I wouldn't have done the same thing. In an alternate universe, I wonder what kind of friends Kiersten and I could have been. Probably the kind that would have ruined everyone's lives and laughed about it.

"Sylvia's at the counter." There's nothing else to say about the Capstone. I gesture behind me. "I'd lead in with groveling if you want a snowball's chance in hell."

"Thanks," Kiersten says. "And, um. Sorry about Rhodes. And what I did. You were cute together."

"We really were," I say.

"I'd talk to Sarah," Kiersten says over her shoulder. "I had to stop talking to her when I finally took a good look at her and thought I was looking at myself. Let's just say I've learned a few things, too."

Boxes line the residency hall walls, all scrawled with Sarah's bubbly handwriting.

Sniffling echoes out from the dorm room Sarah shares with Rhodes. The thought of seeing Rhodes again vibrates over my skin, but I only hear one set of small, familiar footsteps echoing from inside.

I tap on the door one, two, three times, then step inside.

Kiersten's right: Without being attached to me, or Rhodes, or Kiersten, Sarah's a ship without a sail.

She stands in the middle of the dorm room she shares (*shared?*) with Rhodes, in a white T-shirt and blue jeans. She's cut her hair off into a flattering pixie cut; all hints of pink are gone and it's back to its original peroxide blond. Her side of the room is nearly stripped down to the studs, all shoved into giant leaf bags and old boxes poached from the back of the liquor store down the block.

"What the hell is going on?" I clear the room to pick up Sarah's dad's cassette player off the almost-empty desk. A mountain of scabby, cracked crystals sit in a pile nearby, and the surface of the cassette player is raw with the ordeal of picking them off. "Are you moving home?"

"You need to get out of here. I'm trying to do this—" Sarah gestures for the cassette player in my hands. She doesn't have to answer. It's too late in the year to change room assignments.

"Before Rhodes gets back?" I hand it over.

She glares over her shoulder and doesn't say a word.

"Does she know you're moving home?"

"It's better this way," Sarah says.

It hit me after my conversation with Kiersten: *Sarah* had my locker combination memorized.

She knew the extensive history of the Ingrams' relationship with June Baker.

Through Rhodes, Sarah knew what kind of a mutiny it would cause among the Capstone/Ocoee Festival leadership to prove that Rhodes and June were complicit in a little nepotism. Kiersten wouldn't have been equipped for that. She was as much of a newbie to that whole crowd as I've been. Even if she'd been the one to overhear the conversation with Randall, it only makes sense that it would be Sarah to run the ball.

By the time the reality settles into my bones, there is nothing else: only the distinct feeling of facing down something you've sort of known since the beginning.

The agony and ecstasy of being right about something terrible.

"So, do you feel better about yourself?" I go straight to it. "Rhodes lost her chance at a scholarship, but she's not even upset about it because it helped her figure out what she wants to do with her life. I won the Capstone anyway, and Kiersten isn't talking to you anymore."

"Is that what you came to do?" Sarah sniffles into her hands. "Rub it in?"

I knew this version of Sarah was in there somewhere, that one day the blurry facts, and half-truths, and sneakiness would be my problem instead of someone else's. I always knew Sarah was the kind of person I only wanted in my foxhole, that she's not the person you want on the other side of enemy lines. I just never wanted to believe it was possible that we could ever be anything other than friends.

"I don't remember a time that you weren't my friend, Sarah. I need to understand why you did this."

"I DON'T KNOW, OKAY?" Her voice rattles the walls. "I don't know."

"Nobody does anything for no good reason," I say.

"I just don't want to talk about it," Sarah says. "I'm allowed that."

"Cut it out, Sarah Wade. No more precious-Sarah-is-so-fragile, let's-not-apply-pressure-because-she'll-break bullshit."

"Nobody mattered here except the two of you," Sarah spits out. "There was no other competition for the scholarship, no other competition in the visual arts program. Just Iliana and Rhodes, the best of the best."

"Not you, though," I say. I'm beginning to understand.

"Not me! I'm just as good an artist as either of you. I got into the Conservatory as a sophomore, same as you. I got into the Capstone based off *my actual grades*." Sarah shoves her pillows into another leaf bag, one at a time. "You never took me seriously, though, because you two have always been so freaking obsessed with each other."

"You really think all of this back-and-forth between Rhodes and me was about you? The fact that we've always been at each other's throats doesn't mean anything other than what it exactly is—that we hated each other, and we wanted each other out of the way. It never meant anything about what you can or can't do.

"There is so much context there, so much history between Rhodes and me, and you'll never understand it."

"Never understand it!" Sarah laughs, but there's no humor. "Are you kidding me? I could write a complete history on the two of you, week by week, month by month, semester by semester. I've been caught in the middle of it every step of the way, and it has been a complete nightmare."

All I can do is roll my eyes. "Oh yes. Caught between two girls that hate each other. That's the story you tell yourself, right? Little, misunderstood Sarah; big, mean Iliana. Bitter, tragic Rhodes."

"Oh, don't even start, Iliana—"

"Here's the thing I've figured out: You *liked* us fighting over you. As long as I'm pissed because you're throwing it in my face that you're hanging out with Rhodes, I'm trying to pull you back to me. Let's be honest here: When you figured out that we were talking online, and we didn't know who the other was, you felt threatened."

"WHO ELSE AM I SUPPOSED TO BE?" Sarah throws the leaf bag in her hands into the hall. "You said it yourself! No one compares to either of you here. I have been living in your shadow for longer than I can even remember. If—if you found each other, and actually loved each other, where would I even begin to fit?"

Sarah's chin trembles. She swipes at her cheeks with her forearm.

"I guess I thought if I could win the Capstone Award, you'd finally see me as equal to the both of you." She shakes her head. "I couldn't pull myself together after your fight. I couldn't stop crying to give my project presentation, and the Capstone board didn't care."

"So if you didn't get it, we couldn't, either."

"Don't think I never saw all the ways the two of you could have worked as friends. You know like I do—opposite isn't always bad. It can be complementary. I saw it, but you were so freaking determined to hate each other."

That first night, the night Rhodes and Sarah met, could have been yesterday.

You'll love her, Sarah said then.

You're nothing alike, but I just see it, Iliana. The three of us are going to have so much fun—

I hated Rhodes for it. I hated Sarah for it, and I hated the idea of anyone taking her away from me. In this moment, I understand everything.

"Was it worth it?" I'm an asshole for even asking, but I'm not sorry.

She cringes, and glowers, and shakes her head.

"Will we come back from this?" she asks.

The answers are in front of both of us.

No, we'll never come back from this. No, it wasn't worth it. But I know there's only one thing left for me to do before I go.

"I'm sorry, Sarah. I'm sorry you lost your chance at the scholarship. I'm sorry I wasn't better to you. I'm sorry I floated your new Barbie down the drain when we were seven and—"

"Come on, Iliana," Sarah says, wiping at her face. "That was when we were little."

"But it's the way it's always been," I say. "Even if I eventually fix stuff with you later, I always crashed into you to get what I wanted. I'm sorry."

Sarah lets go of the bag in her hands to stand straight, my sister for as long as I can remember. She doesn't cry, doesn't speak, doesn't move.

For a long time, she doesn't look at me.

She neither accepts my apology nor apologizes herself, and I just have to be okay with that.

Without another word, I help her move the last of her bags into the hall on my way to the stairs. Rather than head for the car, I make my way up to Studio B instead.

CHAPTER 31

RHODES

`Username: n/a`

Studio B is in disarray.

Turpentine fumes hang around the ceiling tiles, chairs are scattered, and in the center sits a cornucopia spilling onto a card table. Wax fruit catches whatever light it can, and fake ivy dangles halfway to the floor. It's still Christmas break, just for another day, which means campus is still surrendered to winter intensives.

Somehow, Randall had the good sense not to ask me to help aide this year.

A series of dings cuts the silence from the bag that lies on the table next to my leg. It's probably Griffin, reminding me that I'm supposed to be in Homewood in ten minutes. There's a blanket with our name on it next to a bonfire, and ribs from the barbecue place on the corner, and a water bottle half filled with Stoli from Dad's liquor cabinet.

It's Griffin's friends and Griffin's food, and even if I'm in a marginally better place emotionally, I still can't stomach the thought of watching anyone else fall in love.

I twirl the ring on my right hand with my thumb, then drag my hands through my hair.

No. I'm not going.

Even if I'd rather go sit in a crowded mall than be alone another minute, I'm done putting myself through things I hate because it makes everyone else feel better. Griffin will understand—sometimes, it feels like he's the only one nudging me forward, encouraging me to care for myself in the same way I go out of my way to please everyone else.

Cheshire—Iliana, I guess—would agree with him.

I pull my phone from my pocket and fire exactly that into a text to Griffin, then hit send.

Thinking of Iliana stings in the same way it always does.

I haven't seen her, or spoken to her, since we returned to Birmingham from Nashville and school let out for Christmas break.

She's come up in my mind again and again—in the decision to stay in Birmingham for the holiday rather than drag tail back to Nashville to watch Mom drunk-text her boyfriend while Dad's sucked into the five thousandth rewatch of *Die Hard* on the couch. I thought about her while shopping for Christmas gifts. I thought about her when I'd catch my reflection in the shop windows, wondering what she'd look like loaded down with bags next to me—pissed, probably, and lecturing me about late capitalism and consumerist holidays, but I'd take it over this silence any day.

She's the last thing I think about at night.

The first thing I think about in the morning.

But tonight, instead of meditating on radio silence, I picture the studio filling with soft light from the hall. I know the shape of Iliana's silhouette like I know my own, and it isn't hard to call to memory the scent of her shampoo, or the sound of her voice, or the feel of her skin.

My phone pings again, pulling me out of my little fantasy:

Grif.ingram 7:17p: you sure? I hate you being alone so much

ring.ram 7:18p: omg you are pitying me

ring.ram 7:18p: you're being gross. stop

Grif.ingram 7:18p: I'm just looking out for you

ring.ram 7:19p: thanks I hate it

Grif.ingram 7:19p: whatever

ring.ram 7:19p: now you can make out with your new girlfriend without feeling bad about me third wheeling. Happy birthday or something.

The studio door creaks at the hinges, and it's hard to separate what's real from a product of my imagination.

I drop my phone into my lap.

Iliana's silhouette in the doorway isn't backlit like I imagined it; there's no light from the hall to cast onto the floor, and pale silver-blue light from the windows in the studio across the hall cast a halo of curls into relief against the dark. It caresses narrow shoulders and falls on familiar curves, and it's only just strong enough to glint off the backs of the chairs closest to the door.

It's a permutation of my original fantasy, and I like this one better—it feels more real, somehow. This isn't healthy, though, falling head over heels into daydreams and wishful thinking. Hope can only fly unchecked for so long before it needs to be anchored into something absolute.

I clear my thoughts and take a breath, but the figure in the door doesn't disappear when I try to blink her away.

She's so much *more* than I remember, too—which means the Iliana in my dreams is only a fraction of the vital, breathing girl who stands before me now.

I don't remember how to speak anymore.

Iliana-slash-Cheshire stands in silence, the girl I've hated and the girl I've loved all rolled into one impossible package.

This night, these clothes, this skyline through the studio windows: *This* is how I imagined revealing my identity to Cheshire—to Iliana.

"It was Sarah," I say, apropos of nothing. It's just a guess, maybe an educated one, but Iliana's nod confirms it. "I came back from dinner and saw her boxes out in the hall, so I came up here instead."

There was no way it could have ever been Kiersten, not really.

She didn't have skin in the fight like Sarah did.

"Kiersten came up to Sylvia's," Iliana says. "She admitted to wanting to break us up, but she swore she'd never try to sabotage us. I came up to ask Sarah about it, and I barely had to press her for information." Iliana steps farther into the room. I stuff my hands into my armpits. "I think she's been holding on to it all for a while. She just kind of upchucked it everywhere."

"Pretty par for the course," I say. This is so *natural*, like every conversation she and I ever had over Slash/Spot direct messages. I go on: "I want so bad to be like, 'I thought I knew her! This is so unlike her!' But honestly—?"

"It felt like a matter of time before something like this happened," Iliana says, finishing my thought. "It's wild, thinking about a best friend in past tense."

"*You* were my best friend." My voice shatters. I clap my hand over my mouth.

"You were mine," Iliana says.

She moves to sit next to me on the table.

Mine.

One word is enough to steal my breath.

Mine indeed.

"Deep down, under everything, I had this fear that Cheshire would be you," I say.

"I'm sorry," Iliana whispers. "I should have said that before, properly, but—"

Apologies feel wholly necessary while you wait on one, almost as if they're some kind of magical incantation that'll make the pain go away. But hearing it from Iliana now, it takes something from me rather than giving me what I needed.

I pull my bottom lip through my teeth, and Iliana reaches between us to touch my face.

Iliana, friend and rival.

Lover and enemy.

I drop the weight of my cheek into her palm. It was never supposed to be Iliana, but it could have never been anyone else.

"Rhodes, I am *so* in love with you," she whispers. "I should have told you that night. And then I should have told you when the night in the studio happened. Then I should have told you at the condo. Then I should have told you at the art show. When Kiersten found out about our history, she threatened to tell you herself and I got desperate—I just wanted a chance to prove myself before I shot it all to hell."

She meets my eyes as she speaks.

Iliana smiles, but there's nothing happy about it. "I screwed up every time I turned around. I was careless."

"Were you ever going to tell me who you were?"

"I—" Iliana pauses to mop at her cheek with the back of her hand. "I was afraid of *this*, that you'd find out who I was before I was ready and then hate me for it. But yes. I planned on telling you."

It isn't hard to forget the past, to imagine that we're simply here, together. And *yet*.

"I just wish we could, I don't know—" she sighs, and pops her lips together.

"Pretend it didn't happen?" I laugh. "I bet you do."

Iliana drops her hand into her lap, and already I ache to be touched again.

Everything feels so final.

"It's going to be a part of us for the rest of our lives," I whisper. "No matter how much we wish it away."

"So that's it, then?" Iliana angles toward me to meet my eyes. Hers are wide, uncertain. There's more uncertainty in that gaze than I've ever seen from her. "It happened, and it's over."

"No," I say. Iliana's eyes are rimmed pink, and I hand over a wadded paper napkin from my back pocket. "That's not what I mean at all."

I'll forgive her, and keep on loving her, but our past isn't something I'll pretend never happened. For good and for bad, this is the story that could only ever belong to us. In this moment, I know the answer to my own question. Yes, I can forgive Iliana.

Iliana moves closer to me. Whenever I imagined the first time I was meeting Cheshire—*Iliana*—face to face, I imagined it like this: The first touch would be a soft, slow brush of fingers, eyes closed so I could catalog the tactile wonder that is Cheshire's—*Iliana's*—skin.

For so long, it was only loving a mind.

Words and pictures on a screen.

Every night I imagined a thousand and one scenarios that would lead to this moment, and each time I allowed myself to be engulfed by the mere notion of physical contact. It would crash into me, and I'd let the current pull me under and wash me out to sea.

As expertly as my imagination walked my heart through this in a thousand different ways, it was nothing remotely close to the reality of Iliana's fingernails cautiously grazing the top of my arm, or the soft bloom of her breath against the curve of my throat.

But this isn't a work of my imagination; this is real life.

Iliana touches me, and my hands are the first part of my body to remember it works. I thumb the moisture away from Iliana's cheeks. I touch her hair, follow the path from the corner of her jaw to the base of her skull, and let my fingers trail down her back. I hold on to her like I've never held on to anything, as if she will lift off into orbit and I'll never see her again.

Her apology might have taken something from me, but choosing to forgive her was to accept it back. It's a *choice* to move forward.

Making these decisions for myself is new territory for me, and choosing to love Iliana is a beautiful place to start. There's an entire lifetime's worth of conversations we need to have, plans for next week and plans for the future, where we're going and how we're getting there.

But for now, I'm going to kiss the girl in my arms until she doesn't want to be kissed anymore. We're going to hold hands, whisper about what's in store, and dream about the future.

ACKNOWLEDGMENTS

This book would not be here without Victoria Marini and the rest of the team at Irene Goodman Literary Agency; Nicole Otto; Weslie Turner, Madison Furr, Erin Stein, Natalie C. Sousa, Carolyn Bull, Dawn Ryan, Hayley Jozwiak, Jie Yang, and the rest of the team at Imprint/Macmillan. Your fingerprints are all over the pages of this book, and I am filled to the brim with gratitude for your work.

To Victoria Ying: You are incredible. Thank you for bringing Iliana, Rhodes, the Red Queen, and Alice to life!

I'd like to thank my husband Daniel, and our boys, Levi, Rhys, and Parker. You are my light; you give my life color and demonstrate love in more ways than I could ever enumerate. To my dad, Terry, and my mom, Donna: You knew I'd do this one day, and you sacrificed everything to see it happen. To David, my stepfather: You taught me what it looks like to choose your family and to love them fiercely. To Maribeth and Scott, Ellen, Nathan, and Brooks: You are my people, and I love you. To David and Lucille: You have celebrated every milestone in the creation of this book, and it has meant the world to me to have you in my corner.

To Kristin Brophy, Chelsey Papadopoulos, Jennifer Hawkins, Kes Trester, Tia Bearden, Kristin Walters, Sarah Lyu, Amy Oliver, Ashley Leath, and Beth Branch: You believed in this book when I didn't. You saw what this book could be, and you have loved me through the darkest periods of my life. I don't know where I would be without you.

I would also like to thank Sonia Hartl, Rachel Lynn Solomon, Emily Neal, Laura Lashley, Christine Lynn Herman, Kosoko Jackson, and the rest of my Pitch Wars family; Eric Smith, for being the first person to believe in this story, when it was just a seed of a thing; Rachel Strolle, Ashley Blake Herring, Rachel Hawkins, and Victoria Lee for your early support; Steve, Maria, Carina and Gaby Manning, Jason Myers, and the rest of my DFWCon/DFW Writers Workshop family—I don't know how I would have gotten by during my time in DFW without you.

Finally, I will be forever grateful to Ms. Dianna Hyde, my English Composition 101 professor at Jefferson State Community College. You saw the writer in me before I saw the writer in myself. In all these years I have never forgotten the encouragement you spoke over me while I sat in your class.

ABOUT THE AUTHOR

Anna Birch was born'n'raised in a rural area on the outskirts of Birmingham, Alabama. She traded thick forests and dirt roads for the heart of the city, where she now lives with her husband, three children, and dog. She loves knitting, brie, and hanging out with her family. *I Kissed Alice* is her first book. Follow her on Twitter @Almost_Anna or visit her site at annabirchbooks.com.

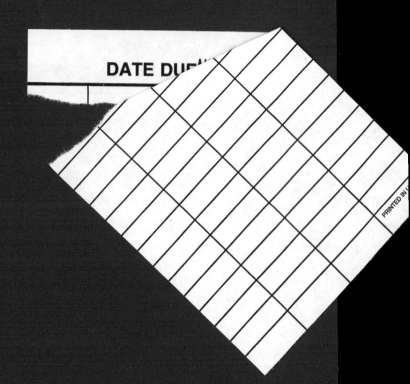

DATE DUE

PRINTED IN